# THE SHEFFIELD AVENGERS

## Tony Barnard

ISBN: 978-1-326-08086-0


PublishNation, London
www.publishnation.co.uk

*This book is dedicated to the Ship's Company of HMS Sheffield 1982.*

# Acknowledgments

I would like to thank the many members of my family and friends for their unwavering support during the writing of this book and to those who have given me advice and answered many detailed questions. You all know who you are. Thank you.

I would also like to thank the following organisations for their kind permission to use their material:

The Imperial War Museum for granting a licence to use the photograph of *HMS Sheffield* on the front cover

Book cover design by DSM Design Ltd

Fabulous Music Ltd for granting the Print Licence to use the extracts from the lyrics of *'Bargain'* by The Who in Chapter Twelve.

# Author's Note

*"The Sheffield Avengers"* is a 'what if' story set against a factual historical background. The information and dates are as accurate as possible but the sequence of events has been altered to suit the narrative.

Whilst certain political and military figures are historically correct, their actions and dialogue are fictitious. All of the other characters in the book are not based on any individual either alive or dead. For the avoidance of doubt, Steve Barraclough and Andy Shaw are figments of my imagination and are not based on any British serviceman who served in the South Atlantic campaign in 1982.

*"Operation Plum Duff"* was planned and carried out by the British forces during the Falkland s War but not in the way that it is depicted in this book, *"Operation Mikado"* was planned but the plan was never implemented.

*"The Sheffield Avengers"* is a tale of not just the skill and courage of Britain's Special Forces but also of the relationship between one of Britain's greatest industrial cities, its people and the warship that bore its name.

Tony Barnard
October 2014

www.sheffieldavengers.com

# Characters

## The British
Margaret Thatcher, Prime Minister
William Whitelaw, Home Secretary
John Nott, Defence Secretary
Sir Henry Leach, First Sea Lord
Admiral Sir John Fieldhouse, Commander-in-Chief Fleet
Rear Admiral 'Sandy' Woodward, Task Force Commander
Brigadier Peter De la Billière, Director Special Air Service
Captain Steve Barraclough, Special Air Service
Captain Alan Archer, Special Air Service
Lieutenant Andy Shaw, Special Forces Pilot
Lieutenant Chris Bell, Royal Navy Pilot
Leading Air Crewman Phil Taylor
Jessica Evans, Secretary
Angus McPherson, Royal Marine
Matt Dempsey, SIS Agent
Andrew Devon, Businessman
Sir Patrick Moberley, British Ambassador Tel Aviv

## The Argentines
Lieutenant General Leopoldo Galtieri, President
Admiral Jorge Annaya, Commander-in-Chief Argentine Navy
Brigadier General Basilio Lami Dozo, Commander Argentine Air Force
Philippe de Souza, Argentine Chargé d'Affaires, Paris

## The French
Francois Mitterand, President
Charles Hernu, Defence Minister
Gilles Arnaud, Aerospatiale Contractor

**The Chileans**
General Augusto Pinochet, President
Lieutenant Colonel Marcus Di Maria Prefectura Carabineiros de Chile
Captain Eduardo Suarez, Prefectura Carabineiros de Chile
Paulo Coelho, Farmer
Isabella Coelho, Nurse

**The Russians**
Major Andrei Gordovsky, KGB

**The Israelis**
Menachem Begin, Prime Minister

**The Peruvians**
Fernado Berlaunde Terry, President
Maria Torres, SIS Agent

# Prologue

## Sheffield

The name *Sheffield* is Old English in origin deriving from the River Sheaf whose name is a corruption of *shed* or *sheth*, meaning to divide or separate whilst *Field* is a generic suffix deriving from the Old English *feld*, meaning a forest clearing. It is very likely that the origin of the present-day city of Sheffield is an Anglo-Saxon settlement in a clearing beside the confluence of the rivers Sheaf and Don founded sometime between the arrival of the Anglo-Saxons in this region approximately in the 6th century and the early 9th century.

Sheffield's situation set amongst a number of fast-flowing rivers and streams surrounded by hills containing raw materials such as coal, iron ore, and millstone grit for grindstones - made it an ideal place for water-powered industries to develop. Water wheels were often built for the milling of corn, but many were converted to the manufacture of blades. As early as the 14th century Sheffield was noted for the production of knives as this passage from *"The Reeve's Tale,"* one of *"The Canterbury Tales"* written by Geoffrey Chaucer demonstrates:

*"Ay by his belt he baar a long panade,*
*And of a swerd ful trenchant was the blade.*
*A joly poppere baar he in his pouche;*
*Ther was no man, for peril, dorste hym touche.*
*A Sheffeld thwitel baar he in his hose.*
*Round was his face, and camus was his nose"*

By 1600 Sheffield was the main centre of cutlery production in England outside of London, and in 1624 The Company of Cutlers in Hallamshire was formed to oversee the trade. Around a century later,

3

Daniel Defoe in his book *"A tour thro' the Whole Island of Great Britain*, wrote:

*"This town of Sheffield is very populous and large, the streets narrow, and the houses dark and black, occasioned by the continued smoke of the forges, which are always at work: Here they make all sorts of cutlery-ware, but especially that of edged-tools, knives, razors, axes, and nails; and here the only mill of the sort, which was in use in England for some time was set up for turning their grindstones, though now 'tis grown more common."*

Invention and innovation have always been the hallmarks of Sheffield industry, in the 1740s Benjamin Huntsman, a clock maker in Handsworth, invented a form of the crucible steel process for making a better quality of steel than had previously been available. At around the same time Thomas Boulsover invented a technique for fusing a thin sheet of silver onto a copper ingot producing a form of silver plating that became known as Sheffield Plate. Stainless steel was invented in 1912, at the Firth Brown Laboratories in Sheffield and these and other developments have helped Sheffield to gain a worldwide reputation for steel and in particular for the production of cutlery. The *'Made in Sheffield'* endorsement became a global mark of quality, strength, consistency and craftsmanship. These attributes also apply to the people who are born and grow up in this great city as well as any warship that carries its name.

## HMS Sheffields

The City of Sheffield was late in having a fighting ship named after it. Nottingham's first ship was built in 1703, London's first man-of-war in 1636 and Newcastle's first dated from 1653. However, by 1982 two Royal Navy warships have been named HMS *Sheffield* after the city.

The first, C24 was built by Vickers Armstrong on the Tyne in the North East of England and was launched on 23$^{rd}$ July in 1936. She was a Town Class light cruiser which saw service in World War Two

4

from the Arctic Circle and the Atlantic to the Mediterranean. After the war, the ship underwent a refit which was completed in May 1946 and *Sheffield* then alternated between duties in the West Indies (where in 1954 she served as flagship of the 8th Cruiser Squadron) and in home waters and the Mediterranean. There were further refits in 1949/50 and 1954. She went into reserve in January 1959 and became flagship of the Home Fleet until September 1964, when she was placed on the disposal list. Her equipment was removed at Rosyth in 1967 and was then broken up at Faslane in the same year.

The second ship, D80 is a Type 42 Guided Missile Destroyer laid down by Vickers Shipbuilding and Engineering at Barrow-in-Furness on 15th January 1970, launched by Her Majesty the Queen on 10th June 1971 and commissioned on 16th February 1975. During its construction an explosion killed two dockyard workers and the damaged section of hull was replaced with a section from an identical ship, *ARA Hercules (D28)* which was being built for the Argentine Navy.

D80's motto is *Deo Adjuvante Labor Proficit* or *"With God's help our labour is successful."* Displacing four thousand eight hundred and twenty tonnes, four hundred and ten feet in length and forty seven feet across the beam she carries a complement of two hundred and eighty seven members of crew. The ship is fitted with two Rolls-Royce Olympus Tyne engines which give a cruising speed of eighteen knots and two Rolls-Royce Olympus engines for high speed running at thirty one knots. The ship is armed with the British Aerospace built surface-to-air GWS30 Sea Dart missile system which provides defence against both aircraft and missiles and is also equipped with a 4.5 inch (144mm) Mk.8 gun. In addition, the type 42 was fitted with a helicopter flight deck and hangar which provided it with a potent anti-submarine weapon and significantly extended the destroyer's radar capability.

The principle role of the Sheffield Class Type 42 destroyers is to provide area air defence for a task force and since their introduction into service they have constituted the Royal Navy's principle anti-air warfare capability but they also have the secondary role of confronting surface and anti-submarine targets.

The ships of the Royal Navy have always enjoyed a special relationship with their affiliated towns and cities but without doubt the people of the City of Sheffield have always been at the forefront with their support for their *"Shiny Sheffs."* This tradition started with the first HMS Sheffield which when she sailed from Vickers Walker yard bound for World War Two service, the ship gleamed with stainless steel – a gift from the City of Sheffield. Many of the fittings that would normally have been made of brass were made of stainless steel and manufactured by Sheffield companies. These included railings, stancheons, staghorns and even the ship's bell – the first stainless steel bell to be fitted to a ship and manufactured by Hadfields of Sheffield which now hangs inside Sheffield Cathedral. These additions quickly led to the ship being christened with the affectionate nickname, *"The Shiny Sheff."*

When decommissioned in 1967, many of the stainless steel fittings from the first *Sheffield* were added to the new *Sheffield*, thereby enduring the name, keeping their distinction and thus ensuring that this unique Royal Naval tradition continued into a new era.

## June 1968 Lake District, England

They had travelled by coach from Sheffield. The sixteen boys from Tinsley Secondary Modern School in Sheffield were on an outward bound course in the Lake District staying at the Youth Hostel in Windermere.

For fourteen year old Steve Barraclough it was the first time that he had been away from home. Not that he had any concerns about this as he was a resilient, self assured and outward going lad from a working class family from the Tinsley area of Sheffield in South Yorkshire.

The objective of the trip, the boys had been told by their Headmaster, Paul Davies in the school hall the day before they had departed, was to foster a spirit of competitiveness and achievement through teamwork where individual talents and leadership skills had an opportunity to surface. These life skills would provide a good grounding for them prior to starting their 'O' level or CSE courses in the autumn.

During the week they had learnt to read Ordnance Survey maps, use a compass, to lay and follow trails, how to tie bowline, sheep shank and reef knots and best of all how to light a camp fire and cook sausages and baked jacket potatoes wrapped in aluminium foil. For hours every day they had sailed in Enterprise and Mirror dinghies on Lake Windermere learning how to rig the boat, tack, jibe as well as righting the boat when it capsized by standing on the centreboard and heaving backwards.

The Enterprise was a two-man, sloop-rigged sailing dinghy designed by Jack Holt in 1956 with distinctive blue sails and the Mirror designed by Barry Bucknell in 1962 with its own characteristic red sails. The little yachts with their coloured sails zig-zagging across the lake looked like a scene from *'Swallows and Amazons'*, the well known Arthur Ransome childrens' story set in the Lake District in the period between the two world wars.

The last day, was however, to be the highlight of the trip. The boys were divided into eight teams of two. Steve was partnered with his oldest friend from school, Andy Shaw and the plan was to race the boats around Hen Holme island renamed *'Wild Cat Island'* after the Ransome story, and navigate a course laid out by marker buoys.

The sky was grey and overcast and there was a fresh breeze across the lake and at the half way stage Steve and Andy were in second position. All they had to do was to tack around the marker buoy and head for the finish but as Steve released the rudder to 'go about' so he could catch the wind on the other side of the boat when a sudden strong gust caught the sail and the boom swung round fiercely catching Andy on the right side of his face just under the temple and in that instant the boat capsized and their world turned black.

Steve surfaced coughing and spluttering in the cold water and looked for Andy so that they could both stand on the centreboard and haul the sail out of the water as they had been trained to right the boat. *Where was Andy?* Steve searched frantically around him but there was no sign of him on the surface.

*"He must still be underneath the water"* he said to himself as he desperately tried to lift the sodden, heavy blue sail to see if his friend was trapped underneath but there was no sign of him. Steve started to panic and although still choking and feeling sick he duck-dived back down into the dark water and under the upturned boat.

The visibility was practically zero but he could sense someone frantically kicking and struggling in the upturned hull of the boat. He lunged forward, his own lungs starting to hurt. He felt the body shape in front of him and grabbed it around the waist and pulled with all his strength and in doing so he freed the left foot that had become trapped behind the oar that was secured on the inside of the boat. Clasping his friend in a bear hug he kicked furiously upwards his own energy sapping but the grip on his friend remained firm. The two of them broke the surface and still Steve did not let go as he trod water furiously until a few seconds later two strong arms lifted Andy clear of the water into the instructor's vessel where he was immediately laid horizontal, his airways cleared and breath blown into his deflated lungs. Steve hauled himself out of the water and sat shivering at the back of the boat as the instructor worked on his stricken friend.

Suddenly Andy started coughing wildly and bringing up a large amount of water and the instructor relaxed as he moved him into a sitting position, took his own jacket off and placed it around his shoulders. As the instructor took control of the idling outboard motor and made for the shore, Andy turned to look at Steve and spluttered:

*"We'll always be mates Steve. I just hope that sometime in our lives I have the chance to pay you back for what you have done for me today."*

8

# 1982 Argentina

It had been going on for six years now. The Guerra Sucia or the *'Dirty War.'* Kidnapping, murder, torture these were the tools of the state sponsored violence carried out by the Argentine government on its own population.

People, some opponents of the government and innocent others, simply 'disappeared' in the middle of the night never to be seen again. Three years ago Amnesty International had claimed that fifteen thousand citizens had been abducted, tortured and possibly killed.

The military junta had seized power from Isabel Peron and was determined to repress any criticism of its regime. The *junta*, which dubbed itself "National Reorganization Process", systematized the repression, in particular through the way of "forced disappearances" (*desaparecidos*), which made it very difficult to launch law suits as the bodies were never found.

The Generals organised a nationwide system, from an overall national scale to a very local one, to track down the so-called "subversives." The regime had regularly used physicians in the interrogation and torture sessions of the individuals captured in this sweeping net.

Life was hard and miserable for the ordinary Argentinean citizen and the economy was in a precarious position. In 1981 inflation rocketed to over 600%, the gross domestic product fell by 11.4%, manufacturing output by 22.9% and wages by 19.2%. Tension and popular protest was rising and the trades unions were gathering support for a crippling general strike. The junta realised that they had to deflect this criticism of their regime and unite the population behind a patriotic and populist cause. The seeds of catastrophe were sown.

# 1982 Great Britain

It was a symbolic number. Three million people. The largest number of unemployed since the 1930's. For over two years the recession had deepened overseen by Margaret Thatcher's Government. Thatcher's political and economic philosophy emphasised reduced state intervention, free markets, and entrepreneurialism. She wished to end what she felt was excessive government interference in the economy. Influenced by monetarist thinking as espoused by Milton Friedman, she began her economic reforms by increasing interest rates to try to slow the growth of the money supply and thereby lower inflation. She also placed limits on the printing of money and legal restrictions on trade unions, in her quest to tackle inflation and trade union disputes, which had bedevilled the UK economy throughout the 1970s. In accordance with her anti-interventionist views, she introduced cash limits on public spending and reduced expenditures on social services.

These policies had started to attract criticism from some followers of the previous Conservative leader, Ted Heath in the Cabinet the so-called "wets", expressed doubt over Thatcher's "dry" policies.' However, the Prime minister was as resolute as she always had been. For example, on 19 January 1976 she had made a speech in Kensington Town Hall in which she made a scathing attack on the Soviet Union stating that the Russians were bent on world dominance. She had said that the men in the Soviet Politburo do not have to worry about the ebb and flow of public opinion. They put guns before butter, while we put just about everything before guns. In response, the Soviet Defence Ministry newspaper *Krasnaya Zvezda* (*Red Star*) gave her the nickname "Iron Lady" which soon became synonymous with her image.

Civil unrest in Britain resulted in the British media discussing the need for a policy u-turn. At the Conservative Party conference on 10th October 1980 held in Brighton, Thatcher addressed the issue directly, armed with a speech written by the playwright Ronald Millar which included the lines:

*"You turn if you want to. The lady's not for turning." I say that not only to you but to our friends overseas and also to those who are not our friends."*

Following the 1981 Defence Review, the Royal Navy's amphibious capabilities had started to be downgraded. In addition following Foreign Office advice, the Royal Navy's ice patrol ship, HMS Endurance along with forty four Royal marines of naval party 8901, the garrison ashore in the islands were withdrawn. These two naval units may have been small numerically but there were hugely important symbolically and consequently they inadvertently sent the wrong message to unfriendly people watching from the mainland.

The stage was, therefore, set.

# Chapter One

## Saturday 1st May 1982: Falkland Sound

It was definitely getting worse. The rain was relentless now being pounded against the toughened glass windows by the biting South Atlantic wind. Rear Admiral John Forster 'Sandy' Woodward stared out from the bridge at the darkening skies overhead. His location in the glass-fronted Admiral's bridge meant that he could exercise strategic control over the fleet without interfering in the Captain's tactical command of the vessel. He was fifty years old and in command of the South Atlantic Task Force of sixty five Royal Naval and Fleet Auxiliary surface ships under the Commander-in-Chief Admiral Sir John Fieldhouse who was based at Northwood in West London and who controlled the submarines in theatre directly from there by satellite. The task force contained the two light aircraft carriers *HMS Hermes* and *HMS Invincible*, over twenty destroyers and frigates and a host of support vessels carrying a British brigade with full equipment.

Huge crowds had turned out to cheer them on their way in that early April morning in an outpouring of patriotic fervour. Not since the 1956 invasion of Suez had such a massive British force set out to sea. Also watching the event with interest was a man in dark glasses from the Secretariá Inteligencia del Estado (Argentine Security Intelligence Service) from the Argentine Embassy in London.

As they left the harbour Woodward had observed the crowds from his bridge vantage point on *HMS Hermes*, waving Union Jack flags and cheering and one banner attached to the port wall caught his eye:

*"Good luck navy – give 'em hell"*

He had thought then and still thought now that they had no idea what was install for them. This was without doubt a bold and courageous endeavour but one that was full of risk and uncertainty.

They had just entered the waters around the Falkland Islands after steaming south from Ascension Island with the Total Exclusion Zone being imposed by London the day before. They had been tracked all the way from the Bay of Biscay to the equator by Soviet trawlers, TU-95 'Bear' reconnaissance and intelligence gathering aircraft and spy satellites in polar orbit that were all undoubtedly providing photographic reconnaissance and intelligence to the Argentines. Sometimes the aircraft would fly as low as thirty to forty metres above the Royal Navy vessels. The communist superpower had decided to overlook the differences of ideology by aiding such a right wing regime to further their own cause.

*"Such is realpolitik"* thought Woodward.

Meanwhile on Ascension Island at about 22.50 local time, the evening before, eleven fully laden Victor tankers of 55 and 57 Squadrons took to the air accompanied by two Vulcan bombers. The number of tankers was required to deliver fuel to one aircraft which would be making the flight all the way to Port Stanley Airport three thousand eight hundred and eighty six miles away, the equivalent of London to Karachi, to deliver its load of twenty one, one thousand pound medium capacity bombs on the airfield. At the controls of Vulcan XM607 was Flight Lieutenant Martin Withers of 101 Squadron, flying the reserve Vulcan.

As they climbed to cruising altitude it became clear that there was a problem with the lead Vulcan. They could not pressurise the cockpit, which was essential to reach the cruising altitudes necessary to reach the Falkland Islands and complete their mission. When told that they had the lead of the mission, a long silence fell over the cockpit which was only broken by Martin Withers words:

*"It looks like we've got a job of work fellas."*

At 04.30 the air around Port Stanley Airport was ripped by the detonation of XM607's twenty one bombs hitting the airfield. Their job done XM607 and its crew flew north on the return leg of its epic mission. Withers had decided for security reasons not to contact the British fleet below instead he radioed with great satisfaction the one word message that meant the success of '*Black Buck 1*':

*"Superfuse."*

Woodward's gaze fell to the swelling sea. Dark, inky blue, the freezing water would kill a man within minutes, *"Bloody weather"* he murmured under his breath. His ships had been arranged in a fairly standard formation. and he had fielded a picket line of three Type 42 guided missile destroyers which were relatively small ships each displacing about 4,000 tonnes. On the right was *HMS Coventry,* out to the left was *HMS Sheffield* and in the centre lay *HMS Glasgow* with the three ships presenting a very wide surface-to-air missile defensive front.

The role of a picket ship was to be the first line of defence and to protect the task force. The principle being that if an incoming enemy aircraft 'popped up' and got a contact, the odds were that the pilots would release their missiles at the first ship they caught on their radar screen. Being a picket ship was a calculated risk and they were almost entirely dependent on their own missile and self-defence systems to survive an attack.

Approximately eighteen miles to the east of the picket line lay the second line of defence, the frigates *Arrow, Yarmouth* and *Alacrity* and the big but older, destroyer *Glamorgan.* Behind this second screen lay the two carriers protected by their own 'goalkeepers' as he called them; two Type 22 frigates whose primary roles was to provide close anti-aircraft defence. *Invincible* had *Brilliant* and through the mist and squall Woodward could make out the unmistakable shape of his watchman, *HMS Broadsword* like a grey ghost appearing through the squall. Both *Brilliant* and *Broadsword* had been fitted with the new anti-missile system Sea Wolf, the Royal Navy's only point-defence weapon system. During trials the system

14

had actually hit the high velocity 4.5 inch shell being used as a target so in theory with a maximum velocity of Mach 2, the Argentine anti-ship missiles should be a far easier prey.

News of the success of the Vulcan raid had been relayed to him from Northwood. Whilst the first raid had not put the airfield out of action it undoubtedly had a huge psychological impact on the Argentines as it demonstrated that Buenos Aires itself or any mainland target was within the striking capability of British land-based aircraft.

The twenty three thousand tonne *HMS Hermes* commissioned in 1959 had been due to be decommissioned next year after a Government defence review but the outbreak of hostilities with Argentina had changed all that and she was now the flagship of the British task force that had set sail from Portsmouth just twenty five days before. The ship was carrying eight British Aerospace Sea Harrier FRS.Mk1 jets of the Royal Navy Fleet Air Arm, four Harrier GR.Mk.3 jets of the Royal Air Force and ten Sea King MkIV and MkV helicopters.

Woodward looked left out of the bridge windows and could just see the *Invincible* with its distinctive ski slope flight deck. *HMS Invincible* was under the very capable command of Captain JJ Black and carried 801 Naval Air Squadron consisting of eight Sea Harriers of the Fleet Air Arm. *Invincible* had been built in Barrow-in-Furness by Vickers Shipbuilding and Engineering and commissioned in 1980.

It was only in February, a few months earlier, after several months of negotiation, that the Australian Government announced that it had agreed to buy *Invincible* for £171 million as a replacement, under the name *HMAS Australia* for the Royal Australian Navy's *HMAS Melbourne*. However, the Argentine invasion of the islands had changed all of that.

*"Two aircraft platforms"'* thought Woodward:

*"It wasn't really enough to provide the vital air cover and he knew it. There was no margin for loss. The success of the campaign lay in protecting the two carriers.* The sixty five naval vessels *of the British task force huddled in Falkland Sound would be 'sitting ducks' without the necessary protection provided from the air."*

*"It is all about air cover. We shall be entirely dependent on the Sea Harriers and, no, we have not really got enough."* said the Chief of the Naval Staff, Sir Henry Leach in the Prime Minister's office on the evening of Wednesday 31$^{st}$ March just four weeks earlier. He had been waiting in the corridor for fifteen minutes. He usually strode around Whitehall in a business suit but this time, just back from an official engagement in Portsmouth, he was waiting outside the Prime Minister's office in the House of Commons dressed in full naval uniform. Inside, as the Argentine fleet sailed towards the Falkland Islands, Margaret Thatcher discussed the impending invasion with a small number of Defence and Foreign Office officials, including the Secretary of State for Defence, John Nott. As they carefully weighed the options available to them they learnt that the Admiral was waiting outside. Leach, a straight-talking, forceful personality was ushered in.

*"But can we do it"* pressed the Prime Minister, her blue-grey eyes piercing into his face. Leach was quiet, calm and confident in his simple reply: *"I believe that we can retake the islands."*

There was no one in the Royal Navy in 1982 that had a better understanding of the dangers of operating ships far from home without air cover than the First Sea Lord. Despite his own background as a gunnery officer, he had discovered a keen interest in naval aviation particularly as personal tragedy had had a deep effect on him. On 10$^{th}$ December 1941, his father John Leach, Captain of the battleship, *Prince of Wales* was killed when his ship capsized and sunk together with the battlecruiser *Repulse* after being hit by bombs and torpedoes fired by just eight Japanese Mitsubishi G3M Naval Type 96 strike aircraft. It was only when eleven Royal Air Force Brewster Buffalo fighters scrambled from Sembawang airfield in

Singapore entered the fray and deterred another wave of Japanese attacks that further catastrophe was avoided.

Leach then added simply: *"And we must!"*
*"Why,"* replied the Prime Minister quizzically.
*"Because if we don't do that, in a few months we will be living in a different country whose word will count for little."*

She looked up at him and her lips momentarily pursed into a thin smile. He went on to inform her confidently and assertively that a task force led by the two aircraft carriers *Hermes* and *Invincible* with destroyers, frigates, landing craft and support vessels could be ready within forty eight hours with her permission.

*"Then make the necessary preparations."*

When Leach and the others had departed the Prime Minister took a sip of the glass of whisky and soda with no ice that was on her desk. It was *Bell's* her favourite brand, and she contemplated deeply. What she had omitted to tell the Naval Chief and the Defence Secretary, was that the President of the USA, Ronald Reagan had telephoned her earlier that day to convey the belief of the US Navy that they considered a counter-invasion by the British to be *'a military impossibility.'*

That had only been thirty days earlier. Since then the task force had been assembled at break neck speed with instructions to make for Ascension Island as soon as possible. No more had that frenetic activity been more prevalent than in Portsmouth, one of the great naval towns of the British Isles. Amongst the masts, cranes and towers that filled the horizon, crowds had been watching quietly for the last few days as convoys of trucks rolled through the dockyard gates in a constant stream of activity. Red flags fluttered at the top of the masts of the ships that were in the process of being loaded with munitions. The flight decks of the two operational British aircraft carriers were cleared to receive the squadrons of the Fleet Air Arm's Sea Harriers and Sea King helicopters.

Over the weekend of 3<sup>rd</sup> and 4<sup>th</sup> April, apart from the hectic efforts of the Royal Navy and all the dockyard workers, effectively the whole army in southern England had been mobilised to move the war reserves to the Fleet. A key role in doing this had been played by The Territorial Army in transporting equipment and stores to Devonport and Portsmouth. It had taken just three days to assemble the task force which was now setting out from Portsmouth harbour on 5<sup>th</sup> April. The ships' crews lined the deck sides to face the now vast throngs of flag-waving, cheering people – friends, relatives and well-wishers all gathered to bid them goodbye and good luck. As the strains of bands playing *'Rule Britannia'* started to fade, Robin Warman of BBC Radio Solent reported:

*"I have been reporting on naval matters for several years and it was remarkable to see ships, many of which were on the point of being scrapped, being restored and readied for war by workers, some of whom had redundancy notices in their back pockets. Whatever the rights and wrongs of the conflict, it was a real feat to get the Task Force together to win a war eight thousand miles away."*

Three days after the departure of the aircraft carriers and amid similar scenes of high emotion, 3 Commando Brigade sailed from Southampton aboard the government-requisitioned cruise liner, *Canberra*. Since the disbandment of 16 Parachute Brigade in 1974, 3 Commando Brigade was Britain's only thoroughly trained and prepared all-arms force capable of carrying out immediate amphibious operations. The use of the forty five thousand tonne cruise liner *Canberra* was ideal for the troops as she alone would be able to transport some four thousand men in much greater comfort than any ordinary troopship. During the voyage down south significant changes were made to the vessel, carpets were ripped up and glued to the windows to prevent light from showing at night, the ship was fitted out so that refuelling could be carried out whilst at sea, gun emplacements were fitted around the ship including Blowpipe missiles and they were carrying out submarine avoidance practice at regular intervals.

Almost immediately the troops began training exercises and weapons drills on the deck. *Canberra* had a Promenade Deck that was possible to run around and this was used by the troops to keep themselves fit in combat gear with their full packs on. The Promenade Deck had a composite cement surface on top of the steel so it was a bit like rubber and would flex but after a week of a couple of thousand soldiers running over it in combat boots it became more like a sandy beach. As the task force steamed south towards the Falkland Islands, the military made full use of the ship's facilities. There were two restaurants aboard, the first class restaurant was reserved for officers and the other was used by everyone else. All meals were served on pressed trays but there were no complaints about the food as it was significantly better than they were all used to. Different bars became pubs for different levels of troops and morale was being regularly boosted with quiz nights, tugs of war and other competitive games on decks between different divisions.

Whilst all the preparations by the British armed forces had been going on, frantic diplomatic efforts were taking place with the American Secretary of State, Alexander Haig undergoing torturous but clumsy and confusing rounds of shuttle diplomacy. The Argentines however were proving to be intransigent. The military junta led by General Leopoldo Galtieri was in a corner. The administration had only been in office for four months but was already hugely unpopular. The economy was in deep trouble. Throughout the previous year inflation had sky-rocketed to over 600 percent, GDP was down 11.4 percent, manufacturing down by 22.9 percent and wages in real terms by 19.2 percent. Within Argentina the junta calculated that the recovery of the 'Malvinas' as they called the islands would not stifle internal dissent but at least it would unite the nation for a time. It would serve as a vindication of military rule and cleanse the reputation of the armed forces after the horrors of the *'dirty war.'*

For now, the gamble had seemed to pay off. Since the invasion of the islands codenamed *Operación Rosario,* the anti–junta demonstrations had been replaced by fervent patriotic supportive crowds. Galtieri was now riding the wave of popular support; his military adventure to capture the Malvinas had been successful and had caught the public's imagination and deflected them from their everyday grievances. Only last night the crowds outside the Casa Rosada in the Plaza de Mayo had stayed half the night chanting with ecstatic delight *"Argentina! Argentina! 'Viva Malvinas.'* With the noise reaching a crescendo Galtieri beaming from ear to ear had stepped outside onto a balcony and waved to the crowds below. It was reminiscent of the scenes in Buenos Aires when Argentina had last won the FIFA World Cup in 1978.

There was no going back now. Argentine reinforcements were flooding into the islands on a daily basis. At the army's main staging centre in the port of Comodro Rivada-via, six hundred miles west of the Falklands, the soldiers continued to arrive, one company after another, bundled up in their padded, dark olive winter uniforms. In addition, the Argentine rulers had ordered their only aircraft carrier, the *Veinticinco de Mayo* and most of the rest of the fleet out of Puerto Belgrano in anticipation of a British blockade. The *Veinticinco de May*, with the English translation of $25^{th}$ of May which is the date of Argentina's May Revolution in 1810 had previously served in the Royal Navy as *HMS Venerable* and the Royal Netherlands Navy as *HNLMS Karel Doorman*. The ship had been built by Cammell Laird in Birkenhead during the Second World War for the Royal Navy as a *Colossus-class* aircraft carrier but only saw three years service before being sold to the Dutch.

On the long twelve day journey South from Ascension Island to the Total Exclusion Zone, the two hundred mile radius around the islands, Woodward had studied the aerial threat arraigned against his fleet. Intelligence gleaned from Jane's *'Al the World's Fighting Aircraft'* indicated that the Argentine Air Force had already taken delivery of five Super Etendard aircraft armed with Exocet air-to-surface missiles. This aircraft weapons system represented the most serious threat to the Task Force ships and it was fairly obvious that these valuable and limited resources would certainly be targeted against the two carriers. Although the Super Etendard was capable of air-to-air refuelling which would extend its maximum effective range easily, this would make it too vulnerable a target and therefore the best 'threat reduction' tactic lay in ensuring that both *Hermes* and *Invincible* remained a minimum of four hundred miles from the Argentine mainland. He was also acutely aware as were the commanders back in Northwood that unless Port Stanley was retaken by mid-June, logistical constraints and the weather would combine to prevent the British troops from completing their mission although there was little talk in public about the gruelling timetable, in case the enemy could deploy significant delaying measures, the clock was ticking relentlessly against him and his task force.

Two hours later Woodward's Task Force found himself in the middle of a major attack by the Argentine Air Force, the Fuerza Aérea Argentina or FAA. They were anchored about seventy nautical miles to the east of Port Stanley. This was a deliberate tactic that would increase the distance for the attacking aircraft by about one hundred and fifty miles putting them at the absolute limit of their fuel range and preventing the use of afterburners which would have given the Mirages and Daggers a huge speed advantage over the subsonic Harriers.

Waves of strike aircraft covered by interceptors had begun to attack the British ships. The FAA clearly intended to launch almost all of its strike force into action today. The first two flights of fighters ingressed at medium altitude but failed to find the British force, reached their 'bingo' fuel limits and had to turn back. However, now the Argentines had found their targets and were pressing forward with their ongoing attacks.

Sir Henry Leach's assessment had been correct thought Woodward, *'It was all about air cover. We have got only two platforms both of them, pitching and rolling in these fierce seas – their presence was paramount to the mission."*

He had stated earlier in a conversation with his superiors at Northwood: *"Loose Invincible and the operation is severely jeopardised, lose Hermes and the operation is over. One unlucky torpedo, bomb or missile hit, even a simple but major accident on board, could do it."*

It was this very uncomforting thought that now occupied his mind. He was only too aware that if Hermes or Invincible was hit the Royal Navy would be publicly disgraced and that he would almost certainly be court-martialled whether 'important enough' to take all the blame or not. If one was lost the British expeditionary force would be doomed because the jets could only stay in the air for a limited time period before needing refuelling.

He knew it would be sometime before a third carrier would be available. *HMS Illustrious* was being rushed to completion at the giant Swan Hunter shipbuilding yard on the Tyne. Teams of shipyard workers were working around the clock to complete the fitting out process so that she could commence sea trials. He was also aware that the other British commando carrier, an earlier sister ship of *Hermes, HMS Bulwark*, that was laid up in No.3 basin Portsmouth Dockyard had undergone a survey to assess her suitability for deployment and work had already started to take her out of mothballs.

*'It could all take weeks, maybe months'* thought Woodward
*"And by that time the war could be over."*

Still things were going well. The ageing Skyhawks although being flown with great skill and bravery by the young pilots of the Argentine Air Force, were technically inferior to the Sea Harriers of *Hermes* and *Invincible a*nd they would endeavour not to engage them in a 'dog fight. Argentina was the first foreign user of the Skyhawk in it s different variants and they had received over two hundred of them since 1965. However, the United States had placed an embargo since 1977 under the Carter Administration due to the *'Dirty War'* which covered not only spare parts but the sale of arms and training of its military personnel. Therefore, by 1982 they were ageing and many had been cannibailsed to keep the forty eight in the air that were deploying against the British. Many of these were not operating with one hundred percent functionality with a number of mechanical faults and the ejector seats were simply not working but despite these defects and the lack of electronic or missile defence, they could still prove to be a dangerous opponent.

Lined up against them were the twenty British Aerospace Sea Harries of the Fleet Air Arm. They had only been in service for two years and this was to prove a real 'baptism by fire.' The Sea Harrier was a modified Harrier 'Jump Jet' featuring a slightly different cockpit layout and the Blue Fox multimode radar, something that other versions of the Harrier did not possess. Overall the Harrier was a more technically advanced aircraft than anything that the FAA had available. Although it only had a short range, it could fly combat air patrol (CAP) over the fleet for forty to sixty minutes, a significant time advantage over the Argentine attackers, who had at best, only a few minutes to find and engage their targets. Woodward had decided that during the hours of daylight his task force would try to maintain continuous CAP coverage over the fleet with two Harriers armed with AIM-9 Sidewinder air-to-air missiles. He was well aware however, that with the limited number of Harriers available until reinforcements arrived on the two cargo vessels *Atlantic Conveyor* and *Atlantic Causeway* which had been requisitioned by the UK government, the Argentine's best tactic was to strike the fleet while the Harriers were diverted or on deck refuelling.

The British pilots knew that the Sea Harrier fights best low and slow. With its huge manoeuvrability advantage, it can stop in midair, hover and then veer off sharply in new directions. The Sea Harrier was able to outmanoeuvre the Argentinean conventional aircraft by using a technique known as 'viffing' (from vector in forward flight). By adjusting his exhaust nozzles to reverse the thrust, the pilot can cause the plane to experience a 2g deceleration and veer to the side creating the impression of stopping at twelve thousand feet! In combat situations, a sudden 'viff' was causing the pursuing Argentinean fighter to overshoot and so from being the attacking aircraft it becomes the attacked as it 'leapfrogs' over the Sea Harrier. Once in front of them, the British Harrier pilots were able to rely on sophisticated electronics to make the kill. The forward-and-down-looking nose-mounted Ferranti 'Blue Fox' radar system spots the target at distances of up to forty miles and a TV-like display screen on the windscreen flashes the computerised tracking data that tells the pilot when to fire. The Sea Harriers were carrying the latest version of the Sidewinder air-to-air missiles. The AIM-9 which has a wide-angle 'boresight' – the pilot only has to aim in the general direction of his target, within forty degrees and press a button. The missile does the rest, homing in on the target with an infra-red sensor that detects the enemy's hot engine or exhaust nozzle.

Woodward had seen two confirmed kills already today by his Harriers flying CAP with the two stricken Argentine jets trailing black smoke quartering down into the ocean beyond the horizon. They had been vectored in by controllers on HMS Glamorgan and the pilots had decided to perform the hook manoeuvre which comprised of the lead aircraft flying head-on to the target and the wingman to split and swing around to attack the targets from the rear. Standing beside Woodward on the flight deck was the BBC correspondent Brian Hanrahan with his distinctive yellow headphones recording a report that would be despatched for the nightly news back home. *"I counted them all out and I counted them all back again"* shouted Hanrahan into the microphone through the gusting wind. Woodward smiled because he knew that this clever piece of journalism had got the journalist around the reporting restrictions placed by military intelligence, so that he could say that all the British Harrier jets had returned safely without saying how many there were.

Overall, the day had gone well thought Woodward. The task force had lost no planes and suffered only minor damage to one ship. He sipped the steaming mug of tea that had been handed to him by his personal Leading Steward.

*"Bloody weather"* he muttered."

# Chapter 2

## Sheffield, South Yorkshire: 1961 – 1972

Steve Barraclough and Andy Shaw had always been close.

They started school together at Tinsley County Infants and Junior School in September 1961 looking smart in their slightly oversized blazers and crisp white shirts and blue and yellow striped ties as they followed their mothers down the cobbled street from their terrace houses in the same street where there was constant struggle to keep the windows clean because they quickly became stained bright orange form fumes from the steelworks.

The terraced houses were the classic two up - two down built in the mid 19$^{th}$ century that were so common to the working class areas of cities across the country particularly in the north and midlands. Both Steve's and Andy's followed the usual model. You walked in off the street into the front room and directly facing you was a door to the back room. The stairs ran from the very back of the second room up to a small landing and the two upstairs rooms, one of which had been divided to take a bath room. In both their houses and many of their neighbours, almost all the original features had gone and so it was impossible to know what the downstairs fireplaces had been like, the design of the range or even the doors, for all of them including the front door had that 1950s makeover which involved a sheet of hardboard which was nailed on. Outside at the rear was a yard with a lavatory and beside it a gate to the alley.

Both Steve's and Andy's house had a best room at the front and all the rooms downstairs had a square of carpet, with lino which stretched to all the corners of the room. Upstairs there was only a rug to put your feet on when you got out of bed, the rest being bare floorboards. In winter the curtains would stick to the old sash windows, especially when it had been snowing. Steve would often sit on his bed with his elbows pushing against the window staring outside at the frosty bank and frozen canal glittering under the bright moonlight. The only warmth was his paisley pyjamas and the one hot water bottle that he shared with his brother, Paul.

They both followed Sheffield Wednesday. They didn't really have any choice as both their families had always been 'Wednesday' supporters rather than Sheffield United or *The Blades;* their bitter enemies from across the city and rivals in the steel city derby. Sheffield Wednesday is the only football club in the English league with a day of the week in their name. The club was initially a cricket club named *'The Wednesday Cricket Club'* after the day of the week on which they played their matches. The footballing side of the club was established to keep the team together and fit during the winter months. The reason the games were played on a Wednesday was due to the team being formed by local butchers who had a half day finishing on a Wednesday. The club was formerly known as "The Wednesday Football Club" until 1929, when the club was officially renamed "Sheffield Wednesday Football Club."

Steve and Andy both enjoyed a passion for motor bikes. From the age of fourteen they had managed to acquire and store an old BSA Bantam 125cc which was no longer roadworthy in an old shed on the perimeter of the giant Tinsley railway marshalling yards. The two of them would ride the bike secretly around the waste ground often falling off and suffering grazed knees and elbows which they passed off as street football injuries to enquiring parents.

They both shared a love of rock music. At the age of sixteen they saw *Jethro Tull* supported by *Procol Harum* at The City Hall, and also *Pink Floyd* and Alvin Lee's *Ten Years After* at the same venue. Also in February of that year they had travelled to Leeds by train to see *The Who* in the refectory at the University. They had underestimated the popularity of the gig and the three hour queue to get in and ended up like many others who failed and took to the roof of the building that evening to hear and feel the music. The album *"The Who Live At Leeds"* that was released soon after became Steve's all time favourite and *Live at Leeds* became a critical smash,

26

with Steve hearing on *BBC Radio One* later that year that *The New York Times* had acclaimed it as: *"The best live rock album ever made."*

Despite their shared upbringing in the same neighbourhood and shared interests they were very different characters. Steve was physically larger and stronger from a very young age and was always the one to get into scrapes in the playground and in the street whilst Andy was quieter and had few friends other than Steve and kept himself out of trouble preferring to sit and read during the breaks in the school day.

One afternoon after school Steve had been playing for the school football team at another school across the city and was walking back through the park as he had spent the bus fare on some chocolate. He was still wearing his school blazer but not the tie which had been roughly shoved into his duffle bag with his football kit. Suddenly he heard a shout behind him: *"There's a Tinsley tosser"*

He instantly knew that this meant trouble but something kept him from running but he didn't remember making a conscious decision to stay. They soon arrived and quickly crowded around him, six or seven boys about his own age, pushing and shoving him between them but Steve didn't say a word. The first punch came then it quickly escalated into a frenzy of kicks and punches. He tried to cover himself as the blows rained down, it seemed to go on forever but it was probably less than a minute.

*"Go on leg it"* said one of them but Steve just stood there his hands trembling and trying to ignore the bruises which were no doubt all over him They then ran away laughing and Steve started to walk on but then he heard shouts and the sound of running. *"Oh shit they're coming back"* he said to himself.

Again he refused to run and he tried to protect himself as the kicks and punches came in with even more force this time. There was a general effort to get him on the ground and although Steve couldn't really defend himself he backed up against a wall and had no intention of going down and eventually the attackers grew tired of the assault and finally ran off.

Steve arrived home battered and shaken with some of his clothes torn but he was not crying. He felt like it but he didn't. He was bleeding from cuts and scrapes all over and his lips were cut and swollen in several places and his right eye was starting to swell up nastily. When he entered the house everyone was out so he cleaned himself up in the bathroom the best that he could and he would tell his mother that the football game had been rough and badly refereed and that his blazer had got ripped climbing over a fence. She would go mad and mend it but that would be the end of it.

The following morning, although he was stiff and bruised he did go to school. It was his first lesson that the body can actually take a good deal of punishment. As he walked down the road he recognised one of his assailants from the previous day coming the other way. About twenty yards away he recognised him. He was alone and Steve felt strangely superior to him. If he and five or six of his mates could not break me then what chance did he have on his own? He must have come to the same conclusion because he suddenly ran across the road through the busy traffic to avoid him but Steve ran after him and cornered him against a fence. Without hesitation he hit him hard in the stomach and as he bent over he brought his knee up sharply into his face splitting his nose and then he hit him on the back of the head and the lad crumpled to the ground. He then put his shoe into a muddy puddle and stamped on the back of the boy's blazer as he lay face down, a process that he repeated three or four times.

*"Tell your mates that this is a message from the Tinsley tosser"* he said as he calmly turned and walked away.

Despite their closeness, Andy had one overriding ambition that he did not share with his best friend; in fact Steve was fed up of him talking about it. Ever since he could remember he had wanted to fly. He had a single minded desire that bordered on obsession to become a fighter pilot. His father, Tom had been in the Royal Air Force

28

during the war as an engineer working on Spitfires stationed at RAF Eshott near Felton in Northumberland from 1942-1945; home of 57 OTU, where its role was to turn newly-qualified pilots into finely-honed fighters.

Tom had enthralled his young lad with tales about the twenty to twenty-two year old men from all nationalities who were all trained at Eshott. Despite the fact that many young pilots never made it home due to the high accident rate at the time, bravado, courage, determination and competition was rife amongst the budding Spitfire pilots. Tom had also taken Andy to RAF Finningley near Doncaster throughout the 1960's to watch the Battle of Britain re-enactment airshows and although Steve had joined them on more than one occasion he often confided to his friend that it was a bit boring.

*"Bored! "How can you be bored?"* Andy had shouted incredulously at Steve one year against the deafening noise of a BAC Lightning which broke the sound barrier as it screamed over the crowds during a display. Steve just shrugged his shoulders and thought about who *'The Owls'* were playing that afternoon.

At another show in the late 1960's Andy witnessed a Vulcan scramble when six of the unmistakable V bombers took off one after the other and the ground literally vibrated as did all his internal organs. The Avro Vulcan was a four-engined nuclear bomber based on a delta wing concept. It became the cornerstone of Britain's independent nuclear deterrent against the Soviet Union prior to the introduction of the Polaris Missile submarines which passed the responsibility for nuclear deterrence to the Royal Navy from the RAF in late 1969.

Andy had therefore decided to join the Air Training Corps (ATC) at the age of thirteen something Steve could not understand and had no intention of joining with him. The ATC was a British cadet organisation sponsored by the Royal Air Force and supported by the Ministry of Defence. Andy took part himself in all the activities including sport, hill walking, parade drill and rifle shooting. But it was the flying experience that he craved and as soon as he was old enough he undertook the elementary flying training at a local Volunteer Gliding Squadron in Air Cadet gliders.

Steve's father, Alan, had been born in the Attercliffe district of Sheffield. He and his brother Frank were *"Cliffe Kids."* He had served in the army during the war. He had been a *Desert Rat* serving in the British 7th Armoured Division in North Africa. He had fought in all of the major battles in the North African campaign culminating in the second battle of El Alamein when the British forces under the command of Lieutenant-General Bernard Montgomery delivered a decisive defeat to the German Afrika Korps commanded by Field Marshall Ewin Rommel.

After being 'demobbed' he had returned to Sheffield and joined the firm of Viners, the celebrated cutlery manufacturing business based in a large five storey factory in Broomhall Street where he had now completed over twenty years service. The company had been started by Adolphe Viener in 1901 who had emigrated to Sheffield from Germany. One of his sons, Ruben Viener, became the driving force and the firm prospered in the 1960's with a modern factory in Sheffield and subsidiaries in Ireland, France and Australia.

The stamp on the cutlery *'Made in Sheffield'* was synonymous with craftsmanship together with enduring and consistent quality. However, as the business grew, far eastern imports, initially of a far inferior quality but at a price that substantially undercut domestically produced goods, started to flood in to the UK from the mid 1970's. There was now a chill wind of change and uncertainty blowing through the Sheffield steel industries and even the famous name of Viners was not immune to it.

On one wet Tuesday March night in 1971 Andy's dream was shattered. They had been three of them, Andy in the lead on his 1962 Norton Navigator 350cc twin, followed by Steve on his Triumph Tiger 90 350cc with the bright yellow petrol tank, twin Amal carburettors with chrome bell mouths and upswept twin chrome megaphone exhausts. It was typical of Steve thought Andy to make as much noise and visual presence as he could particularly accelerating the bike as it passed by the bus stop outside the school where lines of fellow pupils waited on a daily basis. Bringing up the rear was another school friend, Ricky riding his slower Lambretta LD 150cc Scooter.

Andy's bike however was in pristine condition. On passing his test his father had bought him the bike which had been in various boxes of bits from Syd Smith's motorcycles in Attercliffe Common in the city for his seventeenth birthday. Tom had promptly stripped it completely down in the garden shed and had rebuilt it to factory standards using his engineering skills. To be honest he confided to Andy's mother that: *"It had been a labour of love really"*

Norton was Andy's father Tom's favourite manufacturer. To him it embodied all that was excellent about the British motorcycle industry. He had come to love the marque during the war years when he used to ride RAF Norton machines around the air base at RAF Eshott collecting and delivering spare parts for the Spitfires that they were repairing or servicing. .Launched in 1960 at the Earls Court Motorcycle Show the Norton Navigator was a development of the Norton Jubilee. As well as bring bored out to 349cc it also gained the Norton Roadholder front forks with eight inch brakes to replace the Jubilee's lightweight front end. The down tube on the frame was also stiffened to improve handling and deal with the power increase to 22bhp at 7,000rpm. The bike would however remain as his father had said in *'bog standard original condition'* unlike what he called Steve's *'boy racer'* Triumph.

It had been a good evening they had been hanging out at the teenagers' favourite venue, *The Bistrotheque Coffee Bar* on Sheffield High Street and were returning home at about 9.30pm. The driver of the white and blue Ford Anglia never looked right as he pulled out of the side junction. Andy had little warning, he braked hard but although he lost some speed the bike skidded and as he tried desperately to avoid the car, its bumper clipped his front wheel and sent him sprawling along the rough tarmac across the road where he separated from the bike but the momentum propelled him on rolling him over and over until his left arm collided with a reflector post at the edge of the road forcing his elbow to bend the wrong way and snapping it instantly.

Steve and Ricky pulled up sharply. While Ricky started to berate the startled car driver Steve ran to his stricken friend across the road. He was badly shaken up and winded but otherwise seemed ok except that his left arm was hanging uselessly by his side. Andy's adrenaline was keeping him going but as it wore off and the pain started to come in waves he leaned against his best mate for support as they waited for the ambulance which Ricky had shouted across to say was on its way. For a moment Andy's mind went back to the summer three years before when once again his friend had been there when he needed him most.

After spending a few days in the Northern General Infirmary and an operation to place a steel pin in his arm, Andy was allowed home and returned to school the following week with his arm in plaster which was very soon covered with signed statements of good wishes from all his fellow classmates.

Months of physiotherapy sessions followed and by the end of the year Andy had forgotten about his bike which had been 'written off' by the insurance company and was more concerned about his first real girlfriend Jessica , who had recently joined the lower sixth at his school after her parents had moved to Sheffield. Her father was a well regarded metallurgist who had worked at the British Steel Corporation steel plant at Port Talbot in South Wales but had been asked to transfer to Sheffield and to the Corporation's River Don works where he became the manager of the laboratories.

Jessica was tall with auburn hair and brown eyes, with a soft Welsh accent. She was immediately the centre of male attention in the common room at break times with many vying to be the first to 'chance his arm' but after a few weeks Jessica had succumbed to the quieter but equally self assured Andy. During the next few months Andy and Jessica were never separated and Steve saw less and less of his best friend. One night Steve and Ricky bumped into Andy and

Jess coming out of the cinema, called 'The Palace' but which they had nicknamed *'The Bug Hut'* which was situated next to the Tinsley Working Mens' Club but Andy hardly acknowledged him totally lost in another world with Jess.

Andy and Jess had taken to walking together hand in hand at the weekends along the tow path of the old Sheffield and Tinsley Canal up to the Sheffield Canal Basin, close to Sheffield City Centre. The basin dated from 1814, when the canal opened to connect with the River Don Navigation, allowing canal boats to reach the heart of Sheffield for the first time. It used to be a busy, thriving transhipment point for many years, but trade declined as more goods were moved by rail and later by road. Now as Andy and Jess walked along the weed-infested tow path the canal had declined into a forlorn and unwelcoming state.

The water was black with an oily film across the surface and here and there large metal objects protruded from the opaque depths. A few narrow boats were moored along the route that they walked but most were boarded up rusting away with paint peeling of their hulls. Tall, dark, brick-built warehouses lined the edge of the canal but some of them had broken windows and faded painted signs and these were starting to be covered at ground level with sprayed graffiti. It was a sign of the start of industrial decay and dilapidation. But on Saturday mornings as they walked along they could still hear the loud clanging of metal and thumping and rumbling of large machinery and an unpleasant noxious smell periodically entered their nostrils.

*"Next weekend let's go somewhere nicer"* Jess said to Andy one Sunday morning.
*"Ok"* he replied *"I'll ask my dad for suggestions."*

So the following Saturday lunchtime the two of them found themselves on a bus travelling out of Sheffield City centre and after about eight miles they got off at the village of Bradfield and then walk a mile or so up to the picturesque Dale Dike Reservoir. They walked along a well-defined footpath through woods and open fields until they reached the edge of the reservoir. They sat on a grassy bank in the early summer sunshine and breathed in the warm fresh air.

*"This is not the original dam"* said Andy suddenly *"It was rebuilt in 1875 because the original dam was the cause of the Great Sheffield Flood that devastated parts of Sheffield on 11th March 1864, when it broke as its reservoir was being filled for the first time. Two hundred and thirty-eight people died and more than 600 houses were damaged or destroyed by the flood."*

*"How on earth did that happen"* replied Jess with genuine interest.

*"As far as I know the immediate cause was a crack in the embankment but the source of the crack was never determined. As I understand it the dam's failure led to reforms in engineering practice, setting standards on specifics that needed to be met when constructing such large-scale structures. We talked about it in a local history lesson in school last year."*

Jess lay on her back and closed her eyes whilst Andy was sat upright with his arms around his knees and staring intensely at the water in front of them and he suddenly shuddered.

*"What's the matter?"* Jess enquired

*"Oh nothing"* he replied *"I was just thinking of something of another time and another place. Come here, can I have a kiss?"*

Over the next few weeks they often returned to the reservoir bringing a small picnic and a blanket to sit on and whiled away the hours talking and enjoying each other's company.

*"I feel that this is our special place"* said Jess one Saturday afternoon as she put her arms around Andy's neck and kissed him. Their embraces recently had become ever more passionate and inevitably that warm afternoon they made love for the first time on the grassy bank overlooking the glassy but very deep waters of the reservoir.

*"He's gone completely soft in the head."*

Ricky said to Steve one day as they walked to the shed in the school car park where their motorbikes were stored during the day.

A couple of weeks later at the onset of the school holidays, Steve began to feel restless and more and more irritable. He simply wasn't happy with life and just felt that he was drifting along. He now found school boring, there was just too much reading involved in doing A levels and he wanted some excitement. He was also fed up with having no money. He had seen a young bloke driving a light blue Mark 2 Triumph Spitfire with a giant red fibreglass radio aerial trailing behind it through the city centre the other day and he had for the first time in his life been jealous.

*"I want one of those"* He thought to himself and I would fit one of those new eight track tape stereo systems and then I could play my favourite 'Who' album at maximum volume with the roof of the car down. That evening he talked to his father after he returned home after his shift had finished at Viners and told him how he felt.
*"Get a job then son – join an apprentice scheme "*replied his father, *'I'll have a word with the personnel department at work and ask Paul to see if there is anything going at his place."*

Steve however, was not convinced. He loved Sheffield. For the last seventeen years it had been his home and he wouldn't have wanted to have grown up anywhere else but now he wanted out. To be honest he found that the sight of the rows and rows of giant black warehouse factory buildings that lined both sides of the road on the way from Sheffield centre to Tinsley slightly unnerved him. It seemed permanently dark here as he stared out of the windows of the bus and the smell and fumes were often acrid and hurt the back of your throat. *"Sheffield is a great city but I want more than this right now and I know I can achieve more but I don't know how – I just feel trapped right now"* He said to himself a little too loudly so that the old man next to him said:

*"What did you say son"*
*"Oh nothing mate"*

Steve squeezed past him and ran down the stairs and jumped off the bus at the next stop and decided to walk the remainder of the journey home. A half an hour later he saw the giant cooling towers of the Blackburn Meadows coal burning power station situated on the River Don between Sheffield and Rotherham in the distance. As he approached the Tinsley viaduct his mind was made up.

*"I want to achieve something. I want my family to be proud of me. I am strong and determined and I will work hard but it will not be in one of those bloody dark factories for the rest of my working life."*

He was in the same state of mind a few days later when he found himself wandering past the Army Recruitment office in Sheffield town centre. Steve had had no military ambitions as a child other than playing war games with model soldiers and Airfix kits that himself and Andy had made. He enjoyed military history mostly about the Second World War and his father had often told him tales of his adventures in the desert which had enthralled him but he knew nothing about the modern military and its equipment

He stopped at the window to stare at the action-packed posters settling on one depicting the Parachute Regiment. He had heard that the '*Paras*' were some of the toughest and most highly trained soldiers in the world that was all he knew about them, Steve began to wander if he could get through the training. *"It would probably do me some good and maybe I will get to see a bit of the world and get me out of Sheffield for a few years or I will end up in an apprenticeship in some factory he thought."*

He entered the building and started to look around and an old sergeant in army uniform approached him and began to chat to him about what he might be interested in.
*"The Parachute Regiment"*
*"Oh I see and do you think you are fit enough lad?"* came the reply

When Steve answered *'yes"* the sergeant chuckled as if he knew something that Steve did not. However, despite that it wasn't long before he was sitting opposite him at his desk filling out application forms. After completing the forms Steve walked out of the building an onto the busy Sheffield city centre street. The magnitude of the decision he had just made had not had any significant effect on him at all and although it was a spontaneous move he felt strangely free of any doubt. He returned home and discussed his decision with his parents that evening and they were happy to sign the necessary forms to grant parental consent.

*"Good for you lad"* his father had said *"It will give you focus and direction"*

Andy meanwhile had decided that he would study for his A levels but had opted to do so not at school but at the local Further Education College as had Jess. He had chosen to study Mathematics, Physics and Geography whilst Jess had opted for the more Arts subjects of English and History. The following January Andy had gone for an interview with the Royal Air Force in Manchester. He had passed all the entry exams and the aptitude tests with credit and he had been told that he had the necessary skill and imagination to deal with the problems that he was faced with and his technical ability was beyond doubt. But then came the hammer blow. Although physically fit and strong and with perfect eyesight he had failed the medical. The explanation was that he could not 'lock out' his left arm due to the slight restriction caused by the steel pin still in his elbow joint.

Andy's world at seventeen collapsed around him. As he travelled back on the train to Sheffield from Manchester his eyes moistened as he stared out of the windows at the green hills as the train raced through the Pennines. He was just inconsolable and for a few months he went into a huge depression which neither his parents nor Jess could shake him out of.

Later in the spring he was sitting in a café with Jess having a coffee when she said to him:
*"You know Andy, there is so much that you can do. Why don't we go to London when we have finished at college? There seems to be*

*so many more opportunities for young people down there than there are in Sheffield right now. I was reading the other day about the salaries that they pay secretaries and personal assistants down there so I have decided that I am going to take a typing course on two evenings a week from now on."*

Andy just nodded his agreement and then stirred another spoon of sugar into his now lukewarm coffee.

After a few weeks of moping about the house, the insurance money from the motorcycle accident came through. The driver of the Ford Anglia had admitted liability and of course there were two close witnesses to corroborate Andy's version of events.

*"Seven hundred pounds. A veritable fortune"* thought Tom.
*"Buy yourself a car lad. Or you can use it to travel when you have finished at college."*
Andy just grunted and mumbled something under his breath and walked out of the room.

That Saturday night he and Jess went to their favourite pizza restaurant in Sheffield town centre.
*"I have decided what I am going to do with the money Jess"* Andy said suddenly:
*"What's that then?"*
*"I am going to learn how to fly"*
Jess almost choked on the slice of pepperoni pizza that she had just bitten into.
*"You what! How on earth do you propose to do that and why would you want to?"*
*"I have thought about it a lot Jess"* he replied.
*"It is all that I have ever wanted to do. I may not make the grade with the RAF now but there are a lot of opportunities in civil aviation."*
He went on to explain that he had read about the boom in package holidays that had now become so popular with the British public and that there were a number of holiday companies partnering with

charter airlines to fly the short haul destinations to various parts of the Mediterranean in particular.

*"First I need to get a Private Pilots Licence"*

Jess just looked at him and smiled

*"You know I will always support you Andy no matter what you decide to do"*

Not long after Andy joined the Doncaster Sheffield flying school which was based at the Robin Hood airfield in Doncaster and he had a session every Saturday and sometimes Sunday morning as well for six months. Tom was really proud of his son's commitment and willingly offered to drive him to the sessions often accompanied by Jess as they watched from the ground. He was learning on a de Havilland Chipmunk T.10 which had been manufactured in the UK by de Havilland initially at their Hatfield plant in Hertfordshire and then transferred to the factory at Hawarden Airport at Broughton near Chester. It was a great trainer aircraft and was also used by the ATC for their Air Experience Flights and by the Army Air Corps and the Fleet Air Arm for primary training.

In order to gain the Private Pilots Licence he had to first pass a medical examination and the restriction in movement in his left arm was not considered a debilitating factor in any way. He then had to successfully complete the course which involved a minimum of forty five hours flying time and pass seven written examinations and then complete an extensive solo cross country flight and finally successfully demonstrate flying skills to an examiner during a test flight. He put his heart and soul into the sessions and read every piece of material he was given diligently. He would make notes after each flying lesson and keep them in a file and ensure that he read them again a couple of times before the next session. But by the end of the year he had gained the licence that he had coveted so much and at the age of seventeen he could finally say to himself

*'I am a flyer.'*

It was twelve months later and Andy was having another session with the Careers Advisor at the college. After listening again to Andy's story he suddenly said:

*"Have you ever considered the Royal Navy Andy?"*

"I want to fly not go to sea" he replied sharply

*"Perhaps you are not aware but the Royal Navy has what is called the Fleet Air Arm which operates a substantial number of aircraft both helicopters and fixed wing."*

Andy listened intently.

*"Would you like me to make some enquiries?"* asked the advisor

*"Yes please sir"* Andy replied eagerly.

A few weeks later Andy received a letter from the Admiralty Interview Board (AIB) inviting him to attend a two-day interview process at HMS Sultan in Gosport, Hampshire. The interview panel were impressed with Andy and his commitment and dedication particularly the personal achievement of gaining a PPL at such a young age. The following month Andy received another letter addressed to him at Raby Street, Tinsley, Sheffield from the AIB. This time he was being invited to Biggin Hill for flight crew assessment and to see if he had the right physical and mental attitude to become a flyer with the Fleet Air Arm. He underwent a series of tests including fitness, eye and general medical as well as flight aptitude and the usual security and reference checks. It was decided that the issue of his left arm which had been flagged up would not be a restriction as far as they were concerned. After all he had already proved that he could fly a light aircraft and so he passed the medical and all of the other tests.

It was, therefore agreed that as soon as he had finished his 'A' levels and had achieved the necessary grades he would join the Royal Navy as a cadet at Britannia Royal Naval College in Dartmouth.

# Chapter Three

## Tuesday 4th May 1982: Falkland Sound

*HMS Sheffield (D80)*, a modern computerised Royal Navy Type-42 destroyer, had been returning to Portsmouth from a patrol in the Arabian Gulf, her crew looking forward to some well earned Rest and Recuperation when the call to join the Task Force came within hours of the Argentine invasion of the Falkland Islands when she was just four days from Portsmouth.

She was the second ship to bear the name. The first was a five hundred and one foot Southampton Class cruiser that helped sink the fifty thousand tonne German battleship *The Bismark* in World War Two and had a proud battle history. When the ship was decommissioned in 1967, many of the stainless steel fittings that had been presented by Sheffield companies, distinct from the traditional brass fittings, that had given the ship the nickname *'Shiny Sheff'* were added to the new Sheffield prior to her launch at the Vickers Shipbuilding and Engineering yard at Barrow-in-Furness on 15th June 1971 thus enduring the name and keeping the distinction.

In the early hours of the morning Captain Sam Salt, as instructed by Admiral Woodward had positioned his ship on 'defence watch', forward radar scouting patrol, around seventy miles south and east of Port Stanley. They were one of three 'picket ships' all Type-42 guided-missile destroyers. *Coventry, Glasgow* and *Sheffield;* each one fitted with *Sea Dart* surface-to-air missile systems. No one liked being in the 'picket line' as you were totally exposed to a submarine or air attack without the protection of the main force around you. No one could be sure how effective the Type-42 destroyer would be in this situation and to make matters more uncomfortable, the Argentineans had previously purchased two identical ships, the ARA Hercules and the ARA Santisima Trinidad, from the British and Salt was in no doubt that these had been used extensively in training sessions with their Air Force.

Salt knew, like every member of his crew that their job was to protect the carrier Invincible. The classic anti-carrier tactic is to strike at the picket and then pursue with the main attack through the hole in the defences that has just been made. The crew on *Sheffield* as with the other two 'picket ships' had to remain focussed and alert. They, like the crew on every other ship of the Task Force, was expecting air strikes against them today particularly after the sinking of the *General Belgrano* two days before which had heightened the Argentinean public's demand for revenge and Galtieri's Junta had to even the score.

Unknown to Captain Salt and the rest of the Task Force the *Sheffield* and a number of other ships were detected by an Argentine Naval Aviation patrol aircraft, a Lockheed SP-2H Neptune at 7.50am. This was not just by the skill of the Argentine navigators who were operating an old aircraft with serious maintenance problems but they were also utilising strategic information that had been passed to their commanders by the Russians using intelligence gathered by the Soviet satellites already in orbit over the South Atlantic. The Neptune kept the British ships under surveillance verifying Sheffield's position again at 8.14 and 8.43am.

Just over an hour later two French-built Dassault Super Etendard fighter aircraft (3- A-202 and 3-A-203) took off from the Rio Grande air base on Tierra del Fuego at 9.45am. Beneath the port wing of each aircraft were fixed extra tanks of fuel to enable them to make the 860 mile round trip. Beneath the starboard wing of each aircraft was slung the radar-homing, sea–skimming anti-ship missile Exocet. The Exocet is manufactured by the French company Aerospatiale and is the French word for flying fish. Each Exocet missile weighs half a ton, with a three hundred and sixty four pound warhead and 4.9 meters in length. With an impact speed of six hundred and fifty knots it is a ship-killer. This speed is slightly under the speed of sound which prevents the Exocet missile from creating an easily detectable sonic boom.

In September 1980, fifty pilots and technical personnel of the 2nd Escuadrilla Aeronaval de Caza y Ataque arrived at Rochefort Naval Base in France. After three months of French language teaching they were sent to Landivisiau Air Naval Base where for about a month they flew training sorties in Morane Saulnier planes and started to become acquainted with their future combat aircraft, the Super Etendard in which each pilot was allowed a maximum of fifty hours flying time.

Attacking a ship with the AM39 air-launched version of the Exocet missile is undertaken in two stages. Firstly the missile is guided by the aircraft's fire control system which provides the missile with the target's coordinates obtained by the plane's Agave radar system. On launch the missile dives to an altitude of thirty meters which is later adjusted and fixed at 2.5 meters by the missile's radio altimeter. Secondly, in the final few seconds of flight, the missile activates its own radar and searches for the target, locks on to it and guides itself to the impact point.

In July 1981 the Argentine pilots and technicians returned to the Comandante Espora Air Baval Base near Buenos Aries and began the preparation for the arrival of the first five Super Etendards, which finally arrived in November 1981. The Argentine Navy had ordered a total of fourteen aircraft and the same number of Exocets but after the invasion of the Falkland Islands on 2nd April the remainder of the order was placed under embargo by the French Government under pressure from the British and the other Common Market member states.

The Argentineans had no previous experience with anti-ship missiles, and the Exocet was a complicated and cranky weapon. The Argentineans had experienced a lot of trouble fitting the Exocet launch system and rails to the Super Etendards. In November 1981, Dassault Aviation, owned by the French Government and builder of the Super Etendard, sent a team of nine of its own technicians (and some additional French Aerospatiale specialists) to work with the

Argentine navy to supervise the introduction of the Etendards and Exocets.

Although France complied fully with the NATO/Common Market weapons embargo, the French technical team remained in Argentina and many in the Task Force believed they continued to work on the aircraft and Exocets, successfully repairing the malfunctioning launch systems. The French Government, however, had supported Britain wholeheartedly from the outset of hostilities, making available both Super Etendard and Mirage aircraft so that the British Harrier pilots could train against them before setting off for the South Atlantic.

On the morning of 4<sup>th</sup> May, the two Super Etendards that had taken off from Argentina were piloted by two senior naval aviators, both of whom had been on the French training mission, Lieutenant Armando Mayora and Captain Augusto Bedacarratz who commanded the mission. They flew in a tight formation and in total radio silence as they left the Argentinean mainland. At 10.00am they rendezvoused with an Argentine Air Force tanker, a KC-130H Hercules which was a converted transport aircraft. The pilots executed the fuel transmission well and kept their Agave radar switched on but not transmitting. Thirty five minutes later, the Neptune climbed to three thousand eight hundred and forty feet and detected one large and two medium-sized contacts at the coordinates 52° 33 55 South and, 57° 40 55 West and immediately passed the information to the two waiting pilots who were flying at a very low altitude, just above the waves using the curvature of the earth to avoid the line-of-sight sweep of the British forward radars; the rather outdated Type 965 which was fitted to the *Sheffield*. On receiving the information they ascended to five hundred and twenty feet to verify these contacts but being unable to do so they flew on in silence for twenty five miles just fifty feet above the waves desperately trying to remain calm and in focus, and not fly into each other or into the sea as their pulses raced knowing that the large contact could only be one of the British carriers - the prime target.

They climbed again and after a few seconds of scanning, the targets appeared on their radar screens. Although Bedacarratz and

Mayora could not identify the individual targets, in these waters they had to be part of the British fleet. They automatically loaded the coordinates into their weapons systems, turned back to a low level and after last minute checks, launched their AM39 Exocets at 11.04 am from twenty to thirty miles away from their targets. They turned for home rapidly, diving back close to the water knowing that they were already riding their luck in avoiding the British Sea Harriers flying on Combat Air Patrol. Not needing to refuel from the KC-130 again which had been waiting for them, they landed at Rio Grande at 12.04pm.

The two launch aircraft had not been detected as the British had expected them to be, and it was not until a trail of smoke was spotted six feet above the sea about a mile away out over the starboard bow by two officers on the bridge coming straight for the ship that a sea skimming missile was confirmed. One of the officers reached for the broadcast microphone shouting:

*"Missile attack! Brace, brace, brace!"*

Five seconds later, an Exocet impacted *Sheffield* amidships approximately eight feet above the waterline on Deck 2, tearing a gash in the hull that measured four feet by ten feet. The other missile splashed harmlessly into the sea half a mile off the port beam. The missile punched through *Sheffield's* outer skin and disintegrated inside the ship. For some reason, the warhead failed to explode, which undoubtedly saved a great many lives but the rocket fuel started a fire which spread rapidly. The main fire-fighting system was rendered inoperable and all power was lost. Fire-fighting efforts began immediately using a human bucket-chain, the only option left.

The Lynx helicopter lifted from the stern and began evacuating casualties and was quickly joined by Sea Kings from other ships of the Task Force. Despite the valiant efforts of the crew to fight the fire, they were beaten back time and again and Captain Salt had no choice but to issue the order to abandon ship. After only forty minutes all the survivors were off the ship.

Twenty British sailors were killed in the attack and twenty four injured – four of them seriously and 242 escaped without injury. The

4th May 1982 had seen the most significant attack on the White Ensign since the Second World War; thirty seven years before. The vulnerability of the Royal Navy and the ships of the Task Force so feared by Admiral Leach just a few weeks before had been mercilessly exploited by the Argentine Air Force.

# Chapter Four

A month or so after Steve Barraclough's interview with the Parachute Regiment a letter arrived addressed to him headed the British Army which contained all the joining instructions and was typed on military paper and contained a free railway pass. Four weeks later just after his seventeenth birthday, he waved goodbye to his parents and brother at Sheffield main railway station and boarded the train with his small suitcase. As the train pulled out of the station he realised that he really did not know what he was getting in to. He had not received any instructions, other than when and where to report and no programme or list of requirements to bring with him.

*"Well then mate this is it "*he thought to himself as he stared out of the passing countryside through the carriage window.

But he had no regrets at all about leaving his home town at this time and he made his way down to the buffet car and bought a cup of lukewarm British Rail tea into which he stirred two cubes of sugar and returned to his seat. After changing at Leeds and at York he arrived at Northallerton which was the nearest main line station to the Garrison.

Steve stepped off and walked along the platform to where he could see a large Parachute Regiment corporal in his distinctive maroon beret holding a clip board barking out instructions for the recruits to come forward and hand him their joining papers. Steve merged with a crowd of other young men. He kept glancing to see how many of them looked bigger and tougher than he felt. They were certainly all shapes and sizes here. Eventually seventy two recruits were piled into the back of several four-ton trucks outside the station and they headed for the Garrison.

Catterick Garrison is located three miles south of Richmond in North Yorkshire and Steve knew that it was the largest British Army Garrison in the world. However, he was not prepared for just how large it was. It was like a small town with a population of over thirteen thousand people with accommodation for both married and single soldiers, libraries, banks, post offices, community centres, churches, supermarkets and recreational facilities.

This was to be a thirty week course. By the time that he had completed twenty one weeks the number of recruits had reduced from the original seventy two to forty eight with some quitting after just a few days and then gradually the dead wood was being weeded out. By week twenty one they were due to complete the challenging P Coy five day course of eight gruelling tests which included the two mile, ten and twenty mile endurance marches, the trainasium assault course, the team event log and stretcher races, the steeplechase and the milling contest where each candidate is paired with another of similar weight and build and are given sixty seconds to demonstrate controlled physical aggression in a contest similar to a boxing match. With gloves, head protection and gum shields. Steve was now in his element. He liked nothing better than a one-on-one situation and he had learnt long ago in the playground and on the streets of Tinsley that you should never lose your head but stay in control and you will win through. The instructors were scoring candidates on their determination and aggression whilst blocking and dodging reduced their points total. Steve was a natural and he was given the accolade of *'top in class'* in the contest which boosted his pride and reputation within the group.

Steve learnt quickly during these weeks that the real power in the training camp was not the commanding officer as most would assume but the Regimental Sergeant Major (RSM) He is chosen for his loud voice as well as for his immaculate bearing and all of the recruits cowered when he walked through the camp. He had the ability to spot a loose button thread or an unpolished brass buckle at fifty yards and everyone dreaded the inevitable 'in your face bollocking' that was the consequential result of such a transgression. In these last few weeks of the course the RSM had become even more strict and if he was 'king' then the parade ground was his 'realm' and there would be hell to pay if the marching and drilling were not done to perfection.

Steve's parents, his brother Paul and his pregnant wife Linda and his best friend Andy all turned up for the passing-out parade and Steve felt a bit awkward because none of them had seen him in uniform before but he knew that they were all proud of him as were the relatives and friends of the other thirty seven recruits who had made it to complete the course successfully.

Steve was assigned to the Second battalion and based at Colchester. After two years Steve applied to become an officer he was formally interviewed by the Army Officer selection Board and was accepted as an officer cadet and went to the Royal Military Academy at Sandhurst in Berkshire. Steve performed well during the course even though he was in the minority twenty per cent of officer cadets that did not have a university degree or A level qualifications and also had the stigma of coming from a working class background with a northern accent but his operational experience, physical strength, determination and commitment enabled him to compete very effectively. It was a very proud day for his family watching him finally march up the steps of the Old College to be commissioned as an officer at the end of the prestigious Sovereign's Parade. Paul whispered to his father who was standing next to him watching the spectacle:

*"Fancy our Steve becoming a Rupert"*

He completed four tours of Northern Ireland, spent time in Belize, the Middle East and West Africa during which time he had been promoted from second Lieutenant to Lieutenant. It was, however, in 1979 and just after his twenty third birthday when he was approached to see if he wanted to join the selection course for the Special Forces – the Special Air Service. The legendary but reclusive regiment that prided itself on extreme physical fitness and stamina. Every applicant undergoes what is arguably the most demanding test of endurance required of any military unit in the world – the notorious six forced marches across the perilous Brecon Beacons, undertaken in darkness at speed, with increasingly heavy back-packs over distances up to forty kilometres.

Steve was fully aware that the selection process or more correctly, the Special Forces Aptitude Test was brutal and conducted at the very edge of human endurance. The fail rate was ninety per cent but he believed that he could do it and he was determined to try. So with twenty one other officers and two hundred and twenty seven other soldiers he set out for the Brecon Beacons.

The first phase is a series of timed marches. An individual effort over demanding terrain carrying a forty five pound rucksack, rifle and water bottle. This very tough month begins with basic military physical exercises followed by a 'beast', a fierce march over Pen Y Fan, the highest peak in the Brecons. It is a timed march officially called 'High Walk' but known universally as 'Fan Dance' in reference to the name of the peak. Steve set off at a good pace determined to keep the lead group in sight but not overdo it at the start.

*"Pace yourself. Remain in control and focus"* he kept saying to himself over and over again.

The drill sergeant instructors with them had told them that at the end of the march was a truck that would take them to the pub before returning them, to camp and it was just a few miles up the track. It was not long, however before the straps of the rucksack began to cut into his shoulders, his knees were already hurting from previous hard tabs and moreover, Steve knew that there was very little chance of the truck being where the sergeant had said it would be. Two miles further on up the steep track the sergeant turned to the lead group and said:

*"Sorry boys but I must have made a mistake and it must be a bit further on but don't worry I know a shortcut. Come on let's get going."*

They followed him through a farm gate and across ploughed fields which made for difficult, heavy walking as their boots sunk into the soft mud. They carried on along sheep tracks that were rutted and uneven and obstructed frequently by barbed wire fences or stiles. Although these obstacles were difficult to climb over they did ease the pain for a few moments while each soldier waited for his turn.

With every mile the load cut deeper into Steve's shoulders and to counter the weight he tried to lean forward so that he spent most of his time staring at the ground or watching his feet or the heels of the person in front of him. The calluses from previous marches rubbed off in solid chunks in these early few miles and exposed tender pink tissue underneath which eventually started to bleed. And Steve like many of the others tried to switch off and ignore these pain signals coming from different parts of his body and just keep going like he was on automatic pilot.

After another ten miles the sergeant instructor stopped and waited while everyone caught up. He had lied about the truck being here too. As he filed past him Steve felt his eyes burning into him as he was looking for signs of cracking.

*"It's just another five miles lads so crack on"* he said without emotion.

Steve tried to shut out the pain and occupy his mind with something else but it was difficult to lock on to one subject for long so he decided to recite the words of one of his favourite *Who* tracks to himself over and over again. After the five miles were up the sergeant stopped again and waited for those in the rear to catch up. Amazingly no one had quit yet and he wasn't pleased. It was clear to everyone that there was no truck:

*"Did I say five miles? My mistake I must have meant ten"*

There were groans throughout the group and expressions on faces changed and teeth were gritted in anger but no one threw in the towel.

*"Fucking sadistic bastard"* whispered one.

They were ordered to get going again and all comments of encouragement between individual members of the group that had been common earlier on now ceased as everyone withdrew into themselves but the group was fanning out with some now lagging far behind but as long as they kept going they were still on the course. The instructors were looking for tenacity and will power and not necessarily fitness. However as the hours wore on it was clear that there were some who looked close to total collapse. Steve kept sipping at his water bottle. He knew that as the body heated up it

51

began to lose increasing amounts of fluid through the process of sweating and even mild dehydration even in very fit people can lead them into making irrational decisions. Indeed under the extreme pressure of a military test, a soldier suffering mild dehydration may start to believe that they cannot afford to stop for a drink or desperate to prove themselves they convince themselves that they didn't need water and carry on. Steve was sure that this distorted logic was now affecting some of the other members of the group.

At each stop the instructors would stare into their faces. They knew the signs of when a man was losing control of his pain. Shortened breath, darting eyes or no reaction to anything at all even if asked a question were all tell-tale signs. One hour further on and it was now completely dark and the strung out group were progressing slowly up a steep incline when suddenly *'the grand inquisitor'* as Steve had labelled the lead sergeant instructor, paused and waited for all the stragglers to catch up. Steve was grateful for the respite and he drank most of the remains of his water bottle but left the last few mouthfuls. The grand inquisitor shone a torch in everyone's face searching for the signs he knew so well but still no one had quit. Then he said coldly:

*"There is no truck"* He let the impact of the words sink in and he could see the heads dropping.

*"Ten miles further on there is a pub. If you get there before closing time you can have a pint but if you are not there for last orders then you are off the course. Alternatively you can wait here and transport will collect you in the morning – make yourself a nice cup of tea and get your head down."*

Steve let out a huge breath and steeled himself ready to push on again. Suddenly the soldier standing next to him said:

*"Fuck this"* and sat down exhausted on top of his back pack.

Almost immediately he was followed by another who just stated:

*"I don't need this shit"* and threw his pack on to the ground.

The grand inquisitor looked around him with a wry smile almost willing others to follow suit. Shortly afterwards, some more packs hit the ground. Steve and a few others started to move off. It was harder now than ever before, no one spoke and the pace was slow.

Breathing was measured and the pain just had a numbing effect. Steve felt like a zombie because he didn't really feel like anything. He was just doggedly focussed on trekking the last distance even if it took all night long he would make it.

It was a moment that Steve would never forget for the rest of his life. As he and a half a dozen others turned the bend in the track ahead, there in a clearing, much to their great surprise was the truck.

*"This is it lads"* said the driver *"You've done it. The pub and the next ten miles was a bluff"*

It would appear that even the grand inquisitor had his limitations. In the back of the truck on the way home Steve and many of the others took their boots off and started tending to their feet because you could not allow your feet to fall apart. The grand inquisitor knew that their feet would be in a bad way so they would have a few days light physical training before the pressure went back on again. Steve looked towards the back of the truck. Those who had quit just sat quietly and stoney-faced. There was no excited banter in that group. They did not bother with their feet as it didn't matter any more as they would have all the time they needed to recover. It was just sinking in to each of them that the relief of dropping their packs minutes before the rest had cost them the opportunity of a place in the SAS.

Following this Steve then embarked on three weeks of map-reading, fieldcraft, survival training and gruelling marches with loads that became steadily heavier and heavier in the hills during which time a number of people were quitting or 'voluntarily withdrawing' on a daily basis as the pressure mounted. This all culminated in the final march – 'Endurance.' This was to be a forty mile long march which had to be completed without stopping and within a certain time whilst carrying a sixty pound rucksack, a rifle and a water bottle. At the end of 'Endurance' there were only nine officers and one hundred and six soldiers left out of the original contingent of two hundred and twenty eight and these had now won a place on 'continuation training' which included the jungle phase in Brunei.

Steve had to then undertake a further hurdle, that of Officers' Week. This was a further week of intensive training and individual tests of determination exercises. A short while later Steve was at the SAS headquarters in Hereford to learn of his fate. He was one of only two officers and twenty one men who passed. He would never forget the moment that the commanding officer extended his hand and said calmly:

*"Welcome to the SAS."*

After joining the regiment Steve returned once more to Northern Ireland. This time he was involved in stakeouts to track down and take out known Provisional IRA killers. He had also spent time in the salty, sticky breezes and heat of the Musandam Peninsula in Oman and the jungle humidity of Belize as well as the freezing cold winter training in Norway. The following year an episode took place in London which was to galvanise the public interest and high regard for the SAS in the UK. On 30th April a group of six armed men stormed the Iranian embassy in South Kensington. The gunmen took twenty six people hostage – mostly embassy staff but also several visitors and a police officer, who had been guarding the embassy. The hostage-takers were all members of an Iranian Arab group campaigning for Arab national sovereignty in the southern region of Khuzestan Province. And they demanded the release of Arab prisoners from jails in Khuzestan and their own safe passage out of the United Kingdom.

The British government and the Prime Minister in particular, had very quickly resolved that safe passage would not be granted under any circumstances and a siege ensued. Shortly after the beginning of the crisis, the British government's emergency committee, COBRA was assembled. The committee is named after the room in which it meets – the Cabinet Office Briefing Room which is situated in Whitehall. COBRA is made up of ministers, civil servants and expert advisors – including representatives from the police and the armed forces. The COBRA meeting continued throughout the second day of the siege and into the night.

Meanwhile two teams were despatched from the headquarters of the SAS in Hereford and arrived at a holding area in Regent's Park barracks. The teams were from 'B' Squadron, including Lieutenant

Steve Barraclough and they were equipped with CS gas, stun grenades and explosives and armed with Browning Hi-Power pistols and Heckler and Koch MP5 submachine guns. Peter De la Billière, the Director of Special Forces met with his other commanders to draw up contingency plans for an assault. They had learnt that the embassy's front door was reinforced by a steel security door and that the windows on the ground floor were fitted with armoured glass so access would have to be achieved elsewhere.

By the sixth day of the siege, the gunmen had become increasingly frustrated by the lack of progress in meeting their demands and that evening they killed one of the hostages and threw his body out of the embassy, As far as Margaret Thatcher was concerned a red line had now been crossed and the SAS were ordered to conduct an assault to rescue the remaining hostages. However, the Home Secretary, William Whitelaw, was warned by De la Billière that they could expect that up to forty per cent of the hostages would be killed during the assault. He had contacted the Prime Minister who was in her official car en route between Chequers and Downing Street but she had pulled over and spoken to Whitelaw and gave her permission for the intervention. There had been no hesitation or procrastination in making the decision that was potentially full of international repercussions in granting authority for British troops to force an entry into a foreign embassy.

The two SAS teams on the scene - Red Team and Blue Team were ordered to begin their simultaneous assaults, under the codename, Operation Nimrod. One group of four men from Red Team abseiled from the roof down the rear of the building, while another four-man team lowered a stun grenade through a skylight in the roof whilst the abseiling teams with ropes secured around chimneys at the top of the building smashed their way into the second floor windows. Blue Team then detonated explosives on the first floor windows and others, including Steve Barraclough entered the embassy through the back door and cleared the ground floor and cellar. The raid had lasted seventeen minutes and involved thirty to thirty five soldiers. The terrorists killed one hostage and seriously wounded two others whilst the SAS killed all but one of the terrorists.

The whole of Operation Nimrod was broadcast live at peak time on a bank holiday Monday evening and was viewed by millions of people mostly in the UK. Both the BBC and ITV interrupted their scheduled programming to show the end of the siege which proved to be a major career break for several journalists.

Immediately after the raid both Red and Blue Teams were despatched back to their temporary HQ in Regent's Park where whilst celebrating their success with cans of cold beer they suddenly received a personal visit from Margaret Thatcher to personally congratulate them on their exemplary performance. Steve had never felt prouder in his life and that moment vindicated all of the hard work, training and commitment that he had made to gaining the coveted sandy coloured beret and the winged dagger badge of the SAS. Six months later he was promoted to Captain at the age of twenty four after having completing the required five years service as an officer in the army.

## Sheffield 1981

In July 1981, Steve was sitting in The Fox House pub on Shirland Lane in Attercliffe. There was a male gathering of the Barracloughs as it was his father's birthday and there were three empty glasses of Ward's Best Bitter that was brewed at the Sheaf Brewer on Ecclesfield Road in the city in front of them.
*"Same again"* said Frank, Steve's uncle.
*"Yeah – why not"* came the reply from Alan and Steve.
However, despite the birthday celebration the mood was sombre.

Frank had just announced that the canteen had closed that day at the Attercliffe factory of Spear & Jackson where he worked making hand and garden tools that carried the famous brand name that was synonymous with steel and the city of Sheffield. It was in 1760 that a draper named John Love and a Wakefield merchant, Alexander

Spear, decided that steel offered a better living than cloth and went into business together. By 1814, the business had passed down to Alexander's nephew John, who took on an apprentice - Sam Jackson - to learn *'ye art, trade or mistery of sawmaking'*. Sam's first job was carrying blades from the forge to the grinding wheels yet, by 1830, he had obviously proved his worth as a new partnership was formed - Spear & Jackson.

*"They've brought in an outside catering company"* Frank had announced. *"They are only going to do a snack service now. Efficiencies and sensible cost savings they called it. You work long shifts and all you can get is a sausage in a bloody barm cake."*

*"The way things are going the whole of Attercliffe will be a giant shopping centre one day because there won't be any manufacturing businesses left - it will all be in bloody Taiwan or somewhere!"* Alan added.

*"That first pint won't even touch the sides"* Paul announced as he joined them at the table in the public bar. Paul was thirty, three years older than Steve but he looked older than that. He had worked in the Melting Shop at Firth Brown Steels' giant Atlas Works since leaving school at sixteen and completing the Apprentice Training Scheme. Initially he had been mesmerised by the workers pouring streams of golden red molten metal out of huge melting pot cauldrons from a high balcony into iron ingot moulds below; the workers silhouetted against the dark cavernous work shop. He had had ambitions of becoming either a first hand-melter who at the time had a Mk10 Jaguar car or better still the sample-passer. He wore a trilby hat and was in charge of all the furnaces in the shop. With over three hundred tons of steel ready to pour. Paul remembered the first time he had seen him take a spoonful of steel and pour it on the floor and look at the sparks. He could tell simply by years of experience whether the carbon and the manganese content balance were right or not. He had the power of yes or no over the pouring of the three hundred tons of steel and every first hand-melter was waiting for his job.

But now the initial excitement had gone and with it all his ambition and dreams. He had come to regard it more like a scene from hell. The work was physically hard in high temperatures with constant exposure to dust and fumes and then there was the noise. There was noise everywhere. The furnaces, the overhead cranes, the internal railway; it was just incessant and Paul felt trapped. He often said to his work mates:

*"If it wasn't for watching The Owls every other week I don't know what I'd do"*

He was often reminded of a poem he had been read at school called the *Sheffield Apprentice:*

*"I was brought up in Sheffield, though not of high degree. My parents doted on me; they had no child but me. I roved in such pleasures as e'er my fancy led. Till I was bound apprentice, then all my joy was fled."*

Although Paul was not an only child he had somehow identified himself with it and it kept drifting in and out of his consciousness during the long working days.

He had got married at the age of just twenty when his girlfriend Linda had became pregnant. He now had two children and lived in the council estate of Park Hill. The estate had been opened in 1961 by Roy Hattersley who was then chair of housing at Sheffield City Council. The concept of the flats had been described as 'streets in the sky.' With broad decks, wide enough for milk floats and large numbers of front doors opening on to them. Each deck of the structure, except the top one, had direct access to the ground level at some point and the site allowed the roofline to remain level despite the building varying between four and thirteen stories in height. But twenty years later in 1981 it was already looking tired and run down, the walls daubed with graffiti and the concrete walkways often smelling like a public convenience.

*"I am bloody glad that you decided to get out of here Steve"* stated Paul as he tossed the evening copy of the *Sheffield Star* newspaper with the headline announcing further redundancies at the giant British Steel Stainless Steel plant adjacent to junction 34 of the M1 in Tinsley on the table in front of him.

*"You've built a great career in the army and we're all, dead proud of you"*

# Royal Naval Air Base: Yeovilton, Somerset 1982

Whilst Steve had been progressing in his military career so had his friend Andy. He had kept in touch with Steve now and again by letter and they had met up a few times back in Sheffield whilst on leave.

Andy had enjoyed his three months at Britannia Royal Naval College in Dartmouth and his parents and Jess had attended the passing-out parade. He had then gone on to the Royal Naval Air Station at Culdrose just outside Helston on the Lizard Peninsula where he commenced his basic air training on Westland Wessex helicopters and then once he had gained his wings he moved on to fly Westland Sea Kings. In the same year that Steve had been invited to join the selection course for the SAS, after completing six years in the Navy, Andy had been noticed for his abilities and it had been suggested to him that he applied to join 846 Naval Air Squadron based at the Royal Naval Air Station in Yeovilton in Somerset which he readily agreed to do. He was accepted and appointed to HMS Bulwark and also in that year he took an active part in the modernisation programme with the Sea King IV. Andy had taken part in numerous maritime counter-terrorism exercises in the North Sea to protect the growing and vital North Sea oil industry which was taking the country nearer and nearer to self-sufficiency.

Andy and Steve crossed paths a few times at Hereford and in Northern Ireland but they had never had the opportunity to be on a mission together.

In 1982 at the outbreak of war in the South Atlantic the Squadron was equipped with fourteen Sea King IVs, prior to which it had operated eighteen Wessex Vs, a well-tried and trusted workhorse. The Sea King IV however, was like the Sea Harrier; it was yet to be tested in combat situations. It was however, an impressive aircraft and had been designed to be a naval helicopter from the outset. With a full fuel load, it could remain airborne for six hours with up to ten troops on board, depending on the equipment that was also being carried. It had state-of-the-art communications and was overall a vast improvement on the Wessex V.

For some time now, the Squadron had been practicing land-based and amphibious operations with the aircraft and procedures and drills had been developed and regularly rehearsed with both HMS Hermes and HMS Invincible. Andy and the rest of the Squadron were confident that both they and their equipment could perform the tasks asked of them when the time came.

# Chapter Five

## Wednesday 5th May 1982: 10 Downing Street, London

The South Atlantic sub-committee of the Overseas and Defence Policy Committee of the Cabinet usually known as the War Cabinet was in a sombre mood.

Despite the sincere regret at the loss of three hundred and twenty three Argentinean sailors lives after *HMS Conqueror*, the nuclear-powered submarine sank the *General Belgrano* two days before, there had been muted jubilation in London at the British success in sinking the powerful Argentinean war ship and also at the skill and bravery of the Royal Navy in rescuing over seven hundred Argentineans from the open ocean despite cold seas and stormy weather.

Any triumphalism that there was which had been captured by The Sun newspaper's jingoistic headline *'Gotcha'* of the two days earlier had rapidly evaporated as the Government and the British population now fully recognised that they were now in a real shooting war and the potential vulnerability of the British forces had been laid bare. The implications from the loss of *HMS Sheffield* slowly began to penetrate the British people's psyche. The Task Force had been despatched from Portsmouth with much pomp and flag-waving and general public and media support but now the realities of war had hit home. This was further exacerbated by the Argentineans who were putting out statements – some true and some false but all with the dual and deliberate purpose of boosting morale at home and of persuading the British public that this was a war that they could not win.

The Prime Minister looked down the table, not looking directly at anyone but engaging them all in her steely stare; William Whitelaw, John Nott, Cecil Parkinson, Francis Pym, Michael Havers, Terry

Lewin and Admiral Fieldhouse. Each of them felt the intensity of her gaze. She clearly had had little sleep having worked in her study all night as she had been considering the US/Peruvian proposals that the Foreign Secretary, Francis Pym had brought back with him from America that had been a result of the US Secretary of State General Al Haig's continuing 'shuttle diplomacy.' She had managed only a couple of hours rest just before dawn in the flat above Number Ten.

*"At this stage I do not want to know the whys and wherefores although I am concerned that a modern warship had so little reaction time; this will be a matter for a Board of Enquiry at another time." "What I want to know and quickly are what our options are? How can we best protect our ships and our forces so that we can complete this mission without further significant loss?*

She turned to Admiral Fieldhouse:

*"How many of these damn missiles do they have and where did they get them from?"*

Since the sinking of the *Sheffield*, there had been frantic diplomatic activity between Britain and the rest of its NATO allies.

Admiral Fieldhouse cleared his throat and addressed the Cabinet, *"Five to a maximum of ten Prime Minister. They came as part of the deal with the French when they purchased five Super Etendard aircraft last year."*

*"I want you to consider all military options."*

The Prime Minister stated looking directly at Admiral Fieldhouse. She knew that he, like all the others in the room, were as aware as she was of the unspoken position of the Russians who although they had been told by President Reagan to *"butt out!"* it would be unlikely that they would remain on the sidelines if the UK launched an attack on the Argentine mainland.

After the sinking of the *General Belgrano* and the large loss of life, Argentina had gained considerable support and sympathy particularly in Latin America. However, this support was not universal; Chile and Columbia did not share this support for their regional neighbour. Chile was Argentina's direct neighbour and was very aware of the territorial aspirations in Buenos Aries. Back in 1978 Argentina had initiated *Operación Soberanía* (Operation Sovereignty) in order to invade the islands around Cape Horn only to stop the operation a few hours later for military and political reasons. However it was well accepted in Santiago that the Argentine government of Galtieri had every intention of seizing the disputed Beagle Channel islands after the occupation of the Falklands and the defeat of the British.

After the War Cabinet meeting was ended the Prime Minister asked John Nott to meet with her in her private study. Her mood was focussed and she spoke slowly and purposely:

*"John I want you to use our resources, clandestinely of course, to block supplies of Exocet missiles reaching Argentina. France is secure. President Mitterrand has already assured me personally that he is with us; that is not the problem but there are a number of potential sellers on the international market who will have to be bought off or their inventory compromised."*

*"Of course Prime Minister" replied the Defence Secretary*

*"I will contact my French opposite number Charles Hernu immediately as I am sure that he can provide invaluable information."*

*"I want you to act quickly and keep me informed of progress John"* the Prime Minister said firmly as the Secretary of State turned for the door.

Later that day, from his office at Northwood, Fieldhouse spoke by satellite to 'Sandy' Woodward and to the Director SAS, Sir Peter de la Billière, Commander who was in Hereford.

De la Billière had joined the regiment in 1955 and commanded 'A' Squadron in Aden and Borneo before taking over command of the regiment in 1972 in time for the campaign in Dhofar. Having won the Military Cross twice, in 1959 and 1966, and a DSO in 1976, he had been appointed Director SAS in 1978. He had supervised the highly visible Operation Nimrod at the Iranian Embassy siege in London on 5th May 1980 to rescue hostages taken by terrorists. Most of their hostages were fellow Iranians but also included embassy police guard PC Trevor Lock, BBC sound man Sim Harris, BBC news organiser Chris Cramer and tourists who had stopped by to collect visas. It later emerged that during the SAS raid PC Trevor Lock had tackled the leader of the gunmen known as Salim and saved the life of an SAS soldier. He was awarded the George Medal for his actions.

*"The PM wants a comprehensive set of options and quickly".*
*"The Super Etendard base, where is it?* enquired Fieldhouse.
*'Tierra del Fuego'* De la Billière replied.

"We have done some research and the Americans have provided some sketchy satellite intelligence. There are basically five options but we have effectively narrowed it down to two – the airfields at Rio Grande or Rio Gallegos. Our firm belief is that it is Rio Grande."

*"On what grounds"* quizzed Fieldhouse.

*"For two reasons. Firstly, the distance to the target area is shorter giving slightly more flying time in the attack zone. But mainly because the Argentine Navy and Air Force have a historic and long-standing and mutual loathing of one another based on the constant squabble over resources, prestige and political manoeuvring. We know that the Rio Gallegos base was handed over to the Air Force south of the country. I am aware that this is supposition but it is extremely likely that the Navy's fiercely proud and independent pilots would not agree to fly from an Air Force base."*

*"Very well. I need a set of comprehensive proposals in the next few days"* and with that Fieldhouse was gone.

Woodward ordered more tea for himself and De la Billière

*"I don't suppose we could do another Black Buck raid"* mused De la Billière

Black Buck was the codename for the initial raid on 1$^{st}$ May flown by the RAF from the UK mainland via Ascension Island using the ageing Vulcan long range bomber with the objective of denying the runway at Port Stanley to the occupying Argentines. Black Buck's plan had been to drop nearly ten tons of iron bombs from sufficient height to penetrate the concrete strip and prevent aircraft from landing or taking off.

*"A rather desperate long shot Peter"* replied Woodward.
Certainly the mission to Stanley had required precision but not on the scale that would be needed to hit five separate, tiny targets which could be dispersed for protection anyway. Furthermore, even if the

RAF managed to hit the runway, the Super Etendards could be transported on low loaders to alternative airfields nearby.

Woodward had called his colleague's thought *'rather desperate'* because as far as Black Buck was concerned the risks were minimal as no Argentine fighters were based at Port Stanley and by flying in low it had not alerted radar to its presence to the last minute thereby denying the Argentines the opportunity to scramble Mirage Jets from the mainland. This would not be the case in an attack on the air base on Tierra del Fuego.

*"No the way I see it, we have only two real options."*
Woodward continued.

*"We cannot attack the air base from the air as it is too far from the Task Force and our aircraft would be considerably outnumbered and we could then be in a position where we have insufficient air cover for the fleet. I believe a missile strike with a conventional warhead is too uncertain and politically inacceptable. No, our only options revolve around a covert Special Forces raid; get in and out quick with the job done and all completely deniable."*

*"I agree. After all the Israelis completed a far more complex hostage rescue operation as well as destruction of fighter aircraft at Entebbe airport six years ago."* added De la Billière

The raid on Entebbe codenamed Operation Thunderbolt had been a hostage-rescue mission carried out by the Israel Defence Forces (IDF) at Entebbe Airport in Uganda on July 4th 1976. A week earlier, on June 27, an Air France plane with three hundred passengers was hijacked by Palestinian terrorists and supporters and flown to Entebbe, near Kampala, the capital of Uganda. Shortly after landing, all non-Jewish passengers were released. The IDF acted on intelligence provided by Israeli secret agency Mossad. In the wake of the hijacking by members of the militant organizations Revolutionary Cells and the Popular Front for the Liberation of Palestine, along with the hijackers' threats to kill the hostages if their prisoner release demands were not met, the rescue operation was planned. These plans included preparation for armed resistance from Ugandan military troops. Israeli transport planes carried one hundred elite commandos, members of the Sayeret Matkal anti-terrorist unit, over two thousand five hundred miles to Uganda for the rescue mission. The operation, which had been put together with only limited planning and rehearsal, took place at night and lasted ninety minutes with a hundred and three hostages being rescued.

The Israelis flew over Sharm al-Sheikh and down the international flight path over the Red Sea, mostly flying at a height of no more than 30 meters to avoid radar detection by Egyptian, Sudanese, and Saudi Arabian forces. Near the south outlet of the Red Sea the C-130s turned south and passed south of Djibouti. From there, they went to a point northeast of Nairobi, Kenya, likely across Somalia and the Ogaden area of Ethiopia. They turned west, passing through the African Rift Valley and over Lake Victoria. Two Boeing 707 jets followed the cargo planes. The first Boeing contained medical facilities and landed at Jomo Kenyatta International Airport in Nairobi, Kenya. The commander of the operation, General Yekutiel Adam, was on board the second Boeing, which circled over Entebbe Airport during the raid.

The Israeli forces landed at Entebbe at 23:00 IST, with their cargo bay doors already open. A black Mercedes and accompanying Land Rovers were cleverly taken along to give the impression that the Israeli troops driving from the landed aircraft to the terminal building were an escort for a returning General Amin, or other high-ranking official. The Mercedes and its escort vehicles were quickly driven by the Israeli assault team members to the airport terminal in the same fashion as Amin. Along the way, two Ugandan sentries, who were aware that Idi Amin had recently purchased a white Mercedes to replace his black one, ordered this procession of vehicles to stop. The commandos shot the sentries with silenced pistols, but did not kill either of them. As they pulled away, an Israeli commando in one of the Land Rovers that followed the Mercedes noticed that the sentries were still alive, and immediately killed them with a burst from his assault rifle. Fearing premature alerting of the hijackers, the assault team was quickly sent into action. Five Israeli commandos were wounded and one, commander Netanyahu, was killed. All the hijackers, three hostages and forty five Ugandan soldiers were killed, and eleven Soviet-built MiG-1's of Uganda's Air Force were destroyed.

"Yes they did" replied Woodward, "but I genuinely cannot see the possibility of us successfully landing a C130 Hercules transport aircraft on the airfield at Tierra del Fuego without being detected – it would be a suicide mission!"

*"I am not so sure" mused De la Billière*

*"But don't forget the Americans were undoubtedly reassured by this successful raid and when they tried to carry out a similar incursion into Iran a couple of years ago to rescue fifty three American embassy personnel held hostage in Tehran the whole escapade was a total operational and diplomatic fiasco."* Woodward commented and then after a few moments he continued:

*"Peter I want you to set up a close working group to look at this in detail. I know it will not be easy as the airfield will be very well defended but it is our only realistic option."*

## Wednesday 12th May 1982: Buenos Aires

*"We simply have to get more Exocets"*
General Galtieri said as he thumped the table with his fists.

He was fifty six years old and the child of working class parents who were poor Italian immigrants. He had enrolled at the National Military Academy; the *Colegio Militar de la Nación* in El Palomar, Buenos Aries at the age of seventeen to study engineering and his early military career had been as an officer in the engineering branch. But after twenty five years as a combat engineer he had become Commander of the Argentine engineering corps before rising to become a Major General in 1977 and Commander-in-Chief in 1980 with the Rank of Lieutenant General.

He had been an enthusiastic supporter of the military coup that started the self-styled National Reorganisation Process in 1976 and during this time the death squad known officially as Intelligence Battalion 601 reported to him. *The Batallón de Inteligencia* 601 was a special military intelligence service of the Argentine Army whose structure was set up in the late 1970s, active in the 'Dirty War' and Operation Condor (the campaign of political repression involving assassination and intelligence operations). Its personnel had collected information on and infiltrated guerrilla groups and human rights organisations, and coordinated killings, kidnappings and other abuses.

*"We cannot replace our stock, the British have persuaded their Common Market and NATO friends to place an embargo on us"*
stated Brigadier General Basilio Lami Dozo.

*"You are naive my friend the Russians will assist us"* countered Admiral Anaya

*"I am naive! It is not my fleet that has ignominiously returned to port after the sinking of the General Belgrano"* retorted the Air Force chief.

The tension in the air was electric.

*"What the hell do you know?"*

*Anaya spat the words out contemptuously:*

*"I have been planning this for months...."*

*"Yes you have"*

*Interrupted Lami Dozo:*

*"And in your analysis you said that the British would not fight us if we invaded the Malvinas – you have continued to underestimate them. It is my brave and courageous pilots who are taking the fight to the British not the sailors on the Veinticinco de Mayo who are* now cowering in our ports."

*"Enough"* shouted Galtieri once again banging his fists hard on the table. *"We have them on the run, we have found their weak point with the sinking of their destroyer Sheffield and we need to exploit it and quickly. Our Air Force must not seek to engage their Sea Harriers which continue to out manoeuvre our aircraft but fly strategically outside of their combat patrols and use this weapon from a distance which is our advantage. We only have to sink the two carriers and the Malvinas are ours forever."*

He looked directly at Anaya requesting an answer.

*"Despite the arrogance shown by my Air Force colleague my strategy is still robust. Overtly the Russians will not be seen to assist*

*us but they will help us for two reasons, one, that they would delight in delivering a psychological blow to a senior member of NATO and they would be extremely keen to gain access to unique naval facilities in the South Atlantic. I understand that they have assets in the French company that we need to do business with."*

"*I want those missiles*" replied Galtieri

"*Make it happen.*"

"*I already have as I envisaged we may be in this scenario*"

*smirked Anaya glowering at Lami Dozo. "Five Exocet missiles will be arriving in Buenos Aries in about ten days time – now your flying aces can win the war for us Brigadier General!"*

General Galtieri turned to his naval chief and beamed.

## Friday 7th May 1982: Paris

Five days earlier Philippe de Souza, the Argentine Chargé d'Affaires in Paris had met with Major Andrei Gordovsky at the elegant George V Hotel, just off the Champs Élysées in Paris.

"*The maximum is five*"

Gordovsky stated with a matter of fact shrug of his huge shoulders. He was a bear of a man. A veteran of numerous Soviet army campaigns having finally being invalided out of Afghanistan at the end of 1980 after his transport plane was shot down by mujahedeen fighters under the control of Ahmad Shah Massoud in the Panjshir valley probably by a CIA supplied Stinger missile that had started to find their way into the hands of the Afghan fighters.

"*You will have to negotiate the price and payment directly. Our fee as it were as the 'honest broker' is in the special requirements that have been discussed*"

He picked up the large glass of vodka in front of him and drained it in one swallow. The vodka helped dull the nagging pain that came from the steel pins that had been inserted into the lower part of his spine.

De Souza took a deep breath. He knew that he had to deliver, the consequences of failure were not comprehensible but he was also a genuine patriot

*"Was this really in the interests of my country? Were we not selling our souls to the devil in some kind of Faustian deal that would bring a short term advantage to his country but long term obligation? Was this not some kind of Trojan Horse that could provide the Soviets access to the potential vast unexploited mineral and energy resources of Antarctica?"*

De Souza sighed deeply. It was not his call to make. Yes he regarded himself as a patriot and had sworn to serve his country but he distrusted the Military Junta and regarded them as politically opportunist and with personal ambitions that took priority over the needs and welfare of his fellow citizens. He, like them were expendable assets to be used and discarded when it suited their plans

*"I am just the messenger"* he thought to himself. But he was not naive and had realised that if the Malvinas adventure should fail for any reason there would be political fallout and he was glad that he had already put in motion the plans to bring his wife Elena and young son Luis to France. He had an intuitive bad feeling about both his and their future in Argentina.

# Chapter Six

## Friday 7th May 1982: The Élysée Palace, Paris

On the same day that Philippe de Souza, the Argentine Chargé d'Affaires in Paris had meet with Major Andrei Gordovsky at the George V Hotel, the president of France was sitting at his desk in his private office in the Élysée Palace when the phone on his desk rang. The heavily guarded mansion and grounds are situated at 55 Rue du Faubourg Saint-Honoré at its intersection with Avenue de Marigny. The historic building dating back to 1722 had been the official presidential residence since 1873 during the period of the Third Republic.

The current president had been in office for just under a year having beaten his opponent, Valéry Giscard d'Estaing to become the first Socialist president of the Fifth Republic. To date he had seldom used the private apartments at the Élysée preferring the privacy of his own home on the more unconventional Left Bank. However, he also had arranged for a discreet flat to be available in the nearby presidential annexe, Palais de l'Alma in which to house his mistress which accounted for his being at his office in the Palace on this occasion.

President François Mitterrand picked up the phone for the call that he had been warned to expect.

*'Mr President I need your help once more......"*

The telephone call had lasted an hour and Mitterrand had been mentally and physically exhausted at the end of it

*"That bloody iron woman"* he had shouted at his aide, Jacques Attali after the conversation was over.

*"She is impossible. She has just given me, the President of the French Republic, precise instructions!"*

But despite his protestations he had been persuaded to ensure that the British received the secret codes that if applied to the missile would render the Exocet deaf and blinded and would require it to be returned to the factory in Toulouse to have new electronics fitted.

## Tuesday 11th May 1982: Paris

Matt Dempsey was sitting in his parked silver Renault 4 on rue Cimarosa. He looked at his watch he had been here for over seven hours now. He reached for another Gauloises cigarette from the blue crushproof packet on the dashboard. Matt had converted to smoking the cigarettes with their dark, strong tobacco and distinctive aroma after learning that two of his music idols, John Lennon and Jim Morrison had both been fans of the *Gauloises Bleues* and he also believed that it helped to blend him naturally into his adopted environment. The car's radio was tuned to La Voix du Lézard, Matt's favourite station as it played contemporary Rock music, the majority of it being either English or American. The volume was turned down low however, so as not to draw any attention to himself or the parked vehicle.

Matt was thirty six years old and had been in the British Secret Intelligence Service (SIS) for ten years. It is more frequently referred to in the mass media and popular parlance as MI6 although this was a name used as a flag of convenience during the Second World War when it was known by many names. His natural gift for languages and his inherited Gallic features from his natural French mother had made him a perfect fit for his role in France. Generally life was good, he had a smart flat in the Opéra district of Paris and a journalist girlfriend, Josephine who worked for *Paris Match* magazine and his work schedule was usually varied and interesting.

But Matt hated 'stakeouts,' they were just so boring. There had been no sign of his target since he had entered the building after a long lunch at 2.30pm. That was over five hours ago. Still he had only another thirty minutes or so of his shift and then one of his colleagues would take over. He let his mind drift to Josephine and the dinner date they had planned for late that evening, they were going to his favourite restaurant a smart and very busy Bistro situated just behind the giant *Galleries Lafayette* department store on Boulevard Haussmann. Maybe she would even ask him if she could stay over again tonight at his apartment; his pulse began to quicken as he thought of her fragrance *'Je Reviens.'*

A sharp tap on the door window startled him out of his reverie. Matt glanced up and saw a slim, smartly dressed, olive skinned Latin-looking gentleman with jet black hair sleeked back from his forehead and an unlit cigarette dangling from his mouth. The man gestured with his hand and mumbled:

*"Avez-vous une lumierè monsieur?"*

Matt wound down the window and reached for his flick lighter on the dashboard. As he did so there was a sudden movement. Matt caught a glint of something in the early evening light and then there was a sharp stab of pain in his chest as the razor sharp stiletto pierced the centre of his heart and he slumped dead over the steering wheel. The man casually lit his cigarette with the flick lighter and replaced it on the dashboard and sauntered away.

Moments later the side door of the Argentinean embassy opened and Matt's intended 'mark' walked past the silver Renault with the sleeping driver and continued down the street until he reached the line of taxis, approached the one at the head of the queue, spoke to the driver and climbed into the back of the car.

With his 'tail' now removed, Philippe de Souza sat back and chose a newspaper from the pocket behind the driver's seat. The headline in *Le Figaro* stared back at him

*'La guerre dans les îles Malouines ne va pas bien pour l'Argentinains'*

Arriving in the smart, exclusive restaurant on the left bank Philippe paid and tipped the taxi driver generously. On entering the restaurant his eyes quickly scanned the room until he saw the man dressed in business attire at a table towards the rear of the dining area. He strode to the table and shook the man's outstretched hand vigorously with a two-handed gesture used by well acquainted friends.

An hour and a half later, the two men parted company but not before Philippe had taken an envelope from the inside breast pocket of his jacket and slid it across the table where it was immediately picked up and concealed by his dinner guest.

The deal was done. Philippe stood up and shook hands once again with the contact that Gordovsky had set him up with. He innately distrusted the man and his easy *bonhomie* in greeting had all been for show. He had met a few Arabs like him who held no allegiances and changed their loyalties like the wind blowing the desert sand and it was only the strength of the wind or in this case the guarantee of a substantial 'arrangement fee' being deposited in advance in a numbered Swiss bank account that had secured his commitment.

Nevertheless the merchandise would be in Buenos Aires in twelve days time via a complicated web of intrigue, feints and blind alleys.

# Chapter Seven

## Thursday 13th May 1982: London

John Nott had moved very quickly since his private meeting with the Prime Minister on 5th May. Monsieur Hernu, the French Defence Minister, had indeed proved to be an invaluable source and Nott now had every purchaser of Exocet missiles, date and size of the order and the anticipated remaining stock.

The task was to now commence a worldwide campaign involving all of Britain's allies in NATO, the European Common Market and all friendly nations to ensure that Argentina did not manage to secure any further supplies of the deadly air-launched French built missile.

## Friday 14th May 1982: Frankfurt

Andrew Devon ran a successful oil and gas engineering parts business from his offices located in a skyscraper in the Bankenviertel district of Frankfurt supplying clients both in the burgeoning North Sea operations as well as those in the Middle East and Africa. Devon however, was also an arms dealer. He who was well known to the British authorities who had decided that according to a senior intelligence officer:

*"It was time to call in a few favours."*

Devon had been left without any 'wriggle room' after the visit from two senior officers from MI6 who had travelled to Germany to meet with him; initially under the guise as executives of a North Sea oil rig maintenance company. He was not enamoured with the task that he had been set, he knew that it was not without considerable danger and personal risk. The 'mysterious' murder of Matt Dempsey in Paris a few days earlier had even been reported in the West German press as being probably a random robbery gone wrong but Devon was under no illusions as to who could have been behind it.

His task was simple and straightforward. Backed by a £16 million draft handled by the Whitehall branch of Williams and Glyn's Bank, he was to draw in the Argentinean buyers who were currently scouring the world, into believing that he could supply thirty Exocet missiles from Middle East suppliers with whom he had contact. He was to then protract the negotiations for as long as possible, keeping the Argentineans 'on the hook' and at the same time tying up their resource which could have been chasing real sources of supply.

*"It will all be over in a couple of months"* Devon thought to himself as the two English visitors had departed his office.

*"It can't be that dangerous"*

*"Cover your tracks and leave no trail. Just play it carefully and then those bastards are off my back for good"*

But he noticed that his hand was trembling slightly as reached for his gold lighter and the pack of Dunhill International cigarettes on his desk. He went to the back wall of his office and removed a painting revealing the wall safe that lay behind. He punched in the code number and the door swung open. He reached inside of the felt-lined safe and retracted a small note book with handwritten entries.

He reclosed the safe and replaced the painting and flopped into the swivel leather chair behind his desk. He started to slowly flick through his contact book to begin the complicated web of events that he had to conceive and initiate. He grabbed the handset of the telephone on his desk and started to dial.

## Friday 21st May 1982: Port Elizabeth, South Africa

The freighter *Marios Santos* was at anchor at the main container terminal in Port Elizabeth and was preparing to set sail in twenty four hours time. Her destination was logged as Montevideo, the main shipping port in Uruguay with a transit time of about twelve sailing days away. Lined up on the dock were stacks of different coloured containers, red, green, white and grey stacked up to twelve high; one upon the other. One of the three gantry cranes was lowering containers one by one into the hold of the ship. The sky was already darkening and the dock flood lights had come on. The day shift would be making way for their night shift colleagues within the next half hour. There would be a fifteen minute delay as there always was when the shift changed over.

The man from SIS put down his binoculars and glanced again at the notebook in his hand.

*"Third row from the right and three up, the one with the yellow slash No 2010789 he said into the small radio in his other hand."*

It hadn't been difficult to track the shipment. With the information from the French every stockpile of Exocet missiles that existed around the globe was researched and every asset in place had been utilised to check residual stocks and location. It had come down to four suspects South Africa, Israel, Libya and Peru. But it was the South African connection that had reared its head first. The CIA had tailed an Argentine target to a clandestine meeting four days before and observed him in discussions with an official from the South African Defence Ministry. A series of tapped phone conversations had revealed the sale of four Exocet missiles to the Argentineans and these had been traced all the way to the container standing in the stack at the dockside in Port Elizabeth just a few days later.

Five minutes later four shadowy figures broke the surface of the murky dark water near the dock side. They moved quickly and silently scaling the rope ladder that had been left over the dock wall that no one had noticed during the day. Clad all in black rubber and with faces blackened and with waterproof back packs and weapons slung over their shoulders they were using pencil torches to locate the right container stack. Two men fanned out and took cover amongst the shadows of the containers but there was no one around with the flood lights revealing an empty quayside with just the sound of clanging machinery a hundred meters further up the dock. The other two quietly climbed the container stack using rubber suckers attached to their knees and hands and reached the third from the floor. They checked the number with a quick flash of the torch and then placed a small charge of plastic explosive around the seal and the latch. They retraced their steps back to the dock floor and retreated into the shadows.

Thirty seconds later there was a dull thud. No one moved. Two minutes expired and then the two black clad figures re-climbed back up to the container. The latch was destroyed and the container door swung easily open. Once inside they reclosed the door leaving just a crack where the shadowy light could seep in. In front of them was a large long wooden packing case about eighteen feet long. They both removed the rubber covered steel crowbars from their waterproof backpacks and started to work at the top of the packing case. Two minutes later the wood had splintered and the top was carefully lifted off revealing two stacks of two missiles. A black gloved hand slowly and carefully slid along the body of the first missile feeling for the flap that contained the control housing. Having found it a special key was inserted and the waterproof flap sprung open revealing a small keyboard. A sequence of numbers and letters was punched in and a red light blinked twice in the half darkness. The flap was resealed and the exercise repeated on the remaining three missiles. The two black figures pushed the door roughly back into place and fastened it with a new seal. It would hold together but the damage could not be hidden but the container would be loaded that night anyway and it would be a few days before the forced entry was discovered.

*"What did it matter anyway"* thought the man with the binoculars as he observed the retreat of the four black figures down the rope ladder and back into the water

*"The task had been done. These missiles would still fire but they were now totally mute rendered deaf and blind by the disabling codes supplied by the French. They would not be able to hit a proverbial barn door unless they were sent back to the factory in Marseilles to be reset"*

He smiled and made his way back to his parked car.

However, that smile would have fast disappeared from his face if he knew that at that same moment some four thousand miles further north on the African continent, at the Okba Ben Nafi Air Base in Libya, seven miles form Tripoli, a Soviet transport plane was taxiing for take off. Its destination was Peru and it was carrying five French-built sea-skimming missiles in its cargo bay. From there the cargo would be collected and taken to Buenos Aries by an Argentine military cargo aircraft. The complicated web involving Philippe de Souza, Andrei Gordovsky and a number of other Argentine, Russian and Libyan actors together with shadowy, anonymous middlemen and 'deal makers' all initiated by Galtieri's fist banging the table in the meeting of the Junta was being played out.

## Monday 17th May 1982: Buenos Aires

*"We have just heard from the Russians"* said Admiral Anaya to the other members of the Junta.

*"They have successfully launched the Kosmos 1365 satellite which has been positioned over the South Atlantic and they will now start to supply us strategic information about the British Task Force as they promised as part of their deal with us."*

*"Excellent"* replied Galtieri *"Please keep us all informed of all the developments."*

## Monday 10th May 1982: SAS Headquarters, Hereford

The intelligence cell at the headquarters of 22 SAS was a hive of activity. The Director SAS, Peter De la Billière had requested the planning for a direct assault on the Argentine Air Base. At the same time, just back from Northern Ireland, the whole of 'D' Squadron was being despatched to the South Atlantic aboard the Royal Fleet Auxiliary ship *Fort Austin* to undertake operation PARAQUAT, the recapture of South Georgia.

But it fell to 'B' Squadron to fulfil the operational mission that had been devised. According to De la Billière's plan, codenamed Operation MIKADO, the entire Squadron would be loaded on two C-130 Hercules transport aircraft which would crash-land on the runway at the Rio Grande Air Base in Tierra del Fuego. The objective was simple, to seek out and destroy the five Super Etendard aircraft that would be parked on the airfield and destroy or disable all the stocks of Exocet missiles that they found before disappearing into the night in a replica of the type of operation carried out by the Israeli commandos six years previously.

Unfortunately, the available intelligence was minimal. Getting the Squadron on the ground by landing the two Hercules aircraft on the runway was the easy part. Tierra del Fuego and the Rio Grande airbase lie in an extremely remote part of the world. Its name is Spanish for *'Land of Fire'* and it sits at the southernmost tip of the South American mainland. The climate in the region is very inhospitable with snow even possible in the summer months. About a third of the island is covered by forest of a kind that is unique in the world for having developed in a climate with such cold summers. Tree cover extends very close to the southernmost tip of South America. Winds are so strong that trees in wind-exposed areas grow twisted by the force of winds, and people call the trees "flag-trees" for the shape that they need to take in the fight with the wind. With an area of eighteen thousand, five hundred and seventy two square miles the island is divided approximately equally between Argentina and Chile. The Argentinean provincial capital is Ushuaia and on the Chilean side it is the garrisoned settlement of Porvenir which is about one hundred and sixty miles from Rio Grande which is on the Atlantic coast and only twenty one miles across the Strait of Magellan from the Chilean port of Punta Arenas.

De la Billière's plan made two major assumptions, one, that the Chileans would give the SAS a friendly welcome and that the two C-130s, if they survived the landing and the subsequent firefight could fly into Chilean airspace after the raid. If however, the aircraft were too badly damaged then the second assumption was that the Argentinean defence forces would not pursue 'B' Squadron on to Chilean soil. These assumptions were, however, based on safe historical fact. Relations between Argentina and Chile had not been good for some time. In the 1960s and 1970s sovereignty claims by Argentina over Picton, Lennox and Nueva Islands in Tierra del Fuego led the two countries to the brink of war in December 1978. Mine fields were deployed in some areas of Tierra del Fuego and bunkers built in the Chilean side as a consequence of the threat of an Argentine invasion *Operación Soberanía* (Operation Sovereignty) in that year which was halted at the last minute for a variety of reasons.

However, it was this operation that had spurred the development of the defences at the Rio Grande air base when a counter attack could have been expected from across the western border.

Since the election of the Thatcher government in Westminster, the long period of isolation imposed by the previous Labour administration and David Owen, the Foreign Secretary, Britain had become recognised as a loyal friend always willing to assist Santiago however unpopular General Pinochet's regime was in international circles. Although Chile's armed forces were numerically inferior to those of Argentina, there was a general recognition in London that Pinochet's forces could be relied upon to be a formidable ally if given the right equipment and now that the embargo on arms sales had been lifted, this could be a reality.

In the absence of air transportation, assuming that the two aircraft would become unserviceable after the crash landing, the Operation Mikado plan required the SAS troops to tab fifty miles due west, at night and without the benefit of navigational aids, across entirely featureless swampy territory to neutral territory. As long as this trek could be completed in darkness there was no aircraft at Rio Grande that was capable of pursuing them at night. Punta Arenas across the Magellan Strait held the only air base for hundreds of miles and was the priority destination which would be reached via the town of Porvenir which although the main Chilean development on the island was in reality a small, shanty-style town with rundown shacks on the outskirts and smarter, wooden houses, some two-storey towards the centre. This, however, would not be easy as the flat, featureless countryside would provide few hiding places as the surviving members of the SAS squadron and the aircrew made their way as fast as possible away from the pursuing Argentine forces.

The essence of the plan was presented to the War Cabinet and approval was made for the insertion of a small group of Special Forces operatives by a Sea King helicopter so that vital intelligence and detail on the ground observation could be carried out. Until this was available it was agreed that the plan should continue to be worked upon but at the same time preparations and rehearsals for this audacious attack should be carried out immediately.

# Wednesday 19th May 1982: Lima, Peru

In their search for replenishment stocks of Exocet missiles, the Argentines were prepared to deal with any ally and had been fishing in many international waters to try and secure the precious cargo they so desperately required. Overtures had already been made to South Africa and Peru both with some success or so it had seemed. But it was with some surprise to the military Junta that their initial contact with Isrex, the Israeli provider of defence and security products and systems in Buenos Aires proved positive. Unknown to the Argentines, the president of Israel, Menachem Begin had nurtured a deep hatred and resentment of the British that went back to the British administration of Palestine when he had been the head of Irgun, one of the armed Zionist groups fighting the British to secure the creation of the state of Israel.

A subsequent meeting on the 12th May had been hastily scheduled, but this time held in the offices of the Argentine Air attaché in Lima, the capital of Peru; Commodore Andres Dubos together with the head of the Argentine Air Force and member of the Junta, Brigadier Basilio Lami Dozo where negotiations were successfully concluded. The Israelis would immediately supply additional fuel tanks for the Argentine fighter bombers with which to attack the British fleet, since without them the Argentine pilots could not reach the Falkland Islands and return to the continent. The paperwork was sorted out with the Peruvian President Fernando Belaunde Terry authorising his Peruvian Air Force representative to sign purchase orders in blank and destination certificates so that the triangulation operation could go ahead. The role of Peru was crucial and pivotal to the Argentines as it was vital for the plan to succeed for Argentina to secure the agreement of another country that could triangulate the supply operations since it was well known that Israel had very close relations with Britain through trade and the influential Jewish community in the UK and could, therefore, not be seen to be openly supporting Argentina. The meeting concluded with an agreement between all the parties that if this shipment could be carried out without a hitch then the Israelis would be prepared to negotiate the potential supply of Exocet missiles.

The Israelis air lifted the fuel tanks to the air base at Callao which is also the main port of Peru which lies just seven miles to the west of the capital Lima. From here they were transferred into two Aerolineas Argentinas Boeing 707s and they arrived in San Julian, Santa Cruz on Sunday 16th May. Brigadier Lami Dozo was delighted. He could not wait to tell that arrogant pig Anaya, that it was his operation that had been successful and it would be him that could equip their brave Argentine pilots with the means with which to destroy the British fleet and regain the Malvinas once and for all. However Lami Dozo was unaware of how alert the British had become and how widespread and pervasive the operation put in motion by John Nott two weeks earlier had become.

Maria Torres was standing next to her car by the perimeter fence of the air base in Callao. She had a black scarf tied around her head with a pair of large sun glasses perched on the top and wore a beige trench coat tied tightly at the waist. Around her neck was a Nikon camera with a long telephoto lens. She had been working on and off for British intelligence for two years now. It was always low level surveillance work or servicing dead drop letter boxes and the few days a month brought in much needed additional income to help her continue to finance her studies at *Universidad de Lima*. Having an English mother and a Peruvian father she had been bilingual in Spanish and English since her early teens and it was her intention to travel to Europe to seek employment once her studies were completed. It was her command of the English language that had made her stand out and she was approached one day by a mature student in the coffee bar who after a number of subsequent meetings arranged her recruitment. She lifted the camera and steadied the long lens with her left hand and focussed on the three aircraft some hundreds of yards the other side of the fence. Whatever it was that they were transferring between from the hold of the first military looking transport plane to the holds of the two civilian aircraft was being done quickly so she pressed the button and the motorised shutter clicked away until the film was emptied. Two minutes later she got back into her car, placed the camera on the passenger seat and drove off.

The British Ambassador, Sir Patrick Moberly, had obtained the meeting with the Israeli Prime Minister through the normal channels. Whilst the Israelis were curious about the request they had assumed that it would be something to do with the worsening situation in The Lebanon. Sir Patrick was an old school diplomat with a career spanning thirty years in the British diplomatic service and had been Ambassador to Israel for just over a year. It was not an easy time for Anglo-Israeli relations and he knew that his job was to represent the views of the British government which were often at variance with those of the Israeli government.

After the normal pleasantries and the pouring of tea Begin looked over his glasses and said to the veteran diplomat:
*"How can I assist the British government today?"*
Sir Patrick did not reply but simply slipped an envelope from his inside left breast pocket of his pin striped jacket and slid it slowly across the table to the man on the opposite side. Begin picked up the envelope and opened it and took out a photograph that had clearly been taken from distance and enhanced but still depicted its subject with complete clarity. He was staring at an Israeli Defence Forces jet parked next to two Boeing 707 of Aerolinas Argentinas and crated goods were being transferred from one aircraft to the other. He turned over the photograph and written on the back were the words 'Callao, Peru, 16th May 1982.' Begin was absolutely furious but managed to maintain his complete composure despite a redness starting to appear on his neck which did not go unnoticed by the experienced diplomat. Sir Patrick then rose slowly and offered out his hand to the president opposite him and said quietly:
*"I assume that I can report back to London that this will be the last of the Tel Aviv-Lima-Buenos Aires military supply flights."*
The two men shook hands briefly and Sir Patrick turned and opened the door to leave without another word being spoken between them.

# Chapter Eight

## Evening Monday 17th May 1982: South Atlantic

The Sea King IV helicopter of 846 Naval Air Squadron, serial number ZA 290 had been stripped down of all non-essentials and fitted with extra fuel tanks that would extend its range was sitting on the deck of *HMS Invincible* whom accompanied by *HMS Brilliant* and *HMS Coventry* was steaming west under the cover of darkness at full speed and without radar.

The launch had been set for midnight local time from a position close to Beuchene Island, approximately thirty miles due south of East Falkland. With just under an hour to go Andy Shaw walked around the aircraft conducting a pre-flight inspection focussing on every detail required by the check list. As Andy completed his tasks, the four man Special Forces team started to climb into the aircraft heaving aboard their heavy bergens, weapons and other kit.

The Sea King was capable of carrying twenty seven troops a maximum distance of four hundred miles. However, Andy had flown one of the Sea Kings on the successful raid on Pebble Island only a few days before when a team of fifty five SAS soldiers and a Naval Gunfire Support Officer had been inserted on to the island from *HMS Hermes in 'Operation Prelim'*. For the loss of only one man wounded the SAS had successfully destroyed six Pucara aiircraft, four Turbo-Mentors and a Skyvan. In addition, a large amount of Argentinean ammunition had also been destroyed and the commander of the garrison had been killed. Far more important, though, was the fact that there were no Argentinean aircraft on Pebble Island to interfere with the landings at San Carlos Water, and the enemy's morale had been seriously dented.

Andy remembered well the extraction of the men after the operation. He was flying the third Sea King and was the last to arrive at the rendezvous point. The other two aircraft had already loaded and were airborne on their way back to *Hermes*. He had expected to embark twenty two passengers but after embarking eighteen the eight members of the reconnaissance team of 'D' Company emerged from out of the darkness with all of their kit including four canoes.

*"Shit"* said Andy to Chris Bell his co-pilot:

*"We'll be above the maximum all-up mass for take-off!"*

Chris made some hasty calculations involving speed, time and fuel for the forty mile trip back to the carrier. The wind had veered slightly to the south west ensuring a good tailwind, so the flight would take twenty five minutes. The sums completed they started to jettison some fuel to offload weight and contacted the fourth Sea King held in reserve to collect the canoes and the larger packs of kit. The imperative had been to get off Pebble Island as fast as possible to avoid the very real possibility of an Argentine counter attack. Andy had watched as Chris opened the fuel jettison cocks having first checked that the jettison pipes were clear of the ground. As the fuel level reduced Andy applied full power and Chris increased the rotor revs to the maximum transit limit permitted and the aircraft slowly started to claw its way off the ground. Chris closed the cocks and re-balanced the fuel tanks and waves of relief had flooded through the aircraft as they started the return to *Hermes*.

*"But this trip is a completely different ball game"* thought Andy as he completed his checks. *"We really are going into uncharted waters full of unfriendlies"* but he kept his thoughts to himself. His mind drifted momentarily to Jessica. He had written a letter to her last night after he had volunteered for the mission and he hoped that she would receive it soon and reply although he didn't really hold out any hope of a positive outcome.

*"What a bloody idiot you are"* he repeated to himself again and again, He hadn't realised what he'd had and now he had lost it probably forever and there was now an aching hole which he just couldn't fill.

*"Most people probably never have a relationship like I've had at such a young age and now I've thrown it all away. You really don't deserve her anyway"*

*HMS Invincible*
*At Sea – South Atlantic*

*16th May 1982*

*Dear Jess*
*I have had plenty of time to think over the last few weeks during the long journey south on Invincible. Although we have been busy training every day I haven't stopped thinking about you and our times together particularly at our special place at Dale Dike Reservoir.*

*The conditions down here are very challenging and I don't mind admitting that I have been pretty scared on a few occasions. It now appears that the Task Force is in a difficult position and I have volunteered for a mission into Argentina which by its nature is a one way flight and very risky but it has to be done to save lives and ensure success of the operation to retake the islands.*

*The truth is Jess, that I just miss you. I have come to realise what an idiot I have been and that I made a huge mistake in ending our relationship when we had something so special between us. We have been together for so many years now through 'thick and thin' and I have now thrown that away and I cannot bear the agony of knowing the pain that I have caused you.*

*I will understand if you say 'no' but I really hope that we can pick up again where we left off as I have now come to realise that I love you so deeply – and I would like to make our relationship a permanent one as soon as the war is over.*

*I just hope that I am not too late and that you can forgive me. If you have found someone else then I will just have to accept that and live with the fact that I have been very foolish.*

*Tomorrow I embark on this mission which is without doubt going to be the hardest and most dangerous that I have ever done but I will go with thoughts of you in my heart and I am certain that we will be successful and I will return ok.*

*I hope that you still feel the way I do and can find it in your heart to get over the pain and hurt that I have caused you and that we can be together again once more. Please write back to me soon.*

*I am enclosing a letter to my parents which I would be grateful if you could deliver to them.*

*All my love*
*Andy*

Andy pushed these thoughts out of his head and switched into automatic professional mode which the years of training had instilled in him but as he rounded the aircraft his right hand sub-consciously moved to touch his left elbow which he gently rubbed up and down and a small smile appeared on his face.

*"I'm a naval aviator and I'm Flight Commander on this mission"*
He whispered to himself. He was proud of the nickname of his squadron *'Junglies.'* A name coined in Borneo by British army units whilst the squadron was flying Whirlwind HAS7's from *HMS Albion* against terrorist guerrillas and the ground troops were constantly impressed by their highly skilled jungle navigation.

The objectives of this mission were straight forward. For De la Billière's plan to work and to receive the final Governmental approval, accurate intelligence from on-the-ground was an essential pre-requisite. A team of volunteers under the command of Captain Archer of Six Troop would be inserted into Argentina to undertake close target reconnaissance and then report back. Their priority is to confirm the presence of the Super Etendards and the Exocet missiles and to assess the strengths, weaknesses and readiness of the Argentine defence forces. If the team identified an opportunity to destroy the aircraft without further assistance then they were to do so and would be equipped with this option in mind. If not, then the main assault force would be deployed under *Operation Mikado*.

Andy was aware that a number of options for the deployment of the reconnaissance team had been considered by the planning cell at Hereford including insertion by either parachute or submarine. But both had been discounted early in the planning process, the parachute option could not be achieved without the delivery aircraft being detected by radar, thereby eliminating the elements of surprise and concealment and the submarine option could not be carried out because the necessary diesel submarine was still a number of days away from arriving into the operational theatre. So the only option left is the one-way trip to Argentina for Andy and his two man Sea King flight crew, Chris Bell and Phil Taylor.

At 0115 hours the navigation data was delivered to Andy and his crew already aboard the helicopter. Chris fixed their position into the Tactical Air Navigation System (TANS) as the ski-sloped carrier turned directly into the wind at approximately thirty knots thereby creating a relative wind dead ahead of more than sixty knots. Chris increased the rotor revs to the maximum transient limit and Andy started to gently apply the power and the heavy aircraft lifted into a low hover and moved quickly into forward flight across the edge of the flight deck and away from the ship into the dark, moonless night.

*Operation Plum Duff* was under way.

Everyone on board the aircraft had volunteered. Everyone was fully aware that this was a one-way trip to Argentina. The Sea King would have just enough fuel to drop off the special forces team and then get as close to the border with Chile as possible before being ditching and destroyed as it was mission critical that no evidence was left that could prove the British soldiers had been in Argentinean territory – it was and had to be all plausibly deniable. The aircraft flotation kit had been removed from the aircraft both to save weight and in the event of having to ditch the helicopter en route, it would sink without trace.

However, everyone also knew that the threat posed to the task force from the Argentine Super Etendard aircraft and their Exocet missiles was a clear and present danger as had been so tragically demonstrated by the hit on *HMS Sheffield* two weeks earlier. No one could be sure about the extent of the Argentine stocks of these deadly missiles and whether they would succeed in replenishing them. What they were all sure about was that the task force could not sustain the loss of a carrier and even if the British forces were successfully landed on the islands, they would be stranded eight thousand miles from home and facing a harsh Falklands winter which they could not be expected to survive.

Once Andy knew that he was clear of Argentine radar on West Falkland he maintained a steady altitude of two hundred feet as opposed to the earlier height of just fifty. During this early stage of the journey towards the Argentine mainland they found themselves flying into a strong headwind and they estimated that the flight time to the Argentine coast would be approximately four hours. Chris was constantly making regular sweeps with the Omega radar warning receiver to ensure that they were remaining undetected by Argentine land or ship-based radar systems but so far so good; no contact had been made of any kind. The VLF Omega was the first truly global radio navigation system for aircraft, operated by the United States in cooperation with six partner nations. It enabled ships and aircraft to determine their position by receiving very low frequency (VLF) radio signals in the range 10 to 14 kHz, transmitted by a network of fixed terrestrial radio beacons using a receiver unit and it had became operational around 1971.

However, the weather was now becoming a concern to the naval aviators. As the wind started to decrease, so did the visibility and with about one hundred miles to fly to reach the coast, the visibility had reduced to less than five miles and Andy consequently reduced their flying height back down to just fifty feet. But the situation continued to deteriorate and with every few minutes of flight the visibility was reducing by a further few hundred meters. Finally, at about 0500 they caught sight of the Argentine coast and Andy flew the aircraft due west to intercept the coast at the northern tip of San Sebastian Bay. The visibility now was no more than a mile and as they flew closer to the southern shoreline he could just make out the waves breaking on the sandy beach at the southern end of the mouth of the bay which was their landfall waypoint.

*"The weather boys didn't tell us about this shitty fog before we left"* stated Chris peering through the glass. As he did so Andy looked under his night vision goggles, the passive image intensifiers that amplified the ambient light but he couldn't see anything clearly at all. These really were challenging flying conditions and he tensed his muscles in an attempt to achieve a heightened level of focus and awareness only too aware that dense cloud or fog can cause a helicopter pilot to become disorientated and lose control of the aircraft and he daren't even think about trying to land in it.

As they flew over the waypoint, Chris fixed their position in the Tactical Air Navigation System known as TANS. In the context of aviation navigation, a waypoint is a predetermined geographical position that is defined in terms of latitude and longitude coordinates. They then turned onto a heading of one hundred and eighty degrees towards their next waypoint, reducing height to just twenty feet and slowing the aircraft to sixty knots. The terrain they were flying over was covered predominantly in short grass and clumps of the marsh grass that is indicative of boggy ground. Andy continued to fly south but reduced speed still further until they were just about hovering. The surface of the ground remained the same providing virtually no external reference points at all to aid navigation.

*"This is a real bastard"* Andy exclaimed through sheer frustration and nervous tension. He was aware that he could not ascend the aircraft above the fog layer as this would expose them to detection by the Argentine Navy's AN/TP3 radar known to be at the Rio Grande base.

Andy made the decision.

*"We're landing now"* he said which was audible to the SAS Captain behind him through the aircraft intercom system so that he could get his team ready. Andy was not prepared to take any further chances with both his crew and their passengers as he really believed that this might be the last chance they got to make a safe landing whilst remaining in full control of the aircraft.

The planned drop-off point for the Special Forces team had been close to the isolated Estancia Las Violetas, an abandoned rural estate about twelve miles to the northeast of the Rio Grande airbase. In the event due to the adverse weather and light conditions they were seven miles short of their intended destination. Captain Archer came into the cabin and Chris pointed out to him their exact location on the map using the coordinates in TANS. The Special Forces team were already disembarking from the aircraft and hauling out their heavy bergens full of kit. All British elite units called their rucksacks 'bergens' which is often mis-spelt as 'bergans'. The term came from the original 1942 Pattern external 'A' frame rucksack that was closely modelled on skiers' rucksacks made or used at Bergen in Norway. The '42 Bergen was replaced by the 1972 Pattern "Rucksack SAS" - also known as the "SAS/PARA" or "Airborne" Bergen. This had a square external frame that was also used for carrying the Clansman PRC 351 and 352 radio sets. From habit, these were also called "Bergens" - despite the fact that, strictly speaking, they weren't because of the shape of the frame and pack. The bergens were packed with spare clothing binoculars, a tripod-mounted scope and night sights, the latter being a variant of the Individual Weapon Sight used in Northern Ireland. In addition each man was carrying enough rations to last the anticipated length of the mission.

Every one of them was carrying M16 rifles with three spare magazines each and an additional two hundred rounds of 5.56mm ammunition. Chris knew that they did not usually tape a spare magazine to the one already in the weapon because it was possible to change a magazine for one in a pouch just as fast as two that are taped together. Also they had discovered that when you are in the field crawling through all sorts to get to the objective, such as mud and water, it all gets into the magazine taped to your weapon and therefore when you changed magazines and inserted the spare one, all the muck got pushed into the receiver which could cause a jam or other mal function just when you didn't want it particularly in the middle of a firefight. The SAS believed that the M16 is a good weapon for short-range work because it was short, light and had a high lethality close in. It was not so good for long-range work, though, and it certainly doesn't have the stopping power of the good old SLR (Self-Loading Rifle). However they regarded the weight saving over the SLR as being worth it, and that went for the ammunition too. Each member of the team took great care of their M16s, as the weapon didn't really like rough handling, which can pose a bit of problem, especially in terrain like the Falklands where it's continually damp and windy. The Americans first touted the M16 as a self-cleaning weapon, and didn't even bother to issue cleaning kits. Naturally, there were a host of jammed guns when it entered service. They then issued cleaning kits very quickly, but not before several of their guys had been killed because of jams. Some of the weapons were fitted with M203 grenade launchers firing high explosive grenades. But their use was limited because although they could throw a grenade over a distance of three hundred meters which is far greater than a man could throw one; it could only go in a straight line and not around a corner like a hand-thrown grenade.

They were also equipped with LAWs, the M72 Light Anti-tank Weapon, an American throwaway rocket launcher. It was very useful for SAS-type operations because it is light, which means several can be carried by one man. It is also accurate and can penetrate armour but the version used in the Falklands by the SAS was only effective against light armour which was perfectly ok for this mission. Because it fires a high explosive warhead, the M72 is potent against targets such as stationary aircraft so if the reconnaissance party had the opportunity to destroy the Super Etendards on the ground then they had the means to do so. Finally they all had white phosphorus grenades which not only burn fiercely but provide a good smoke screen if time was needed to get away and a nine millimetre Browning Hi-Power pistol tucked in a shoulder holster under the right arm.

Webbing and clothing are also important on Special Forces operations, and this was no different for the Rio Grande reconnaissance mission. The contents of a team member's webbing are always a high priority. In addition to carrying rifle magazines and grenades, Falklands webbing included a survival pack, water bottles, a bivvy bag (a Gore-Tex sleeping bag cover) and food. Each one of the team had customized their webbing according to personal taste - for example, some of them carried two 1944 pattern water bottles with metal mugs, which are ideal for making a brew and saving space. Waterproof matches are always a priority and are usually carried in small plastic containers, which are themselves waterproof. Each man also had his own medical kit, though one person in the section also carried a specialist medical bag. Syrettes of morphine were carried around the neck for easy access, and two field dressings were taped to their webbing.

Woolly hats were essential as a lot of body heat can be lost if the head isn't covered. In any environment, but especially the Falklands, it was important to guard against hypothermia which is why they were also all wearing climbing gloves, with the fingers cut out to make handling things easier. Each man wore either green Gore-Tex jackets or windproof arctic smocks, DPM (Disruptive Pattern Material) lightweight trousers which are thin but dry out very quickly after getting wet. A set of quilted green trousers, which were ideal for zipping over the lightweight DPM's were carried in the bergen – these would be essential when lying up in the 'hide' on the reconnaissance mission. Norwegian Army shirts had been a favourite with the Regiment for many years, and the team wore one with a head over - a woolen tube that slipped over your head and can be worn around the neck depending on the weather.

Andy, Chris and the winchman Phil watched as the four man SAS team started to trek off in the direction of the Rio Grande airbase about nineteen miles away. The wind was light but cold and sleet was falling steadily. It would be a hard tab across very difficult terrain carrying all this kit and at night so that they managed to stay concealed from sight. The three aviators' priority now was to leave the area as quickly and clandestinely as possible and fly to Chile.

During the planning of Operation Plum Duff, three potential locations for landing and destroying the aircraft had been chosen from a study of maps and satellite imagery. Chris selected the waypoint in TANS and Andy lifted the aircraft into a hover and moved forward. However, directly in their path was a mountain range and because of the fog he had no option but to take the aircraft higher so that it would safely navigate the mountains. Given the low fuel level and the density of the fog there was no possibility of circumnavigating these mountains but Andy was only too aware that in ascending he would be exposing them to the Argentine surveillance radar at Rio Grande but this was a risk that they just had to take.

A few minutes later the Omega burst into life confirming that they had indeed been detected by a radar system and after just a few seconds Chris confirmed that it had detected the unmistakable signature of an AN/TP3 surveillance radar and the bearing of the signal also showed that this had to be from Rio Grande. The atmosphere inside the helicopter became very tense, with everyone of the crew's nerves on edge expecting something to happen at any moment. What made matters worse was that the Omega was wired into the internal communications system and therefore throughout the climb over the mountain range they could all hear the relentless noise of the radar. Every ten seconds a pulse of sound would break the silence of their intense focus and concentration reminding them that their every move was being watched by the Argentines. No one spoke. The only sound was the pulse of the radar in their earphones. The same thought was on everyone's mind that at any moment an Argentine fire-control radar would lock onto the aircraft. Consequently Phil kept a supply of chaff in his hands constantly ready for deployment but Andy was sure that with every minute that went past they were moving out of the range of the radar-controlled artillery and Roland SAM systems that the Argentines were known to possess at Rio Grande. An interception from a night fighter from the Rio Gallegos airbase would be unlikely because they would be over the border in Chile before that could be scrambled and intercept them.

Andy clenched and relaxed his fists and forced himself to relax and focus. The long transit flight from *Invincible* to the Argentine coast had been filled with animated conversation but now the silence was only punctuated by essential dialogue relating to changes of navigation or altitude, each of them kept their thoughts to themselves.

Once they had cleared the mountain range Andy steered the aircraft towards the middle of the bay and started a slow descent and almost at once the Omega fell silent and the rhythmic pulses of the Argentine radar faded away. They now found themselves in almost perfect flying conditions that were in complete contrast to those that they had just experienced the other side of the mountain range. Chris made some careful calculations on fuel and they decided to opt for landing site two. The visibility was gradually improving as they progressed and the wind decreased in strength. Gradually in the distance they could all see the landmass of mainland Chile.

With the landing site only five minutes away Chris made a final fuel calculation. According to him they had just enough to reach the first-option landing site although he smiled when he said:
*"We may be flying on fumes when we arrive there"*
*"I hope that you are only joking and that you did pass your maths 'o' level at school"'* Andy snapped back.

The landing site that had been chosen as the best-case option was a small beach approximately eleven miles south of the large provincial capital town of Punto Arenas. Their orders were to remain undetected if possible and avoid capture for as long as possible ideally at least a week to allow the reconnaissance team back at Rio Grande to do their work without unnecessarily arousing suspicions. Then they were to make contact with the British Embassy in Santiago who would arrange for their exfiltration.

Once they had landed Chris and Phil immediately began to prepare the aircraft for its destruction by ditching it in deep water so they set about making holes in the aircraft fuselage at positions that would be below the waterline with a small hand axe and a survival knife. Andy took the aircraft airborne in a low hover and landed on the sea. He planned to rock the helicopter with the rotor until it turned turtle then escape and make his way back to the beach in the small survival dinghy. However, they had not anticipated the flat and calm sea conditions. Furthermore, the Sea King's design gave it a boat-shaped hull to enable it to make water landings and it remained defiantly upright and stable. So Andy took off once more and landed on the beach for Chris and Pete to make even larger holes in the fuselage of the aircraft particularly at its base. Andy took off again but almost as soon as he was airborne the low fuel level warning lights that had been indicating for some time that the fuel level was dangerously low suddenly went red meaning that the situation was critical and the engine began to splutter and fade intermittently. He fought with the controls trying to steady the aircraft as best as he could and made a hard landing back onto the beach which resulted in the undercarriage collapsing and the main rotor blades making contact with the sand dunes.

Andy shut down all the systems and evacuated the aircraft and joined up with Chris and Phil who were running to meet him from the other end of the beach.

*"Bloody hell mate – this isn't Farnborough Air Show"* shouted Chris.

*"Very funny"* Andy replied and he looked at his watch, it was just after six and it would be dawn in about an hour.

*"Come on lets get a move on."*

They all knew that it was essential to burn the critically damaged helicopter to destroy any evidence of their mission. Amongst their kit was two gallons of petrol for their small cooking stove and whilst Andy poured this all around the cockpit, Phil unloaded all their personal kit and Chris smashed the night vision goggles to pieces with rocks from the beach and scattered the remnants into the sea. As they all withdrew from the aircraft Andy threw a distress flare into the cabin and instantly the helicopter was completely ablaze. All three of them grabbed their bergens and started to make their way into the hills beyond the beach.

The terrain was difficult and fairly barren with fallen trees everywhere which were hard to see in the dim light available and they inevitably kept stumbling into them. They had to traverse about another ten miles of this terrain to reach their destination which was a small hill covered with woodland overlooking Punto Arenas. As the light started to improve they made the decision to lie low as it was imperative that they were not seen under any circumstances. They had covered a reasonable distance from the beach and there was plenty of cover available from the fallen trees and shrubs. Andy looked back in the direction of the beach but could see no evidence of the fire, the helicopter must have burnt itself out by now and with luck it would be a few days before the wreck was discovered which should provide them with plenty of time to get clear of the area. They were all wearing the same Disruptive Pattern material Artic smocks and trousers as the SAS team they had dropped off in Argentina some hours ago and so blended into the background well but it would be essential to keep down low to avoid the potential of being seen. They made two small low-to-ground shelters using ponchos which they had pulled out from their bergens. They had all been awake for over twenty four hours now and desperately needed some sleep but they knew that it was important to stay alert to any potential dangers so whilst Chris and Phil slept, Andy took the first watch.

Meanwhile back in Tierra del Fuego, the SAS team had moved swiftly from their infiltration point into the cover of scrub and were preparing to lie low for the remaining hours of daylight. They were laying in an all-round defence that covered the whole three hundred and sixty degree arc. They all knew that it was very important to let their bodies and minds adjust after the noisy flight in the helicopter and take in the new environment. The sights, the sounds the smells and the change in climate and terrain. After a number of eventless hours darkness fell and they started to tab the sixteen miles or so to the their destination lying up point or LUP, a wood covered hill overlooking the Rio Grande airbase from the southeast.

Back in mainland Chile, Andy's mind wandered *"What would Jessica's reaction be to his letter. " Should he have volunteered for this mission which he knew to be a one-way flight? "Get a grip"* he told himself as he sub-consciously recognised the dull ache in his left arm and rubbed it up and down sharply with his right hand. It was now obvious that they could only make their destination under the cover of darkness and the fallen trees and rough terrain would make the going tough, slow and uncomfortable. He estimated that it may be possible to achieve a half a mile or so an hour and with about thirteen hours of darkness they could theoretically make their destination in about two days but time was not important. What was critical was remaining undetected.

Andy managed to get a few hours of sleep. He awoke and the three of them shared another cold snack and started to gear themselves up for another push forward once the light had faded. Chris and Phil confirmed that there had been no signs of activity from the beach and that all had been quiet. There was absolutely no sound other than the three of them talking together in hushed voices and with the light diminished it was time to set off once more. The weight of the bergen, climbing a progressive incline and clambering over fallen trees in the darkness all combined to make the progress slow and painful for all of them. They took their first rest and had a drink of water but then realised they had only made just over one hundred yards. It was obvious to Andy that his estimate of half a mile an hour had been hopelessly over optimistic.

*"We should have kept those bloody night vision goggles"* said Phil stating what the others had also been thinking, *"It would have been a stroll in the park compared to this"*

After about ten hours of desperately slow, agonising progress they came across a small valley which offered them good protective cover and Andy decided that they would call a halt here until the following night. Whilst Chris and Phil erected their survival shelter Andy set off to look for water taking three water bottles with him. It was still completely dark but he followed the line of the valley and eventually came across a small stream. He filled the bottles and made his way back to where the others had now erected their bivouac. The first light of dawn was now breaking on the horizon and Andy glanced back in the direction of the beach. After all this time and effort he reckoned that they had covered not much more than two miles which was not a lot at all. However the objective was not distance he reminded himself but stealth. He felt comfortable that they were far enough inland to risk boiling water and cooking some food which would be heaven compared to trying to get down the cold rations with just gulps of water.

As the three of them eat their first hot meal leaning against their bergens they chatted about what might be happening with the task force some seven hundred miles or so to the east.

The day passed quickly and with the benefit of a hot meal they all slept well in shifts as previously. Once the daylight diminished they packed up and set off once more. They soon reached the little stream where Andy had filled the water bottles the previous night so they replenished them again and washed themselves in the freezing cold water. The rest of the night passed uneventfully and after five or six hours of exhausting walking, most of which was uphill they pitched camp for the third night.

In the daylight they checked that their camp was well screened from view and they spent the day relaxing as much as possible and enjoying some more hot rations. Their daytime reverie was broken by the sight and sound of a helicopter flying south along the coast towards the area of the beach where the burnt out wreck of the Sea King would be plainly visible.

*"Shit"* said Chris

*"It looks like our cover has been blown"*

*"Stay very low"*

During the rest of the afternoon they saw the helicopter making more trips all along the coast.

*"Look there"*

Phil exclaimed pointing towards the beach. Andy turned and followed his outstretched hand. He could clearly see a group of military vehicles carrying engineering and lifting equipment and other plant moving south from the direction of Punta Arenas to the beach area. It was pretty obvious to all three observers that the wreckage of the Sea King had now been discovered.

Back in the UK the news of the discovery of the Sea King had broken. Frantic diplomatic conversations were taking place and the Chilean authorities had released a statement attempting to maintain their neutrality in the conflict. They had informed the Argentine ambassador in Santiago of what had been discovered and assured him that they had not had any complicity or knowledge of this incident. To back up this stance they sent a note of official protest to the British government and ordered a thorough investigation into the incident. It was internationally important to maintain in public Pinochet's declared position on the ongoing conflict over the disputed islands.

## Wednesday 19th May 1982: Outside the Rio Grande Airbase

The Tierra del Fuego town of Rio Grande lies one hundred and thirty nautical miles north of Cape Horn, thirty three miles east of the Chilean border and about three hundred miles from the Falkland Islands. The climate is damp and cool with frost and snow being recorded in every month of the year and during April and May the temperature was usually low with the ground remaining frozen for much of the time.

Captain Archer and his three man SAS team reached their destination on Tuesday 18th May having tabbed the distance of nineteen miles from where Andy's Sea King had dropped them off. It had taken longer than they had thought because the terrain was hard going. It had been rough in the Pampas grass but rougher still when they had been traversing the numerous rocky-sided ravines and maintaining an accurate compass course had been challenging to say the least. The four men were sweating inside their windproof smocks whist outside the sleet and damp was building up and threatening to seep through the seams. Their legs were tired and many had sprained ankles but now they had arrived at the destination it was vital that they kept active to keep warm and prevent serious cold and damp penetrating their bodies' core.

Carrying out detailed reconnaissance missions undercover is a difficult operation and one that is often under estimated by military commanders and planners. The first priority for the team was to establish their LUP, a 'hide'. Military doctrine states that the best place for a covert observation post is on or near the crest of a hill whilst avoiding a topographical crest so as to avoid the possibility of being silhouetted against the skyline. The location decided upon by the Hereford planners was just on the forward slope of a wooded hill above the south easterly approach to the Rio Grande airbase about a half mile from the perimeter fence. The location allowed for a very good field of view from which to observe but not be observed provided that the team adhered to the plan and the rules which they all knew intuitively. They could clearly see that surrounding the air base's entire thirteen thousand yard perimeter was a simple, low, sheep-proof fence, which was almost certainly protected by numerous anti-personnel mines. The Argentine defenders were conscious that many of Rio Grande's twenty five thousand inhabitants were Chilean and the possibility clearly existed that some of these were being used as the 'eyes and ears' of the neighbouring regime so they placed notices in the local newspaper and broadcast on the town's radio and television stations warning of the presence of these minefields.

Captain Archer quickly sorted out 'the stag'. This was their protective guard duty. The term is believed to have originated in the Scottish Highland regiments as those carrying out guard duties were like the stag looking after his does. There were two men on stag, changing every two hours. Their job was to look and listen. If anything came towards them then they had to warn the others and get them stood to as fast as possible. The rest of the team took the opportunity to sleep covering their arcs so they would just have to roll over and start firing if anything kicked off. They also arranged Claymore mines in front of their position so that both men on stag could see them in their field of view and be ready to detonate them with a remote control hand-held device. The Claymore is a directional anti-personnel mine named after a large Scottish medieval sword. Unlike a conventional land mine, the Claymore is command-detonated and directional, meaning it is fired by remote-control and shoots a pattern of metal balls into the kill zone like a shotgun. It was the sentry's job to make the decision to detonate the mines because if the attacker was in the kill zone then the team was in a position to be compromised. The mines were positioned as a protection of last resort but the best protection was concealment. The observation party had three main tasks: to confirm the presence and number of the distinctive French-built Super Etendard Argentinean aircraft at Rio Grande, to assess the strength and state of readiness of the enemy in and around the airbase, and to work out routes into and out of the area for the raiding party whilst remaining concealed and evading enemy contact at all times. If they were unfortunate enough to be discovered then they were to make their way as fast as possible back to the coast and make contact with the submarine.

This was just the kind of clandestine surveillance, conducted from carefully concealed hides at which the SAS had excelled in Northern Ireland. Captain Archer had three tours of the province under his belt and many of his team had spent weeks concealed in trenches along the border with the Republic seeking out members of the IRA and sympathisers who were either bringing in or concealing weapons and explosives or trying to disappear following another bombing outrage in Belfast or Londonderry.

From the moment the *Sheffield* had been sunk, the Argentine Naval Air Service realised that it possessed the means to win the war. All the training that they had carried out against a Type-42 destroyer, calculated to be their toughest opponent, had paid off. They had been practising attack sequences on and the likely defence tactics on their own two Type-42 Destroyers, *ARA Santisma Trinidad* and *ARA Hercules* sold to them by the British some years before. However, they also realised that their success had made the air base at Rio Grande a priority target. The Argentine defenders were convinced that British saboteurs from the SIS, SAS and SBS would be landed on the nearest shore with the objective of infiltrating the airfield and destroying the aircraft and missiles. The announcement of the discovery of the wreck of the Sea King helicopter in neighbouring Chile convinced the Argentines that this aircraft had flown into their airspace at low altitude constantly dodging hills and dropping into radar dead ground. The base commander was certain that this was either a precursor to a major raid or was itself the evidence of an infiltration by saboteurs. He concluded that it had either delivered an SAS raiding party or probably more likely planted a navigation beacon to guide RAF bombers to the target. Rio Grande was undoubtedly a prime potential target for such a raid but he thought: *"Would they be that foolhardy"* He had no option but to suspect that the British might try such a daring tactic.

Immediately one thousand two hundred Argentine marines spent three days conducting an intensive search of the entire area, sweeping twenty five kilometres north of the base and concentrating on two sites, the Estancia Las Violetas and Seccion Miranda which they identified as the most likely helicopter landing sites.

The SAS 'recce' team having now been in situ for three days watched this activity with heightened alert. They were now aware of the discovery of the wrecked Sea King and the statement issued by the Chilean authorities. They were relieved that the main thrust of the search at this time was away from their south easterly position which had been carefully selected by the Hereford planners and had been well worth the yomp that they had carried out three days before. They were also ready to strike camp and move at a moment's notice.

On Saturday 22nd May, the third day of this search activity the Argentines dispatched two amphibious personnel carriers to take troops into more inaccessible areas but despite coming within a few hundred yards of the very camouflaged and dug in reconnaissance party, they found no trace of any intruders. Since no attack had been forthcoming they concluded that if the SAS had been there it was purely a reconnaissance mission and they must have now exfiltrated themselves overland.

They had been in situ for five days now and were now feeling cold, damp and thoroughly miserable considering it as home from home – just like the Brecon Beacons particularly when the cold, clinging fog descended around the air base which it did on a regular basis. The team had clearly identified five Super Etendard aircraft but only four seemed to be operational. The fifth aircraft had never moved and had remained in its protective hangar. However the hangar doors had been left open and the team had been clearly able to see mechanics regularly working on the aircraft and one of its engines was missing. Captain Archer deduced that the mechanics were either affecting a major repair or more likely that this aircraft had been cannibalised to keep the other four operational.

The five days had shown a fairly similar routine with aircraft coming and going all the time but nothing out of the ordinary. The base security patrols apart from the search party activities were regular and frequent and carried out at exactly the same time and in the same manner on each of the days they had been observed. There was, however one peculiarity which caught the observers on the hill by surprise the first time that it had occurred. On each evening at about 1800 hours as darkness fell around the airbase, the Argentines carried out the same procedures.

*"Clever bastards"*

Captain Archer said as he watched two of the Super Etendard aircraft being towed out from their hangars by tractors and out through the air base's main gates with a contingent of troops in jeeps and armoured personnel carriers as an escort. They were obviously dispersing their most valuable assets from any potential British attack on the base during the night either from the air, from the sea by naval gunfire or from a Special Forces team that had managed to infiltrate into the country one way or another.

On the second evening Captain Archer had arranged that the convoy would be followed discreetly by two members of his team on foot at a distance. He figured that they could not be towing those aircraft very far and that the probable destination was somewhere in the small town They had all watched with amazement as the Argentines had painstakingly slowly maneuvered the two aircraft, easing them carefully through the main gates of the air base and then along the road towards the town. The convoy was followed again on the third and fourth evenings and the destination had been the same – it was clearly a regular preventative routine. It was, however, an incredible operation and not just from a security perspective. There was a very large risk of damage to the aircraft particularly as the wing span was thirty one feet six inches and even with the wing tips folded it only reduced to twenty five feet six inches which made it a very tight squeeze between the telegraph poles on the side of the road as well as avoiding any pot holes in the road. Furthermore, the high weight loading on the forward single wheel had to be taken into account and to avoid all of the aircraft's wheels sinking into the road surface; each aircraft had to be emptied of fuel to its basic weight of fourteen thousand pounds and then reloaded in the morning when it returned to the base.

*"They only move two of them* off the base," stated one of the 'recce' team to his Captain standing next to him, *"and they go to the same places every time and at the same time and are moved back just before dawn every time".*

A week before the arrival of the British SAS team on the hill overlooking the air base, the base commander had decided that since the fact that a high proportion of the town's population of twenty five thousand inhabitants were of Chilean origin and obviously sympathetic to that country, there were few opportunities for deception and that the dispersal of the Super Etendards to safe bunkers or camouflaged sites on the exposed airfield would be difficult to achieve in daylight. So he instigated a policy of moving two of the planes at night into the town and concealing them in car parks, guarded by the Marine Logistics Battalion. He calculated that although time consuming these exercises could be concealed by satellite reconnaissance but he had not bargained with the night vision capabilities of the SAS spotters on the hill.

Just after 11.00am on the following morning, Sunday 23rd May, they watched as an Argentine military transport plane landed at the base. No sooner had the aircraft come to a standstill and the engines were shut down then there was an immediate flurry of activity. Two jeeps, an open topped flat bed lorry and a vehicle carrying a large fork lift truck sped across the tarmac and stopped just as the cargo doors were opened from the inside. The observers could see that there were a number of troops inside the cargo bay and they were now manoeuvring some large wooden crates onto pallet trucks and a team of four, one at each corner of the long wooden crate gingerly wheeled the crate down the ramp and onto the tarmac where it was then lifted by the fork lift onto the back of the waiting truck. There were five of them. All were identical in shape and size. The whole disembarkation process took just over an hour and the lorry with the five crates securely loaded then drove across to the far side of the airfield away from the observer team and disappeared inside a hangar and the doors were then immediately closed.

*"I have got a very bad feeling about this"* said Captain Archer as he focused the pair of binoculars handed to him by one of the observers onto the last of the five crates as it had been loaded on to the lorry. He could clearly make out the stencilled lettering on the side of the crate. Each one had been exactly the same. The wording was in both French and Arabic. He could not speak Arabic but he had no difficulty whatsoever in understanding the words *'Aerospatiale'* and *'Missile.' "If they are what I think they are then we are in deep shit"* he grimaced as he handed the binoculars back to one of the team by his side.

The trooper taking the photographic reconnaissance through a long telephoto lens mounted on a tripod finished off another role of film and then emptied the camera and put the exposed film into the watertight and sealed black plastic container and into a zipped pocket in his tunic along with the other four he had already taken.

*"How the hell did they get hold of those"* stated the observer next to the Captain

*"I thought that we had squared things off with the French"*

*"We have. There is Arabic on those crates for a reason"*

Ten minutes later Captain Archer gathered his team around him apart from those on perimeter security:

*"We need to send in a Sit Rep today and await further instructions"* he said to the assembled group of three men all squatting down in front of him to remain concealed.

*"Things are clearly not what we expected. One, we now know that the base is far better protected and reinforced than we had imagined. Two, two of the key targets are dispersed out of the base at night and three, well three is a bloody game-changer for the task force as It looks like the bastards have got hold of five more Exocets from somewhere in the Arab world."*

Captain Archer carefully wrote out the notes for the situation report. His patrol's signaller had been issued with a satellite communications system so he could talk directly with the SAS Directorate throughout the mission. The one-time encryption pads, Morse code and burst transmissions were no longer necessary. The down side was, of course, that he would have to pass on this very bad news directly.

# Chapter Nine

## Saturday 29th May 1982: Sheffield

Jess was sitting in the lounge of her parent's home watching television eating corn flakes. The BBC morning news was reporting on the latest situation in the South Atlantic and various commentators were debating whether the task force could survive the rate of attrition and damage that was being inflicted on them by the Argentine Air Force.

She sipped the cup of tea that was on the table beside her and opened the letter that had been delivered that morning. It was what was called *"a bluey"* in the British armed forces, a free Air Mail letter home.

*"Dear Jess*
*I have had plenty of time to think over the last few weeks..."*
As she read on the tears welled up in her eyes and then ran down her face.

*"...I love you so deeply – and I would like to make our relationship a permanent one as soon as the war is over."*
She let the thin blue paper slip from her fingers and drop onto the carpet and she put her hands to her face and sobbed uncontrollably.

Her mind went back to that Saturday night on 3<sup>rd</sup> April before he had left for Portsmouth the following day. She and Andy had gone out into town for a drink and a pizza. She knew that over the last few months she had been pressurising him into making some commitment but he had always avoided the issue saying that:
*"The time wasn't right for this reason or that"*
But she felt that time was slipping away and that her biological clock was ticking. She loved Andy. They had been together for ten years now. Everyone regarded them as a couple but even her mother had now started to believe that the chances of her daughter walking up the aisle in a white wedding were fading. But she hadn't

anticipated what he was to say as they finished the pizza and he drained the last of his beer:

*"Jess, I just think that we should cool it a bit. I am not ready for marriage and commitment and children and all that means. I still have things to achieve in my career. I am still only twenty seven years old. Why don't we have a break and see how we both feel when I return from the South Atlantic which will be in about six months' time?"*

Jess just felt numb. She was stunned. Without saying a word she got up and walked out of the restaurant and walked to the bus stop and stepped onto a bus a few minutes later. She sat looking out of the window and the tears had just flowed.

A couple of weeks later the pain and hurt had turned into anger and frustration. So when her friend Stephanie called to say did she want to go out that Saturday night to *Crazy Daisy's Night Club* in Sheffield city centre she had readily agreed.

*"I've wasted ten years of my life so I won't waste anymore"* she had thought.

Somehow the last two weeks of pain and sorrow seemed to melt away with every vodka and lime she drank. She lost count of how many she had had and so when a good looking lad came up and asked her to dance she was more than happy. One thing had quickly led to another and in a moment of rashness which she had almost instantly regretted, she had had sex with him in his car in the car park behind the club.

Five weeks later she was pregnant. And now the love of her life was in his roundabout kind of way proposing to her. What's more he was embarking on a mission from which he may not return and he was going without the knowledge that she loved him too. Jess got dressed and telephoned the office where she worked and called in sick but she was sure that she would be ok tomorrow she assured them. She decided to go round to see Andy's mother. She knocked at the door and gave his mother the letter that Andy had written to them and she said that she had had heard from him too and that he was fine. She knew that Andy had told her that they were separating. Just as she was about to say goodbye and turn away she burst into tears and covered her face.

*"You'd better come in dear"* said Andy's mother.

Half an hour later they were sitting together on the sofa in the front room of the terraced house drinking tea, Jess' eyes were red from crying. She had told her everything that Andy had said that night and had also confessed to the regrettable incident that had occurred a few weeks ago and the condition she was now in. She had then passed over the letter that Andy had written to her.

His mother read the letter in silence with a very sombre expression on her face. Different emotions were now racing through her mind. She had always liked Jess and like her husband had long hoped for a white wedding and now this had occurred and to cap it all her only son was now heading off into unknown danger from which he may not return. She turned to look at Jess, her own eyes now moist and said:

*"Don't do anything hasty dear. Take your time to make up your mind what to do and firstly you must tell your parents. I will write to Andy - whether and when he will get the letter I don't know and I suggest when you are ready you do the same."*

Jess thanked her and they embraced each other and Jess walked back to the bus stop and decided to go into town to walk around the shops and have a coffee and just think about things.

## Friday 14th May 1982: Hereford

De la Billière and members of the planning cell were addressing the sixty members of 'B' Squadron and a number of RAF personnel at the Hereford base:

*"They are expecting an attack from the sea so we will give it to them"* he stated to much audible surprise from the assembled group.

*"But"* he continued:

*"This will be just a feint, but a very serious distraction for them nonetheless. Our tactics will be a combined three pronged attack, by land, air and sea. Captain Archer and the other members of his reconnaissance team who are on their way to the air base right at*

111

*this moment will start a whole series of diversionary attacks. This will be followed by a series of sustained attacks by members of SAS/SBS who will come ashore in inflatable boats from the submarine, HMS Onyx. However, the main thrust of Operation Mikado will be the attack from the air by landing two C130 Hercules aircraft of 47 Squadron Special Forces Flight on the runway at Rio Grande. Each of the aircraft will hold thirty members of 'B' squadron SAS equipped with Land Rovers and Triumph motorcycles'.*

The Land Rovers would be the standard Special Forces *'Pink Panthers'* or *'Pinkies'* as they were affectionately known. These were based on the Series 11A 90 Land Rover but adorned with a pink paint scheme which was regarded as being a highly effective desert camouflage especially at dawn or dusk. They were also fitted with a General Purpose Machine Gun and fifty-calibre Browning heavy machine gun mounted at the rear.

There was a stunned silence in the room. This would be, they quickly realised, one of the most audacious operations ever carried out by the British military and certainly so since the end of the Second World War. The planners calculated that by approaching the air base from the west, the Argentine radar would only detect the aircraft at a range of thirty miles which meant a six minute warning for the defending forces.

*"Six minutes"*

The same thought went through the minds of all the members of the squadron as they sat there leafing through the briefing papers. According to the planners, that was enough time for the Argentines to scramble and put all the ground defences on alert but not enough time to be thoroughly prepared or so they thought.

The sea part of the campaign would see Special Forces personnel landed from the Oberon Class diesel electric submarine *HMS Onyx*. The two hundred and ninety foot submarine had been built by Cammell Laird shipbuilders in Birkenhead and commissioned in 1967 and carried eight twenty one inch torpedo tubes; six at the bow and two at the stern. She was the only non-nuclear submarine that was part of the British Task Force in the South Atlantic but her smaller displacement, only two thousand four hundred and ten tonnes when submerged, made her the ideal vessel for landing troops close to land in shallow waters. She was powered by two supercharged V16 – ASR1 diesel engines when running on the surface, and two battery powered electric motors when running submerged. The Oberon Class submarines were very quiet and state-of-the-art conventional submarines; that had proved very difficult to detect when submerged. The submarine's batteries, allowed the ship to travel underwater up to speeds of seventeen knots, but would only last for relatively short periods before requiring a recharge from the main diesel engines. To do this the vessel would have to surface or snorkel and inevitably lose its stealth to a vigilant enemy.

This part of *Operation Mikado* would see two dozen SAS troops taken ashore *from HMS Onyx* a few miles offshore in Gemini inflatable rubber dinghies rowed and piloted by members of the Special Boat Service (SBS). Exiting and then re-entering (E&RE) a submerged submarine is the most clandestine method for coastal insertion and the infiltration of water-borne targets. E&RE is a process by which a team of Special Forces operatives exit out of a slow moving submarine while submerged at periscope depth, swim to the surface and then head for the objective. On completion of the operation, the team return to the water, rendezvous with the submerged submarine, swim down and re-enter it. The process sounds simple and straightforward enough but is fraught with dangers and risks and had been practiced regularly by British Special Forces in the black, cold waters of sea lochs in Scotland.

The procedure works as follows, The submarine with its team of Special Forces troops on board slows to no faster than a couple of knots and no deeper than periscope depth which is about thirty feet. The first man out of the escape hatch about thirty minutes before the team is the casing diver. His job is to make sure the large air bottles distributed at various points around the outside of the submarine that the team will use once they have exited, are all in working order. He also prepares the team's larger operational equipment for release, which is stowed outside the submarine in special watertight bins under the outer casing in readiness to be floated to the surface on nylon lines along with the team when they surface. Finally it is his responsibility to supervise the divers as they exit the submarine and then tidies everything up before re-entering himself and the submarine departs the area.

As E&RE is almost invariably carried out at night, the casing diver works in darkness, moving around the submarine mostly by feel and memory as a light could betray his presence to a passing reconnaissance aircraft, boat or observer on a distant hilltop. In the absence of through water communications he communicates with his colleagues in the submarine by tapping the hull with a three pound brass hammer that he keeps in a leg pocket of his diving suit. The submarine crew are told to keep absolutely silent when the casing diver is outside which gives them a very eerie feeling as his clangs echo throughout the submarine which tell of his progress and the fact that he is still with the submerged submarine.

The Special Forces team then muster under the forward escape hatch in the ceiling of the torpedo storage and firing compartment. The lower hatch is opened first and one man crawls up into the tube. He continues to breathe using a breathing umbilical, a mouthpiece that is connected by a rubber tube to the submarine's air supply. The lower hatch is closed and the tube is flooded and when the pressure in the escape hatch equalises with the outside the top hatch opens and the man exits. When he is free, the upper hatch is closed again, the water is pumped out and the lower hatch can be opened and the cycle repeated until all of the team have exited the submarine. Equipment is carried in a lightweight nylon dry-bag over which is strapped a multi-pouched vest containing everything that is needed for the mission. The main assault weapon is strapped down one side or across the front of the body on a quick release hook and a pistol is fixed into a holster on the lower thigh or hip. On top of all this all personal diving equipment has to be carried which includes fins, mask and a small air bottle of only about ten minutes duration at surface pressure which has a male connection that plugs into the female connection on the large air reservoir bottles outside the submarine for recharging. The bottle is small simply because a larger one would not fit into the escape hatch along with the diver and all the rest of the equipment.

As De la Billiere continued his presentation, Steve recalled that he had carried out this procedure a number of times in Scotland and once before on operational duty. It was like being in a coffin after the lid had been nailed firmly shut, the coffin had been lowered into the ground and six feet of earth had been piled on top of you while you try and stay calm inside. It was definitely not a time to succumb to claustrophobia and Steve had learnt that the trick was to clear your mind, keep still and think pleasant thoughts whilst you waited for the signal from the casing diver that he was ready to open the outer hatch and let you out. He had always used the same focusing technique. He went back to the time he was ten years old and watching the 1966 FA Cup Final of Everton vs Sheffield Wednesday. He was with his father and Paul in their front room watching the match on an old black and white television which his father would hit from time to time to stop the picture from going grainy. After fifty seven minutes *Wednesday* had gone 2-0 up and he would never forget the feeling of euphoria and togetherness as the three of them hugged each other at that moment. The memory was not even tarnished by the fact that *The Owls* had gone on to lose the match 3-2.

The training for Operation Mikado had started in earnest and was intense. Simulated nocturnal attacks were being constantly carried out on RAF airfields from Kinloss in Scotland to Binbrook in Lincolnshire. The rule book for night flying had been torn up as RAF C-130 Hercules aircraft roared low over Britain trying to plant the transport planes onto the airfields' main runways without being spotted by the ground radar. The aircraft were approaching fast and as low as fifty to one hundred feet with the station commanders being told that they might arrive at any time and not to call the control towers. It was exciting but dangerous work for the flight crews. There was no night vision and no runway lights and one occasion the rear aeroplane ended up in front of the other passing each other in their descent without either crew being aware of it and on another occasion on his final approach to a blacked out airfield in Scotland the pilot descended into a thick mist and completely lost sight of the runway. The aircraft plunged towards the ground, terrifying everyone on board and made as hard a landing as possible without ripping the airframe apart. The members of 'B' squadron on board these aircraft were left in no doubt whatsoever that this training was serious and important as suddenly weapons that they had been promised for months suddenly materialised such as the XM 203 'over-and-under' Armalite with a 40mm grenade launcher attached to the underside of the rifle's stock.

However, as the rehearsals progressed, clear disagreement was starting to develop between the flight crews and the air traffic control personnel. Some of the RAF ground staff claimed that they had detected the approaching aircraft from a fair distance out, considerably beyond the distance envisaged in the plan but the pilots were denying that this was possible. Professional pride was at stake here but there was no room for it in a mission such as this. It became obvious to the RAF pilots that from whichever direction that they were to approach the Rio Grande air base, they would have to fly the last three hundred or four hundred miles as low as possible and in the dark.

Furthermore, word started circulating within 'B' Squadron that this was a 'suicide mission' with no reasonable hope of success and dissent was rising. Many now openly voiced that an Entebbe-style raid was not the way to attack a well-defended military air base. This was so completely different, Entebbe was not an air base within a country at war and protected by air-defence radar and surface-to-air missiles. It was a civilian airfield with a well-lit runway and was approached by very innocent-looking civilian aircraft following standard air traffic control procedures until the last minute.

*"This"* some of them said to each other *"Was on another scale entirely."*

De la Billiere, however, was becoming increasingly dismayed as he discovered that the attitude of this unit was at best lukewarm to the whole plan. He had never encountered such a lack of enthusiasm throughout his career as previously the SAS had always 'champed at the bit' at the first scent of conflict. Whether this was due to a lack of leadership, a lack of detailed intelligence or a lack of preparation time he could not be sure at this stage but time would quickly tell. Meanwhile he decided to simply press the team to rehearse harder and plan for all eventualities.

## Friday 21st May 1982: Chile

Andy, Chris and Phil were all now keeping a low profile certain now that the wreckage of the Sea King on the beach had been discovered. They broke the camp they had been hiding in during the day and moved off into dense cover of gorse bushes. They assumed that the Chilean military would now be searching for them from the air during the daylight hours. After hours of slow progress and with about three hours left till first light they pitched camp once more, camouflaging their position the best that they could in the darkness.

After a few hours of sleep Andy awoke and started to improve the camouflage of their bivouac site by building a framework of branches over the tent and covering them with gorse. The day passed slowly until the early afternoon when Phil suddenly whispered:

*"Quiet I can hear something"*

Andy and Phil stared hard in the direction in which Phil was pointing but at first could not see anything but realised by the sound that something was close by.

Andy then whispered *"There"*

All three of them were now very concerned to see an old man who had appeared into view carrying a stick and was shepherding a small herd of goats from the area of the high ground behind them downhill to the coast road. They were only about thirty meters away but fortunately passed on by without being aware of the presence of the British airmen.

*"Bloody hell that was a bit too close!"* exclaimed Andy when the man and the goats had disappeared from view. *"Sooner or later someone is going to stumble into us; we are going to have to get a move on tonight"*

The others all nodded their heads in agreement.

With a few hours remaining till nightfall they cooked a hot meal and returned to the stream to replenish their water bottles. They then broke the camp once more and started on the very hard slog of a trek up a steep incline to the top of a wooded hill. After six hours non-stop they were all exhausted and collapsed at the top, selected the best position they could in the darkness and pitched camp once again and slept till dawn.

Andy awoke at first light and stepped out of the shelter breathing in the cool but fresh morning air. He walked to the top of the hill and looked around. Towards the north east, Punto Arenas was clearly visible only about a mile or so away and there was no sign of any activity along the route that they had walked over the previous five nights. He spent five minutes reconnoitring the general area around their camp site and concluded that they had selected their position well and the bivouac was sufficiently camouflaged. The hill was thickly wooded on the top and they could not be observed from ground level in any direction but they were vulnerable to being spotted from the air so once again he woke Chris and Phil and got them to cover the site with branches and saplings and any undergrowth that they could find to conceal themselves further.

The next two days and nights passed without incident and they settled into a routine of sleeping at night and remaining awake during the day which whilst very boring was a welcome relief to be returning to some kind of normal routine. They talked about their home towns, family, football and women. Whilst Andy talked about Jess he did not tell his colleagues what had happened between them. On the morning of 25th May they awoke at first light to a bright, clear morning. Today was the day they had decided that they would try and make contact with he British embassy in Santiago by telephone from somewhere in the area of Punto Arenas. Andy had reasoned the night before that there must be a public call box or whatever they had here along their route but despite the fact that they did not have any Chilean coins he was confident that they would be able to make the call somehow.

Breakfast completed, they broke the camp for the final time and dug two large holes in which they then proceeded to bury their bergens and all the rest of their kit and then generally tidied the site to hide any evidence of their occupation over the last three days.

*At about 1300 hours Andy stated brusquely:*

*"Right let's go boys"*

The three of them set off down the hill and joined up with the coast road. They were all wearing their Disrupted Pattern Material waterproof smocks and trousers and they felt comfortable that if they just sauntered along they would be less conspicuous to any casual observer. After walking for ten minutes or so they passed a sign that indicated that they were about to enter *'Punto Arenas, Republica de Chile.'* They were passed by several civilian vehicles travelling in both directions and a few civilians walking in the opposite direction but so far no one had paid them a blind bit of notice.

*"Keep an eye out for a phone box"*

Andy said under his breath to Chris just behind him.

*"Yes – no problem. There has to be one around here soon as we are approaching a much more built up area"*

Just at that moment a car travelling in the opposite direction made a U turn in the road and pulled up alongside them. Out of the car stepped a Carabineiros Captain who called to them in Spanish and approached them after introducing himself as Captain Eduardo Suarez of the Prefectura Carabineiros de Chile:

*"Son las tres aviadores Británicos?*

Andy thought quickly even in his pigeon understanding of Spanish it was obvious that he had addressed them as *'British Airmen.'* He knew that neither his nor any of his colleagues' Spanish was up to the mark for any kind of disguise so he replied in English sticking to the agreed cover story the three of them had rehearsed the previous day up on the hill:

*"No. We are sailors from a British merchant ship in the port"*

*"Pero no hay buques Británicos en el Puerto"*

replied the Captain and he then reaffirmed his belief that they were the three missing British airmen.

*"I think that means that there are no British merchant ships currently in the port but how did he know that there were three of*

*us?"* mused Andy but he didn't have time to dwell on the thought before they were all politely asked to get into the car which they did as clearly their ruse had not worked. They were driven swiftly to a facility that contained Captain Suarez's' Commanding Officer, Lieutenant Colonel Marcus Di Maria.

On entering Di Maria's office they were offered refreshments and a casual, relaxed conversation then ensued. However, half and hour later the door opened and they were ushered into another vehicle and driven to a different facility and into what clearly was some kind of interrogation centre where they were told they were to be questioned formally about their presence in Chile.

*"Shit! I don't like the look of this"* said Chris *under his breath as they were escorted into a room* that contained various pieces of equipment which had obviously been used previously for interrogation purposes. Andy felt butterflies in his stomach but said nothing and a few moments later a Commander from the Chilean Navy entered the room and stated in fluent English that the interrogation would be carried out by him and not by any members of the Chilean secret police which Andy had feared. He felt his muscles relax and the knot in his stomach eased slightly.

It soon transpired that the three of them were to be questioned collectively and not individually and it was clear to Andy that this was going to be just a formality. During the questioning which lasted the next two hours, each of them stuck rigidly to the cover story that they had agreed before they had lifted off the deck of *HMS Invincible* eight days earlier. This was that they had been conducting a patrol off the Argentine coast in search of Argentine naval vessels, when the aircraft had suffered an engine failure. Being now a long distance from the Task Force and with the possibility of a second engine failing they had decided to seek refuge in the nearest 'friendly' country. As they only had sea charts at their disposal they had no way of navigating with any real accuracy and had, therefore, just headed west until their fuel situation became critical when they landed and destroyed the aircraft to prevent it falling into enemy hands in the event that they were in Argentine and not Chilean territory. They had then laid up for a few days until Andy had been confident that they were not in Argentina and could then make their way into the town.

The Commander seemed at first to be satisfied with the answers to the questions but then he leaned back in his chair and started to speak slowly saying that he also believed that it was possible that they had dropped off British Special Forces either in Argentina or in Chile which Andy vigorously denied on several occasions They were then left on their own but they knew that the Commander had posted two military sentries outside their door so they just sat there in silence not speaking to each other in case the room had been bugged which they suspected that it had been. The knot was beginning to return to Andy's stomach and he noticed that Phil was constantly tensing and opening his right fist. The time went by very slowly. They were all tired, hungry and in need of a good bath but they just sat around the table and kept their thoughts to themselves.

Some two hours later the Commander re-entered the room and announced that Chris and Phil were to be flown to Santiago immediately and would then be repatriated back to the UK. He then turned to Andy and said that he was to remain and would be transferred to the Punto Arenas airbase. Chris and Phil looked anxiously at Andy but he just smiled briefly and maintained his silence but his stomach tightened once again.

## Saturday 15th May 1982: Sheffield

It was a Saturday morning and Jess had woken early feeling sick like she had done for the last few days. The conversation with her parents a few days before had not gone well.

*"Oh Jessica what on earth did you think you were doing and how did you get into this mess? You are twenty seven years old not a fifteen year old school girl!"* her mother had reprimanded her.

*"After everything we have taught you."*

Jess dressed and got the bus into town and an hour later she was on the bus heading out of Sheffield City centre and after about eight miles she got off at the village of Bradfield and then walked a mile or so up to the picturesque Dale Dike Reservoir like she had done so many times before with Andy. As she walked along the well-defined and familiar footpath through woods and open fields she was listening to some music on her portable cassette player. The blue and silver Sony Walkman with its chunky buttons, headphones and leather case, had been a present from her parents the previous Christmas.

She sat on a grassy bank on the edge of the reservoir in the late spring sunshine and breathed in the warm fresh air and once again tears streamed down her face as the Human League track *'Don't You Want Me?'* played in her ears. She and Andy had gone to watch the band from Sheffield play at the Top Rank in Doncaster the previous November and now she sang along gently to the lyrics that she knew so well as she had played the song over and over again in the last few weeks.

She thought of all the time that she and Andy had spent up here, laughing together, sharing their first work experiences, talking and planning. She also remembered the time that Andy had got furious with her when she went swimming in the reservoir although there were signs on the bank telling of the deep water and its dangers.
*"Get out now"* he had yelled *"You don't know what is underneath the surface and you could get trapped"* and he had ran to the water's edge and dragged her out quite forcibly.

And then she remembered the first time that they had made love.
*"Enough."* She said to herself *"I have made up my mind."*

She would keep the baby. It was her baby. She may have lost the man she loved dearly but she would channel all that love into her child. She would manage, she knew that it would not be easy but there were plenty of single mothers bringing up children these days and her parents would just have to get used to the idea.

# Chapter Ten

## 0830 25th May 1982: Punto Arenas

It had been several hours since Chris and Phil had left the room and Andy had been left on his own but with a tray of refreshments which had lifted his spirits. Dozens of thoughts kept coming into his mind over and over again and none of them were in the least bit pleasant:

*"Would they imprison him?"*

*"Would they hand him over to the Argentines in some barter deal?"*

*"Would London disown him and declare that it was some kind of rogue unsanctioned operation that he had been involved in?"*

It was now early evening when the Commander finally returned and asked Andy politely to follow him outside to a waiting car which took them and the two sentries into the military part of the Punto Arenas airbase. They drove in silence but as they passed through the base Andy was surprised to see a C130 in standard UK camouflage livery but bearing the lettering *'Fuerza Aerea de Chile.'*

*"What the hell is going on here?"* he thought but his thoughts were interrupted by a short tap on his passenger window as the car slowed down in front of a low building on the far side of the airfield and he looked straight through the glass at a familiar face but wearing Chilean army fatigues. It was an RAF Squadron Leader he had worked with at RAF Lyneham. Andy could not conceal his surprise:

*"Ray what on earth are you doing here and wearing that gear?"*

*"I'll explain inside"* he replied with a wide grin:

*"We've heard all about your exploits and we've got a job of work for you here with us. Top brass have said that you are a key asset in theatre so come with me things are moving pretty fast right now and I need to get you up to speed with our operation here."*

Andy's head was spinning but he was delighted to see Ray and he followed him quickly into the building.

## Tuesday 25th May 1982: San Carlos Water, Falkland Islands

The *Atlantic Conveyor,* a fourteen thousand nine hundred and fifty tonne roll-on, roll-off container ship registered in Liverpool and owned by Cunard had been requisitioned by the Ministry of Defence at the outset of the conflict in the Falklands along with her sister ship, *Atlantic Causeway* through the STUFT system (Ships Taken Up From Trade). The decision had been made by the Royal Naval chiefs that *Atlantic Conveyor* was not a 'high value unit' particularly once her cargo had been discharged and so due to the necessity to get her into theatre as soon as possible and due to the fact that there was controversy about whether arming auxiliary ships was legal, she had not been fitted with either a passive or active defence system.

*Atlantic Conveyor* had sailed for Ascension Island on 25th April carrying a cargo of six Wessex helicopters from 848 Naval Air Squadron and five Royal Air Force HC.1 Chinook helicopters from No.18 Squadron. At Ascension Island she had collected eight Fleet Air Arm Sea Harriers of 809 Squadron and six Royal Air Force Harrier GR.3 jump jets and left behind one of the Chinooks to support the logistical operation on the island. On arrival in the Falklands in mid May, the Harriers were immediately off-loaded on to the two aircraft carriers *Hermes* and *Invincible* although she was kept in range of Argentine bombers because the British ground commanders needed instant access to the helicopters that she kept on board. She had landing spots on her improvised 'flight deck' and since her arrival she had been used as a virtual third aircraft carrier by the helicopter pilots. Although the precious Harriers had been taken off she was still loaded with stores and ammunition including six hundred cluster bombs for the Harriers and all of the equipment that was needed to construct an airstrip at the beach-head area in San Carlos Water.

However, with frigates and destroyers tied up protecting the two carriers and the beach-head at San Carlos where the British troops had landed as well as providing naval gunfire support, the Commander of the Task Force, Rear Admiral Sandy Woodward did not have sufficient escorts, particularly those fitted with the Sea Wolf antimissile system to go round. It was Wednesday 25$^{th}$ May, the Argentine National Day. Woodward had deliberately kept the *Atlantic Conveyor* back in the holding area until he felt that the timing was right for a fast run into San Carlos Water to unload their supplies as fast as possible and then retreat back to the relative safety of the Task Force ships. This had to be done in the dark or she would have presented a 'sitting duck' to the Argentine pilots in San Carlos Water which had now become known to the British forces as 'bomb alley.' The precaution had been taken of painting the white superstructure a matt-grey for the hundred mile voyage.

However, unknown to the personnel on *Atlantic Conveyor* two Argentine Super Etendards were making a long sweep north up from the Rio Grande air base on Tierra del Fuego before heading south east for their final approach to the Task Force Battle Group. The pilots had gone a long way round in order to spring the element of surprise on the British ships. Adrenalin surged through the veins of the two pilots of CANA 2 ESC as they released their missiles at about forty miles. As they did they 'popped up' on the radar screens of a number of the vessels at about 18.30. Chaff was immediately released from Brilliant and Ambuscade but the missiles hurtled through the chaff cloud still looking for a target. On board the merchant navy vessel the order was given immediately on receipt of the 'Air Raid Warning Red' signal:
*"Emergency Stations!"*
One of the Exocets hit the *Atlantic Conveyor* ten to twelve feet above the waterline penetrating the ship's hull and entered the C cargo deck where trucks and fuel were stored resulting in an uncontrollable fire.

*HMS Alacrity* and HMS *Brilliant* closed in to help but the order was soon given to abandon ship and by the time the survivors were picked up, a total of twelve men, including the Captain, Ian North, had died. All of the desperately needed helicopters apart from one Chinook that was airborne at the time of the attack and thousands of tons of stores, including ammunition, Harrier spares and tents had to be left on the burning ship.

*"I thought that all the bloody Exocets in the Argies' arsenal had been counted for"* snarled Woodward from the bridge of HMS Hermes to Captain Lin Middleton beside him:

*"They must have been resupplied somehow but from whom and when I don't know"*

*"Damn! Critically we don't know how many they have now got!"*

Later Woodward was back on his Admiral's bridge staring at the wreck of the *Atlantic Conveyor* burning on the horizon through his binoculars. He already knew that there was very little hope indeed of rescuing any of its valuable cargo. He also knew that Major General Jeremy Moore, the commander of the British land forces, would be fuming over the loss of the precious helicopters as his troops would now have to tab the forty miles from San Carlos across the most inhospitable landscape of East Falkland to engage the Argentine troops around Port Stanley.

*"Operation Mikado is no longer a desirable option it has now become the number one bloody priority or we are in deep trouble"* said Woodward to no one but the biting South Atlantic wind.

# Chapter Eleven

## Monday 24th May 1982: Hereford

Whilst the rehearsal training both in the UK and in San Carlos Water continued in earnest, information was continuing to be received by the planning cell at Hereford from the reconnaissance team on the hill overlooking the Rio Grande airbase by satellite communication and the news was received with very mixed emotions.

The news that the team had had visual confirmation that the Super Etendards were indeed at the base was reassuring and meant that any stocks of the Exocet missile were also likely to be there too. However, what was of real concern were the details of the strength and depth of the Argentine defences. It was obvious to the planners that the Argentines had prepared themselves for the possibility of an attack by British Special Forces from wherever it may be launched. Furthermore, they had now received the devastating news that the Argentines had almost certainly been resupplied with another five Exocet missiles.

*"This could be a game-changer"* De la Billière said to one of his aides close by.

The information from the SAS reconnaissance team had been supplemented with some useful but poor quality and cloud-obscured aerial photographs around Rio Grande supplied by the Americans. Although of poor quality they confirmed the fact that the Argentines had prepared significant defences for the air base in the event of attack.

Following the satellite communications call with Captain Archer, De la Billière had taken all the new information into consideration. He had thought deeply and had had a number of telephone conversations with senior military colleagues. Finally the War Cabinet had been consulted and agreement had been reached and permission given for his revised plan because otherwise the odds were now very firmly stacked in favour of one of those missiles penetrating the Task Force defences and striking one or both of the carriers.

Eventually he called his planners and all the operational personnel from the SAS and the RAF together for a critical meeting.

*"Gentlemen"* He started. *"I have called this meeting as we have to make some important decisions and make them today."* He had the immediate attention of everyone in the room:

*"After the sinking of The Atlantic Conveyor, the Admiralty are demanding that we accelerate our planning for Operation Mikado. It is now clear that the Argentines have managed to replenish their stock of Exocet missiles from somewhere and the carriers are now at serious risk. I do not have to remind any of you that if we were to lose either Hermes or Invincible it is game over for us in the South Atlantic and all that that means. It is also evident from the on the ground intelligence that we have now gathered that the Argentines are far better prepared defensively at the Rio Grande air base than we had anticipated. They have deployed four Marine Infantry Battalions to defend the base in anticipation of a Special Forces attack, they have also now established an anti-aircraft unit beside the base and are maintaining regular helicopter patrols along the shoreline. This is a formidable defensive force which cannot successively be engaged by a Special Forces raid. Operation Mikado was always going to be audacious, daring and challenging but now I believe that with the knowledge we now have that the odds are stacked against us and that we would be taking serious and unacceptable risks with some of our most precious military personnel."*

*"So Operation Mikado is abandoned"* asked a trooper standing towards the rear of the briefing room.

*"No! It most certainly is not!"* replied De La Billière with some indignation.

*"We just have to adjust our plans in the light of the new information that is now available to us. We have to accept the real situation that despite our very best methods the Argentines have been resupplied with additional stocks of Exocet missiles and that this could have a very significant adverse effect on our ability to retake*

128

*the Falkland Islands. Our Task Force will not be able to stand the rate of attrition, the weather window was always challenging and the potential loss of one or both of the carriers would be terminal for the whole operation. Clearly we cannot now eliminate the risks entirely but we can and must reduce the odds against us and rely on the speed, strength and skill of our land forces now that they are back on the islands."*

*"So what is the plan?"* enquired the rebuked trooper in a softer enquiring manner.

*"We now know that the Argentines have only four operational Super Etendard aircraft as the fifth has been cannibalised for spare parts. The Exocet missile cannot be air launched from any other aircraft in their inventory. We now know that all the aircraft are dispersed at night in defence of a potential British attack on the air base. Two are camouflaged around the base and two are taken off the base and concealed in the neighbouring town. These two aircraft gentlemen, are our targets with a refined Operation Mikado. If successful we can reduce their strike threat by fifty percent in one clinical operation and spook them into moving the aircraft and the remaining Exocets from the base and possibly out of theatre."*

The room was silent as he continued:

*"The plan is to insert a very small but highly capable team by sea as previously planned. They will rendezvous with Captain Archer's men on the hill overlooking the Rio Grande air base and receive all the local information, topography, troop movements and lay outs that they need. Critically, they will also have one night to reconnoitre the situation and see for themselves the movement of the aircraft and its escorts and the formation of the guards during the night before they are returned to the base the following morning. The key element of the plan is plausible deniability. Stealth is our weapon. There will be no explosions or blowing up of aircraft and there will be no open engagement with enemy forces. The Argentines do not remove the Exocets on these aircraft at night as it would involve a very long and complex operation to replace them and make them operational again in the morning. Our mission is to simply enter the codes that will cause them to mal-function and thereby*

129

*taking them out of the game. As far as we and the rest of the world are concerned British troops have not entered Argentine territory."*

*"What about the remaining inventory of missiles"* stated another member of the group facing their Commander.

*"We will have to deal with those as and when the opportunities present themselves. In the meantime, our ships are more wary now and the combat air patrols and airborne radar surveillance have been stepped up. Furthermore the chaps in the Fleet Air Arm have developed a technique involving using Sea King helicopters to act as decoys, which they are confident will deflect sea-skimming missiles away from our surface ships."*

He did not go on to explain how this worked in detail but it involved the deployment of a helicopter to the right of a targeted ship to seduce the incoming missile away from its parent ship and then, at the last moment, climb rapidly, with the missile hopefully passing harmlessly below and falling into the sea as it runs out of fuel.

Over the last twenty four hours he had also decided that the revised Mikado operation did not require the more strategic skills of the Squadron 'B' Major but of a more hands-on, tactical leadership style suited to a very small and nimble team. He had liked Steve Barraclough from the first time that he had met him and he had played his part along with the rest of 'B' Squadron perfectly in the glare of publicity during the siege of the Iranian Embassy in London two years earlier. Even more importantly, he was a very popular figure in the unit and the men would follow him anywhere and the reports of his work with the squadron in Oman had been exemplary. He had just entered the second year of his second two year tour within the regiment and was the ideal candidate to command the small team.

*"The mission will be undertaken by a team of six men. I have decided that it will be lead by Captain Steve Barraclough who I believe is ideally suited to this challenge and he has handpicked the other members of the team to accompany him. Let me remind you that the objective is to disable the missiles. It is not to cause major damage and chaos. We do not intend to engage with the enemy*

*forces unless absolutely unavoidable. I will keep all of you updated as things progress but that is all for now and the team are being immediately dispatched south and will be liaising with the Task Force as soon as possible and then transferred to the submarine HMS Onyx.*

## Tuesday 25th May 1982: Outside the Rio Grande Airbase

Captain Archer and his men had now been in situ for seven days now. They had been fully briefed on the revised operation Mikado plan and were all feeling pleased that at last some action was getting under way. It had been agreed with the planners in Hereford that once the insertion patrol had rendezvoused with his men then two of them would immediately depart where they would make their way to the coast, retrieve the submersibles left by Steve and his team and then liaise with the submarine as it surfaced cautiously very aware that there would be shore patrols by Argentine aircraft. They were then to return with additional submersibles for the extraction of the remaining six men from the attack and the two that had been left on the hill.

The observation team were relieved that they would soon be on the move again. It had been a miserable mission but a vital one as they all knew. It was just, that for some of them it had been a candid reminder of days spent in a wet, boggy ditch on the border between the North and the Republic of Ireland as they waited to intercept and take out members of the Provisional IRA as they crossed to and forth to carry out their atrocities.

## Wednesday 26th May 1982: HMS Onyx

There were six of them in Steve's team including himself, all members of the SAS. He had worked on previous operations with three of them and the other two were known to him and he was well aware of their capabilities. They were accompanied by two members of the Special Boat squadron (SBS) whose task was to pilot the

Gemini boat and take Steve and his team ashore and return them to the submarine at the end of the operation. Steve did not know these two men but he had worked on previous missions with the SBS and despite their inter-service rivalries he had been impressed with their professionalism and determination. The SBS worked with the Geminis all of the time and it made perfect sense that they should take responsibility for the boat and the insertion on this occasion.

The Gemini was a rigid inflatable assault boat which came in three sizes, 5.2, 6.5 and 8 meter versions. Their hulls were made of glass-reinforced plastic which made them ideal for beach assaults. They were powered by a single or twin140 horse power outboard motors with a top speed of 35 knots. Their low profile engines made them perfect for raids on hostile shores and Steve was assured by the SBS men that they would not be heard or seen during the insertion of his team.

They were all set to go that evening. They checked their equipment and went over the detail of the plan once again whilst they awaited the final authorisation for the operation.

## Friday 28th May 1982: Rio Grande Town Supermarket

The six men had spent the first night and day reconnoitring the area and noting the arrival and departure of the two aircraft. The number and position of the guarding troops and any regular patrols that they carried out. During the day they had laid low keeping themselves and their kit concealed and out of sight and taking turns to catch some sleep and take watch.

The supermarket car park was surrounded by a chain link fence about six feet high with small flood lights mounted on extended poles every fifteen yards or so which lit the car park but left large areas in shadow or semi darkness. They were designed to deter would-be car thieves and thefts from the supermarket not to protect high tech military aircraft. The chosen entry point had been carefully selected the previous night and verified again during the daylight hours. It lay equidistant between two lights and provided the maximum amount of shadow possible. The two men of the wire-cutting detail quietly and quickly clipped out the entry point whilst the others remained alert out of sight in the background.

Once the hole in the fence had been cut Steve and one other member of his team Barry, scrambled through. Barry started to stealthily approach the first parked aircraft when suddenly a man in white overalls climbed down the ladder from the cockpit and he turned as he reached the ground and saw the dark figure coming round the rear of the plane.

*"Qui etès-vous"* he challenged nervously.

*"You traitorous French bastard"* muttered Barry just as another man in matching overalls appeared from the front of the plane where he had been working in an inspection hatch holding a large wrench in a threatening manner and stepping towards him. The British had suspected that although the French government had complied fully with the NATO/Common market weapons embargo, a French technical team comprising of Dassault Aviation and Aerospatiale personnel remained in Argentina and were probably supervising the difficult job of fitting the Exocet launch system and rails to the Super Etendard aircraft and helping to prevent malfunctions.

*"Non arrêt Pierre! Ce n'est pas notre guerre. Pour nous il est juste un travail"*

In response the second mechanic threw the wrench on the ground and backed away from the trooper and joined his colleague standing with their backs to the aircraft. Whilst Steve kept his weapon pointing at them, Barry quickly and roughly gagged them and tied their hands behind their backs with a plastic clip. They were then prodded and pushed quietly away from the two parked aircraft and bundled though the hole in the perimeter fence where they were pulled through by one of the team on the other side.

*"Just do as you are told mate and you will be fine"*

*"Your President has told our Prime Minister that you are to do everything to support us so start helping now"* said another and as an added incentive he prodded the one called Pierre roughly in the abdomen with the muzzle of the 203.

Pierre then had his hands released and was told to take off his overalls quickly. Steve had selected him because he was nearer his size and figured that his colleague Gilles, would be easier to control. He changed into the white overalls and the white cap leaving the French mechanic from Aérospatiale to don his abandoned uniform and have his hands rebound with a plastic clip. Steve attached his webbing across his chest over the white overalls. The contents of his webbing were usually a high priority. However, in this instance he did not want to restrict his mobility and agility so he limited them to spare rifle magazines and grenades, a water bottle and his own medical kit with syrettes of diamorphine dangling from his neck for easy access.

Whilst the operation had appeared quite straightforward on paper – a clandestine, stealthy insertion by a very small Special Forces team to sabotage two aircraft's missiles without any enemy engagement, Steve was well aware of the huge risks involved.

*"What were the odds of remaining undetected"* he had mused and was recalling now.

*"If not what then were their chances of surviving and escaping from a significant force with large reinforcements nearby?'* He tried to shut these thoughts out of his mind and focus on the task at hand. Steve had decided to take his bergen with him. Planning for the unexpected had been drilled into him time and time again. He shouldered his bergen, although he needed to be highly mobile he never went into action without certain pieces of life saving kit.

*'Shit happens so be ready for it.'*

Steve pushed Gilles in front of him and released his hands and gag. *"Just one word and there will be this knife in your back"* he said and Gilles saw the blade glint in the moonlight.

*"It is not our war monsieur. We are here to simply complete our contract so we will not obstruct you."*

Steve re-sheathed the knife and shouldered his back pack and followed Gilles back through the hole in the perimeter fence. They walked silently in single file with Steve trying to conceal his weapon against his side. About twenty five yards ahead of them a group of three guards were standing together talking and smoking cigarettes in a relaxed manner. They rubbed their hands together in the chilly air, their rifles slung over their shoulders, it was going to be another long night of boring duty. Gilles waved casually at the men in the distance and the wave was acknowledged in return with a shout from one of them:

*"Make the aircraft fly faster tomorrow mon ami! We have some large ships to destroy and then the Malvinas will be ours forever"*

Steve and Gilles walked slowly but purposefully towards the parked aircraft nearest to the entry point in the fence. The French Dassault-built Super Étendard was nearly thirteen feet high, forty six feet long and with a wing span of thirty one and a half feet. The aircraft projected an image of menace and potency as the two men approached. As Gilles climbed the ladder into the cockpit area, Steve made his way to the Exocet missile slung beneath the starboard wing of the aircraft. He located the flap that contained the control housing and inserted the special key that he had been given and the waterproof flap swung open revealing a small keyboard. He took the piece of paper that he had carefully placed in the pocket of the overalls and punched in the sequence of numbers and letters that were written on it and a red light blinked twice in the half darkness. Steve closed the flap and motioned for Gilles to come down and join him back on the ground.

They then slowly walked together pretending to be talking quietly towards the second aircraft parked about ten yards away. Half way to the aircraft two guards started walking towards them from where they had been standing behind the fuselage. Steve motioned for Gilles to go ahead and meet with them whilst he just raised a hand in a friendly gesture and sauntered to his right to go around the parked plane from the rear and access the starboard side where he could repeat the process he had carried out a few moments ago on the first aircraft. He was just closing the waterproof flap having seen the red light blink twice at him when Gilles approached him and he saw the two guards start to walk away to the far side of the car park but now directly in front of the aircraft.

Gilles said something which Steve did not understand and as he turned his head towards the Frenchman his left hand accidentally brushed against his assault rifle which he had lent against the body of the aircraft sending it clattering to the ground. He instantly stooped to pick it up but one of the guards saw the weapon and cried out, their eyes met and Steve could see the guards start to unsling their rifles. He instinctively dropped them both with a double tap sending a two round burst straight through the chests of the challenging guards. The four shots rang out loudly in the still of the night. There were shouts from around the car park and a flurry of movement and the noise of boots crunching on the gravel in haste. Gilles cried out in alarm but Steve just ignored him and started to run towards the fence where the hole had been cut sensing rounds starting to lance through the air all around him.

*"Shit –so much for plausible deniability"* he muttered to himself as he dived to the ground aware that the white overalls would stand out making it difficult to conceal himself even in the shadows provided by the street lights of the supermarket car park.

The five men on the other side of the fence some two hundred yards away opened up with blanket bursts of protective covering fire but suddenly rounds were coming in from all directions. An armoured personnel carrier (APC) on the far side of the car park suddenly opened up with its turret-mounted 7.62 mm machine gun, firing wildly in the direction of Steve and the rest of the patrol a few hundred yards behind him. For the next few seconds it was both chaotic and terrifying. Steve was desperately trying to make himself a hard target, keeping low whilst crawling into a fire position. Instinctively he wanted to keep down and wait for it all to end but he knew that it would not and he had to do something quickly and effectively. He could see two jeeps roaring towards him across the car park silhouetted by the overhead lights, one stopped and three soldiers jumped out and started running towards him whilst a fourth remained on board and brought the general machine gun mounted on its back to bear raking the earth not more than ten yards from where he lay. Steve took a deep breath and stuck his head up. There seemed to be no communication between the APC and the other vehicles. Infantry were jumping out of the back of the APC shouting and firing but Steve was convinced that they were not entirely sure what they were firing at but even so there was so much incoming fire from their direction that he was forced to get his head down again. A second APC had now started to manoeuvre itself towards the parked aircraft and a sustained burst from its machine gun sent rounds thumping into the ground getting closer and closer to where Steve lay. He knew that it took maximum fire-power balanced with ammunition conservation to win a firefight but it was clearly evident that the opposition's firepower was far superior to theirs. Open engagement with the enemy on this scale had definitely not been in the plan.

*"This was fast turning to rat shit."*

'Whoosh'

A rocket and then a split second later it was followed by another one that sped over his head from behind the perimeter fence and the two Law 66 missiles slammed into the side of the advancing APC. There was a massive shudder of high-explosive and a huge ball of flame erupted from the stricken vehicle and soldiers were screaming and leaping out of the back and front with their uniforms on fire. It was a scene from hell. A fusillade of machine gun bullets came in bursts from behind him and then a third rocket streaked across the car park and one of the jeeps that that was firing its general purpose machine gun exploded in a massive impact that knocked it on its side and was immediately covered in flames and smoke. There was shouting, hollering and general confusion and mayhem everywhere. Steve realised that things could quickly spiral out of control. Reinforcements would soon be on their way from the air base, command and control would be restored and effective superior fire power would overwhelm them in no time at all. He had to move quickly and decisively.

He pushed himself into a crouched position and released the 40mm grenade fitted below his M203 aiming it in the general direction of the second jeep that had come careering around from the rear of the two parked aircraft and was spraying machine gun fire wildly in all directions. He watched the bomb going through the air and there was a loud bang, screams and then a shower of gravel descended upon him. The grenade had found its mark and a second jeep was now burning on its side with its engine still racing adding to the cacophony of sound and confusion. White phosphorus grenades had also been deployed by the team behind him providing a pervasive smoke screen between Steve and his adversaries. Steve instinctively knew that this was his chance to retreat back the two hundred yards to the perimeter fence and to get away but just as he was about to turn and sprint there were screams and shouting from behind him. A sustained burst of accurate machine gun fire had found targets. One of his patrol, Staff Sergeant Harris was killed instantly when three bullets raked in a diagonal line across his chest and a second trooper was badly wounded in the left arm and shoulder. Steve did not know the extent of the casualties caused to the other members of his patrol but he was certain that if he ran towards them, now in his white overalls despite the darkness and the shadows, he would be a sitting duck and he would bring even more concentrated and accurate fire upon his comrades.

Although it was completely against what his instincts were telling him, Steve knew that he had to go forward and attack this force that vastly outnumbered him. Perhaps it was crazy, suicide even but there was no option, he had to draw their fire and attention and allow his comrades to evacuate and get to the rendezvous point or they would all die or be captured. He would catch them up in due course. Without thinking he changed his magazine. He had no idea how many rounds were left in it but it still felt heavy so he shoved it in his webbing for later. He took a deep breath and shouted:
*"Fuck it! The deniability is completely up the spout now!"*
He stood and turned and as he did so he let loose a long and sustained burst of fire from his M203 straight into the open intake cowling of the port engine on the nearest Super Etendard aircraft. The hail of bullets shredded the delicate turbo fan blades and other parts of the engine ensuring that with no supply of spare parts, this aircraft would take no further part in this war whatever the outcome. What Steve did not know at this time was that this was the aircraft that had launched the Exocet missile that had struck HMS Sheffield so devastatingly amidships just over three weeks before.

His actions took the Argentine guards completely by surprise and his fire cut down two, then three and then four of them as he ran head forward, jinking, then diving to the ground and rolling and then firing a volley of shots once again. After what seemed an eternity but was actually only about a couple of minutes he found himself behind the side wall of a warehouse building on the edge of the car park. He lent against the wall his chest heaving and gasping for breath and at the same time amazed that there were no patches of red on his overalls. Other than cuts and bruises he was unscathed – so far!

He ran along the edge of the warehouse which led away from the car park and the scene of carnage just managing to find his way in the half light emanating from the car park behind him. He clambered on to some large plastic rubbish containers and vaulted over the rear wall landing on grass on the other side. Clutching the M203 rifle in his right hand he just ran in the semi darkness across what looked like a field heading towards a line of trees about four hundred yards away. The supermarket had been built on the edge of the town and beyond lay open countryside. He measured his pace but kept going quickly. He could hear shouts and a commotion behind him but quite far back at this stage but for how long he did not know. All he wanted to do was to get away. He just had to keep going and the take stock, conserve ammunition, identify his position and somehow get to the rendezvous point.

The four surviving members of his patrol had watched their leader in awe and amazement willing him on but expecting him to be cut down at any moment. Fire was still coming in sustained bursts. One of them shouldered his dead comrade and the four of them set off back the way they had come moving as quickly as possible as they knew that the area would soon be swarming with Argentine troops and probably tracker dogs as well. They had to make the journey of three or four miles to the rendezvous point as fast as possible and whilst still protected by the cover of darkness. Once it was light they would be easily spotted by the Argentine patrolling helicopters. They forged ahead in silence. Every one of them apart from the injured man whose arm and shoulder was heavily bandaged, taking a turn at carrying their deceased colleague. Whilst speed was important, remaining undetected was vital. They could not risk another engagement with enemy forces. Although they had conserved ammunition they did not have enough for a major firefight and they would be outgunned anyway and quickly overrun with all that that entailed. Each of them apart from the body carrier covered all of the arcs, weapons ready, nerves and senses heightened to their maximum level.

After an hour of they were about half way. It was exactly two hours to the rendezvous time. The air was chilly but thankfully there was a high degree of cloud cover restricting the natural moonlight but twice in the last ten minutes a helicopter with a powerful search bean had rattled overhead causing them to dive into the bushes and lie low and still. They now had to liaise with the two remaining men of the 'recce' team and then jointly traverse back over the rough Patagonian countryside to the rendezvous point as soon as possible.

## Friday 28th May 1982: Outside the Rio Grande Airbase

The two remaining members of Captain Archer's reconnaissance team had heard the shooting and explosions coming from the town and they could now clearly see balls of fire and smoke belching up into the night sky.

*"What the hell is that all about?"*

*"It must have gone wrong because that was definitely not in the plan"*

As they started to leave their LUP which had been their base for the last ten days they saw a lot of movement on the air base. Troops were running across the tarmac and jumping into the back of at least half a dozen open top trucks, four armoured personnel carriers were manoeuvring near the front gate and these were being quickly joined by jeeps and light armoured vehicles. Major reinforcements would soon be arriving in the town.

*"Let's get our gear and get the hell out of here now"*

# Chapter Twelve

## Saturday 29th May 1982: Tierra del Fuego

All hell broke loose. Flashes and bangs came from all around him and Steve could hear the screech and the distinctive noise of the air displacement as bullets zipped past him.

He had walked, ran, scrambled and crawled for about fifteen to twenty miles away from the supermarket car park and into the surrounding countryside. He had managed to stop behind a rock and stripped of his webbing and changed out of the overalls and hauled on a spare set of fatigues from the side pocket of his bergen. It was a few hours now since he had shot the guards in the car park. He needed to lie up and reconnoitre his bearings so that he could make his way to the rendezvous point but he was not sure where he was and survival was the first priority now.

Suddenly Steve let out a scream as a high velocity round passed through his left thigh. He could see blood pouring from the gaping wound and that there were clear entry and exit points.

*"Shit – that doesn't look too good"*

He said out loud as he cut away the fabric of his fatigue trousers using his combat knife. Adrenaline and training were kicking in and numbing the pain which he knew would not last long. He ripped open the two field dressings that were taped to his webbing and applied them to the holes in his thigh. He was bleeding profusely. He knew that at this rate of blood loss he wouldn't survive long. Using his belt as a tourniquet he tightened it around his upper thigh as much as he could in order to try and staunch the blood flow. Fortunately, the bullet had passed clean through and had missed the femoral artery so the wound was not what was called a 'gusher' as he knew that if that was the case he would have very little time indeed. The pain was searing through his leg now as he reached for one of the syrettes of diamorphine which he had around his neck and quickly injected into his left thigh. On previous operations he had seen what horrific damage even a small calibre round can do to the human body. A 7.62 mm short, the standard AK47 round, hits human flesh at a velocity of seven hundred and fourteen meters per second. The bullet ricochets off bone and rips an erratic course through the body, tearing a ragged exit hole as it leaves.

Steve fell on his back as the felt the chemicals surge through his blood stream and he let out a long breath and pulled himself into a sitting position and leaned against a rock. Rounds were still whizzing around him. He had to get out of here as far as possible whilst under the cover of darkness. Slowly he crawled on his stomach back to the next cluster of rocks dragging his damaged left leg as best as he could. After a while the incoming rounds suddenly stopped. The pursuers, he realised, hadn't seen him. They did not know he was hit. They had just been firing speculatively in this direction as well as a number of others and he could see groups of searchlights in the distance fanning out across the open terrain.

Steve kept absolutely still ensuring that his exhaled breath left no tell-tale vapour trail in the cold air. The temperature was a degree or two above freezing point and he could not afford to get cold and his muscles to start to seize up – he had to keep moving. He hauled himself to his feet and shuffled towards a group of trees on his left. He selected a sapling and took out his combat knife from the sheath on his belt and cut himself a staff of some sorts that would help to take the weight off his injured left leg. He set off slowly and started to climb a small rise towards a ridge. It was slow, painful progress and he just closed his mind to all other thoughts and focussed all his energies and concentration on just staying upright and moving forwards. After about an hour he had made it to the ridge. He collapsed and let his bergen roll to the ground and then propped up against it he took a long drink from his water bottle. In the distance about another mile or two further ahead in a small valley he could see a light and a group of buildings and a faint trail of smoke was climbing upwards from one of them lit up by the night stars. He hauled himself to his feet once again and leaned heavily on the stick with his left hand.

Steve struggled on sometimes limping, sometimes crawling, sometimes stumbling, occasionally loosing his balance on a few occasions as he slowly descended down the valley. In his mind he was back in the Brecon Beacons three years ago on the final stage of the SAS selection course. The last day was a real bastard. How he had wanted to throw his bergen containing the weights and the rest of his kit on the ground when seven of the twelve in his group that day finally said

*"Fuck this. I am not going any further"*

But he hadn't despite every muscle, every sinew in his body screaming with pain. He had been gritting his teeth so hard that he had bitten through his bottom lip. For a split second he had imagined the weight slipping off his shoulders and then the relief of sitting down and ending this ordeal but that thought was cut off in an instant.

*"Yes and I would then spend the rest of my life regretting it and being unable to live with myself for those few seconds of relief"* he had told himself. Somehow that thought had lightened the load and he straightened himself up and turned to the others who around him

*"Who's for reaching the pub before closing time? Last one home buys the round."*

He was now determined that no one would see the inner him. He would not let them grind him down. He thought of his brother, Paul, working everyday in the intense heat and noise of the smelting shop. Smoke, sulphur fumes and graphite dust permeating his surroundings but he didn't quit because he couldn't.

*"If you're coming, then get a bloody move on"* he had said as he strode off, his shattered body taking the strain once more. When the pain signals had started coming in from all parts of his body at once he had just switched off and become an automaton. Even when the vicious bastards had moved the finishing point and they saw the truck that was supposed to take them back to camp about twenty miles away move off again another ten miles further on and loaded his bergen with even more bricks he had not cracked.

He had to get himself back in that zone now. He knew that he had to be reasonably close to the border:

*"Am I still in Argentina or Chile?"* he asked himself

*"Would the Chileans give him a good reception or not? Would the Argentines pursue him across the border anyway in this remote location?* A myriad of thoughts were bombarding his tired brain.

*"Focus"* he almost shouted as if he had received an order from a superior officer as his breath exhaled in the cold night air.

The light coming from what he could now clearly see was a small farm house was getting nearer now.

*"They don't know that I am here. The blood loss is held at a reasonably acceptable level as is the pain at the moment. I need to move now and move as quickly as I can under the circumstances but in a totally covert fashion."*

Two hours later it was just starting to get half light as the dawn approached. Steve was at the entrance to the farm house. Propping himself up against the wall he cautiously peered through the window. There was a small table light on and there was still a glow from an open fire and in front of it lay a dog and asleep in an old wooden chair was an old man, presumably the farmer with two empty wine bottles and a glass on the floor beside him. The dog stirred and pricked up his ears. Steve drew back and held his breath. Nothing. He had to make a move or he would fall down in a minute. It was now or never.

During his time in the SAS he had learnt languages and had a pretty good working knowledge of Russian, Spanish and French. Steve knocked firmly on the old wooden front door. It was weathered and light blue paint was peeling away from it but it was still sturdy enough and the knock seemed very loud indeed in the still night air. The dog started barking and the old man stirred and started muttering and then shouted at the door thinking it was one of his farm hands:

*"You are too early amigo"*

Steve knocked again and the dog was charging around now and the old man got up and shuffled to the door and withdrew the heavy bolts at the top and bottom. The sight that greeted the elderly farmer was one that would stay with him for the rest of his life. A tall, imposing young soldier soaked in blood, his face streaked with mud

144

and camouflage paint and drenched with sweat and exhaustion leaning against the door jamb to hold himself up but with a big smile on his face.

*"My God – who the hell are you?"*

Steve spoke quickly and quietly in Spanish. His tired brain switching into some kind of auto pilot that would temporarily block out the pain but he knew he was close to collapse and passing out. He had one chance.

*"Don't worry my old friend, I mean you no harm. I am English and a long way from home and I have been fighting the Argentinean forces. It is all to do with the war in the Falkland Islands."*

*"Ah the Malvinas. They try to steal your lands by force as well"*

*"I hate those bastards"* spat the farmer through yellow nicotine-stained gritted teeth.

*"You had better come in"*

Steve dragged his battered body through the door and flopped down onto a wooden chair letting his gun and bergen slide to the floor. He relaxed. Even in this state he instinctively knew that the old man could not be a physical threat to him.

The farmer looked at Steve's leg and said:

*"What has happened to you my friend? How bad is it?"*

*"I will survive – for the moment anyway"* Steve replied stoically

The old man grunted and shuffled past him and into a small kitchen off the main room and five minutes later he returned with two steaming mugs of tea. He poked the remains of the fire and threw a few logs on and it soon sprung into life throwing some much welcome warmth and glow into the room. Steve felt the tension in his muscles relax a little but the pain in his leg was now starting to throb badly. The old man rolled a cigarette and put it in his mouth and lit it and offered the papers and tobacco tin to Steve who thanked him but shook his head.

*"Where are we"* Steve enquired after a few minutes.

*"We are only about a mile and a half from the border"* the farmer replied.

*"I have lived here for over fifty years and my father before me and this farm used to be on Chilean territory but the border was never really defined back then and somehow the Argentines have*

*annexed this land as the border was tightened up only a few years ago in 1978 during the crisis."*

Steve was aware that four years ago the Argentines had initiated *Operation Soberania* a plan to seize the disputed Beagle Channel Islands but stopped the operation a few hours later. However, as a result borders on Tierra del Fuego had been tightened up and the line had been slightly redrawn and so the farmer had suddenly found himself in Argentine territory and not that of Chile. The old man had continued to talk whilst smoking and drinking his tea

*"My wife died last year after a long illness. However, a couple of months ago my daughter returned from Santiago where she had been in medical school and had become a qualified nurse and she has been looking after me but I know that she will leave in the summer. This is no place for a young girl. She needs to build a life and a family. I still have my two old friends who live near by who work on the farm."*

Steve suddenly realised that they were not alone in the house and his senses went on alert and just at that moment a young woman in a dressing gown appeared at the top of the stairs:

*"Papa – who are you talking to?"*

*"My God who are you"* exclaimed Isabella as she put a hand to her mouth in a startled surprise as she came down the stairs and entered the room after hearing her father speak to someone.

*"A friend in need"* replied Steve with the broadest smile he could make whilst clenching his fists in pain. Isabella and her father exchanged a heated conversation in Spanish with a lot of arm waving and raising of voices which Steve got the gist of which was that she would do her best to clean him up, he could rest for the day but he would have to move on as he could put them in great danger.

Steve sat on the wooden chair sipping a second warming tea that the farmer had made him in a large chipped white ceramic mug whilst Isabella gently cut away the blood and dirt soaked khaki fabric of his fatigue trousers. She had brought some cotton wool and some hot water with disinfectant in it and Steve had directed to her to some more dressings in his webbing and she was about to try and bathe the wound on both sides of his thigh.

*"This will hurt quite a lot I think"*

Steve looked up at her and just smiled and then every muscle in his body went rigid and he gripped the arms of the wooden chair that he was sitting in with all his strength as she dabbed at the wound but the smile never left his face.

Isabella dressed the wounds as best as she could. At least they had stopped bleeding for the time being and she relaxed the pressure of the tourniquet on Steve's thigh.

*"You will need proper medical attention very soon"* she said quite matter-of-factly in a detached *manner "Otherwise this will get badly infected and you could then be in real trouble"*

Steve sensed that she was still resenting the middle of the night intrusion into her world and that she was genuinely frightened – of him or the situation he was not sure. Both probably.

He unpacked his bergen and retrieved his personal Sabre locator beacon. Struggling up from the chair he opened the front door and placed the beacon on a low wall and switched it on manually. It was the same model that the Harrier pilots were using when flying off *Hermes* and *Invincible* but their version switched on automatically on touching water. Isabella then helped him get out of his outer clothing and assisted him into the chair that her father had just vacated as he went upstairs. She turned out the light and said

*"Try and get a bit of sleep. It will be dawn in about an hour. I will wake you but I do not think that we will be interrupted before then."*

It was only then that Steve realised how incredibly pretty Isabella was. She was tall with raven black hair and piercing sapphire blue eyes. Steve had never really had time for women. Unlike his mate Andy he had never had a girlfriend at school, in fact he did not know a single girl by name during his entire school years and hadn't really spoken to one either. They were simply alien to him but gorgeous and he watched from afar always lacking the confidence to initiate a conversation. During his army career to date there had been a few 'one night stands' and short term relationships but that was all. There simply had not been either the opportunity or the room in his life to have any kind of meaningful relationship. Life was the army and the regiment was life as far as he was concerned.

Isabella left Steve and went upstairs and he heard her resume the conversation with her father but he couldn't make it out and within a few minutes he had nodded off. However, she did not sleep. She sat up in bed thinking about this dangerous stranger who had invaded their privacy and she was sure that the Argentines would come and search for him and they would then be in danger themselves. He had to go and go very soon.

An hour later she crept downstairs. First light was just starting to come through the windows and she went over to where Steve was still slumped in the arm chair with his leg up on a wooden stool fast asleep.

*"There was something about this tall stranger in the blooded uniform"* thought Isabella, *"He seems to exude strength and presence"* and she felt a stirring in her stomach.

*"That's ridiculous'* she told herself *"you've only met him for a few hours and know nothing about him"*

She went into the kitchen and made a pot of tea and then sat on the far side of the room looking across at the sleeping soldier. The firelight flickered light across his face which was still streaked with mud and a little blood had clotted in the growing stubble on his chin and she felt a twinge again in her stomach, something she had not felt since she was a teenager and she moved across the room almost unconsciously and brushed the hair off his face and gently placed a light kiss on his forehead.

*"I can't believe that I just did that"* she whispered to herself but it was all that she could do to stop herself from doing it again. She'd only had one serious but tumultuous relationship in her life which was when she was training at medical college in Santiago. Three years she had been with Marcus but she had never told her father that he had struck her on at least two occasions during drunken rages and finally when she had discovered that he had been repeatedly unfaithful to her, they parted. Since then and with the death of her

mother last year, life had been too busy for any relationships although there had been plenty of offers.

*"Enough of this – we're in serious trouble here. He's got to get away from here and get medical help and fast"*

Isabella then woke Steve by touching his shoulder. He was immediately awake and fully alert and only too aware of the constant throbbing pain in his left thigh. He asked Isabella to pass him his webbing and he injected himself with another syrette of diamorphine.

*"What are you going to do"* she enquired. She was speaking English now very well but with a distinctive accent. She had learnt it at school and then reinforced her knowledge when in college.

*"I am not sure. My colleagues will know that I am alive"* said Steve *"because I have activated my rescue beacon but whether they can do anything to help is another matter. I have to leave from here as the Argentine search parties will be here very soon and you have been very kind and I do not wish to place you or your father in any danger."*

*"I will make some breakfast"* she said and went into the kitchen

She returned ten minutes later with a fresh pot of tea and some toasted bread with some variety of jam on it which Steve did not recognised but wolfed down anyway. It had been a long time since he had eaten anything. At that moment the old farmer appeared and added some more logs on to the fire and pulled up a chair next to Steve and rolled himself a cigarette.

*"Well my friend what are we to do with you?"*

*"I need to get across the border"* said Steve *"and take my chances with the Chilean authorities."*

*"Can you walk far?"*

*"I don't think so"*

*"I thought as much"*

Dawn had fully broken now and the early sun such as it was coming through the windows but it was still very cold outside and there was a frost all over the ground. The old man slurped the tea that his daughter had passed to him and rolled another cigarette and then said:

*"I have a horse and an old cart in one of the barns outside. Take it. Isabella will go with you and show you the way and then she can return with it."*

Isabella turned to look at her father with a very unfriendly expression on her face and there was another heated exchange of words but eventually there was an agreement. Such had been the animated nature of the conversation that Steve had only been able to understand a small part of it. Amongst other things the old man had told his daughter:

*"The British are our friends Isabella. We need them to give the Argentines a bloody nose in Las Malvinas otherwise those fascist bastards in Buenos Aires will become further emboldened and try and seize our territories too."*

Isabella turned to Steve and said:

*"I will go with you and show you the way. It is about an hour because with the cart you have to go on a more circuitous route as the tracks are not good around here and then I will return to my father."*

Steve looked at the old man and said

*"What will you do if the Argentine soldiers come looking for me?"*

*"I will deny ever setting eyes on you. You must take that beacon device with you. There is no evidence that you were here. Isabella has burnt all the bandages and dressings. If they do not go I will persuade the bastards with this and he reached behind a cupboard and brought out an old side-by-side AYA twelve gauge shot gun."*

The old man put on a battered, heavy, short overcoat and a brown wide-brimmed leather hat

*"Wait here and get ready I will be back in ten minutes"*

and went out of the front door into the frosty morning air. Minutes later Steve could here the braying of a horse and the clip clop of its hooves on the cobblestones of the farmyard outside. He heaved himself up and started to put on his outer clothing but lost his balance and fell back into the chair.

*"Let me help you"* said Isabella. The remoteness with which she had spoken to him the previous evening seemed to have disappeared.

150

The old man re-entered the house and said *"All ready"*

Steve went outside dragging his bergen with one hand and his gun slung over his shoulder and the stick in his left hand taking the weight off his injured leg. He could see a horse with a blanket over it and steam rising off his back in the frosty morning air tethered up to an old small cart. It had a faded red, peeling painted body with some designs hand-painted on the side and faded yellow wooden spoke wheels. It reminded Steve of a gypsy cart of the sort that he had seen at fun fairs in his childhood. He bade farewell to the old man and thanked him for his support and assistance and they set off down the bumpy track. It was full of potholes and deep ridges and Steve was in agony as the wooden wheels banged and crashed across the rough surface. He was holding on with his left hand and steadying his M203 with the other continually sweeping the arcs and on constant alert for any sign of danger which he knew must be all around here now. Every bump and rut in the track was agony to him now and there were no more diamorphine syrettes – he just had to grit it out. They were both sitting on the raised bench at the front of the old cart, Isabella had the reigns and was encouraging the old horse along and to get going as fast as it could.

Back at the farm house the old farmer had gone back inside and was coaxing the fire back to life. He sat back down in the tattered armchair and rolled himself a cigarette and just sat there thinking. The truth was he was lonely and he missed his wife terribly. They had never been separated in all those years of marriage and as much as he had appreciated his daughter coming home to help him out; this was no place for a girl of her age and qualifications. He made up his mind to speak to her when she came back with the horse and cart. It was time that she returned to Santiago and resumed her career and found herself a husband, He had seen the way that she had looked at the tall Englishman and the secret glances she had given him when she thought that no one else was looking. The roar of an engine and the screeching of brakes in the yard outside brought him out of his reverie. He grabbed the shot gun that was on the table and went towards the door. There was sharp rap on the door and he opened it and two Argentine soldiers were standing there:

*"We are looking for a British soldier who has murdered some of our colleagues"* they said gruffly looking at him quizzically *"Have you seen him?"*

*"No – there's just me and my daughter here"* he replied.

The soldier at the front stared at him and then looked down and he could see numerous sets of fresh footprints and the cart wheel tracks in the frosty ground.

He moved towards the farmer threateningly *"If you are lying to me old man..."*

*"Get off my land"* the farmer replied and levelled the shotgun towards the chest of the advancing soldier.

*"Don't be a fool old man"* and he reached out to grab the gun and hit the old man in the face hard with his left hand but as he did so the farmer's finger tightened on the trigger and the soldier fell back as the full blast hit him in the chest and ripped it open displaying a huge gaping bloody hole. The other soldier immediately raised his weapon and shot the farmer with a short burst and then ran to the jeep and called his colleagues on the radio.

Ten minutes later Steve saw two army jeeps racing towards them about eight hundred yards behind them down the track. Isabella glanced round to see what he had been looking at:

*"Oh no"* she cried.

*"Get out and leave me now* "shouted Steve as he could sense that they were now taking incoming fire *"I will be ok"*

*"No we need to keep going – its not far now."*

A few moments later Steve could here a series of staccato shots and a dozen-odd rounds tearing into the air and he could see tracer zipping past them and the sound being amplified by the punch of the pressure waves. *Crack. Crack. Crack-Crack Crack.*

He turned round and loosed off a sustained burst of fire at the advancing front jeep trying to steady his aim the best that he could as the cart bounced and rocked along the rough track. Isabella frantically pulled on the reigns and shouted at the horse to go faster but she suddenly screamed and let go of the reigns. Steve took a quick glance at her and saw a deepening red patch on her back just below the right shoulder blade. It all seemed to happen at once, the

152

horse reared up at the sound of the gunfire and the cart suddenly turned over and they were both thrown out. Steve rolled over and over but he did not let go of his weapon. He came to a stop and forced himself into a kneeled position. He was scratched, bruised and every muscle aching and his leg throbbing but no bones were broken and he let out another burst at the jeep which was now only four hundred yards away. Incoming rounds and tracer fire kicked up plumes of dirt all around him and the upturned cart. The natural human reaction to being shot at is to fight, freeze or flee but Steve had taught himself to ignore such instinctive responses so that he could asses how best to deal with any combat situation.

He glanced quickly sideways looking for Isabella and saw that she had crawled back to the cart and was sitting propped against it and sobbing and her top was covered in blood. He swept his head from side to side and saw that the first jeep was now only two hundred and fifty yards away and the second a few hundred yards behind that and then from the right he saw an Armoured Personnel Carrier speeding over the rough terrain towards them.
*"This is going to get ugly and be over pretty quickly"* he said to himself *"Shit! Why did I have to involve this beautiful woman? It's not her war and now I've got her shot and if she survives this firefight I hate to think what they will do with her. You have really fucked up here mate."*

Steve made another long sustained burst of fire at the advancing jeep and then instinctively reaching into his webbing he grabbed a spare magazine and inserted it. Without hesitation he emptied the whole magazine into the oncoming jeep – bullets ripping into the metal body of the vehicle and smashing the windscreen. Suddenly the jeep veered violently to the left and then rolled over onto its side and came skidding to a halt with the sound of screeching metal and with the engine still racing. Steve could clearly see three soldiers jump out of it and start to crawl slowly towards him.

Isabella was still sobbing and screaming hysterically and still sitting upright against the side of the cart which now had pieces of wood broken off it and hanging down as rounds had slammed into it.

*"Get down and underneath the cart"* he shouted at her *"Do it now"*

The second jeep was now closing in fast and the APC on his right was not far away now. *"How many troops would be in that?"* Steve thought. *"Shit!"*

He lay as prostrate and close to the ground as possible to minimise the target that he presented. He clenched his weapon tighter and placed two spare magazines on the ground next to him. He checked his weapon again. The 40mm grenade he had fitted below his M203 when on the cart was still in place.

The second jeep was only one hundred and fifty yards away now and the amount of incoming fire was huge and all of a sudden the horse reared up in pain and agony and then slumped to the ground as rounds slammed into its body. He steadied his aim and as he did so he found himself mouthing the words of his favourite *'Who'* track which had just drifted into his mind:

*"I'd gladly lose me to find you*
*I'd gladly give up all I had*
*To find you I'd suffer anything and be glad...*
*...I call that a bargain*
*The best I ever had."*

# Chapter Thirteen

## Friday 28th May 1982: Punta Arenas

Andy had been at the base for a couple of days now and had been fully briefed in on the situation there and the vitally important role that the British military personnel were carrying out. Britain was desperately short of reliable 'on the ground' intelligence about Argentina which is why such an intense diplomatic play had been going on with Argentina's neighbour, Chile. Chile was very wary indeed of its bellicose neighbour as relations had historically been very tense and suspicious. The invasion of the Falkland Islands therefore, was viewed with very great concern in Santiago. Only four years ago, the Argentine fleet had set sail to seize some disputed Chilean islands which General Galtieri, on the morning of the invasion stated in a broadcast that:

*"This was the first step to recovering Argentina's territory"*

This announcement had left very little ambiguity in their interpretation of Argentina's intent in Santiago. It was clear to the Chileans that as long as Britain retained the Falklands, Chile should be reasonably secure but should Britain lose the war, then Chile could expect to be next and then Argentina would have an overwhelming advantage of secure anchorage to threaten Antarctica.

Chile had over the years gained unrivalled experience at watching their neighbour's potentially hostile troop movements. Supported by a string of signal intercept stations along the border, enhanced by surveillance flights close to the border, Chile's military and intelligence units claimed to know the exact current location of every member of the Argentine military. Britain had therefore agreed with Chile that a small detachment of RAF and Navy personnel could be based at the Punto Arenas base to act as liaison between the Chilean and British military. These personnel would try to be as incognito as possible by wearing Chilean uniforms and name badges and to avoid contact with civilian personnel who shared the airbase but nothing could be done about their Anglo-Saxon looks. In addition the Royal Air Force would be willing to loan some vital equipment to step up still further the quality of the intelligence that could be gathered. This included three Canberra PR-9s from 18 Group, No.1 Photographic Reconnaissance Unit based at RAF Wyton fitted with oblique cameras to overlook Argentina from Chilean airspace and two Sigint Hercules for the collection of technical data. All the aircraft had been painted in fresh grey-green camouflage and with the identification label *'Fuerza Aérea de Chile'* on the fuselage.

The English Electric Canberra is a British first-generation jet-powered light bomber manufactured in large numbers through the 1950s. The Canberra could fly at a higher altitude than any other bomber through the 1950s and set a world altitude record of 70,310ft (21,430m) in 1957. It had the ability to evade the early jet interceptors and had regularly done so while patrolling within Warsaw Pact air space but it was also exceptionally well adapted for photo and strategic reconnaissance use which made it the ideal aircraft for the mission on which it was now undertaking.

# Chapter Fourteen

## Saturday 29th May 1982: Punto Arenas, Chile

The news of the daring, clandestine Operation Mikado and its successful outcome had reached the base at Punto Arenas by accident just hours after the insertion teams had been picked up by HMS Onyx. No Special Forces operation is ever cross-referenced to others in the British military but a tired Flight Lieutenant at Northwood in London had inadvertently added the signal address of the naval party at Punto Arenas to a signal that he had sent out with the sit rep received from HMS Onyx.

The death of Staff Sergeant Harris was regarded with great sadness but mixed with elation and the great daring-do of the British forces. Captain Steve Barraclough was being regarded as MIA (Missing in Action) although this had not yet been officially confirmed for his own safety. His radio beacon had been identified and although there was no question of 'writing him off' at this stage, he was not expected to survive on his own behind the enemy lines. The Argentine forces on the whole of Tierra del Fuego and the mainland coast would now be spooked, radar and other surveillance would be intense and the risks of an incursion by a British aircraft on a rescue mission were deemed unacceptable. The British were now well aware that the Argentines listened intently to news reports, particularly on British television and had gained valuable intelligence from the openness of the reporting. Operation Mikado would remain classified. The official British position would be that no British forces had ever entered Argentine territory during the war.

Steve was not going to be abandoned as an expendable asset but his location and extraction was going to be difficult and there were so many issues at the moment – timing and planning and authority were needed. The other members of 'B' Squadron were 'banging desks' to be allowed to mount a rescue operation particularly now that Steve's rescue beacon had been activated and identified. However, there had been a heated debate about the virtue of sending a valuable troop-carrying helicopter on a one–way mission to Argentina in the first place and there was virtually no chance of another being sacrificed. Since the sinking of the *Atlantic Conveyor* when three Chinooks, five Wessex and a Lynx helicopter were lost there was a critical shortage of troop-carrying helicopters to support the attack on the Argentines on the mainland.

Andy was very proud of his friend but now desperately concerned about his safety. He knew that the Argentine troops would be hopping mad and in no mood to take prisoners and if he was still at large his life would be in great danger and it looked very much to Andy that despite the official line, time could just run out for Steve as his colleagues were left with very few options indeed.

Andy sipped a cup of strong black coffee out of a plastic cup and stared out of the window at the airfield below sub-consciously rubbing his left elbow whilst deep in thought. He couldn't explain it but he had a deep nagging feeling that his friend was in trouble and did not have time to wait whilst the military deliberated on what they could to extricate him. For a moment he was transported back in time once again submerged in the cold, dark, green water of Lake Windermere. He was struggling violently but his foot was stuck fast and he was still drowning as desperation set in. Then just as he felt it was over and that his lungs would finally burst, a strong arm gripped him round the waist and started to haul him to the surface from under the upturned boat where he had been trapped. He broke through the surface coughing and spluttering as sunlight once again shone in his face.

In that instant Andy knew what he had to do.
*"There will be hell to pay but so what"*
he thought as he turned from the window.
*"Some things just have to be done even though I will definitely get binned for this."*

His gaze became more focussed now. Outside to the left of the main airport apron a few hundred yards away was a small heliport. It was used almost entirely by oil company executives flying in and out to the exploration fields off the coast. There were two aircraft already parked there and as he stared a third was just hovering back into position. The crew shut down the main rotor engine and the blades started to slow becoming more and more visible as they cut through the air above. A ladder emerged and the passengers, three men in suits carrying briefcases climbed down and walked across the apron into the small terminal building. A fuel truck rolled up and the ground service crew immediately set about refuelling the aircraft and performing other checks by opening and closing flaps and making adjustments. Then the two crew members descended the ladder. It must be a shift change. Andy knew it was now or never. He drained the coffee in one go and leapt out of the chair, the metal legs grating on the tiled floor as he pushed it away. A few heads turned but then after a second turned away again. Not much was happening on the base.

He walked swiftly down the stairs, a man with an air of intense purpose. Turning left at the bottom of the stairs he opened the door in front of him and entered the room. It was very smoky as there were no windows and some guys were playing pool and chatting. The British military personnel had been encouraged to inhabit this area as much as possible to avoid unnecessary contact particularly with employees of the three domestic Chilean airlines that shared the airport facility.

*"Hi Andy how are you doing?"* said a guy looking up from his snooker cue as he leant over the table ready to break the fifteen red balls set in a triangle as a new game commenced. Andy ignored him and walked straight up to the bar where a tall, broad-shouldered, red-haired Royal Marine in Chilean uniform was standing smoking a cigarette with a small beer in his other hand.

*"A word"* said Andy dragging Angus to one side.

*"I'm going for Steve"* Andy whispered *"Are you with me?"*

*"What the hell are you talking about mate"* replied Angus in his broad Scottish accent slightly bemused.

159

*"I haven't got time to piss about. I am going to get Steve. He's alive and I know where he is and I'm going right now. Are you in or out?"*

*"Why can't the unit get to do the evac?"*

*"Risk on assets"* replied Andy tersely.

Angus looked at his friend incredulously. He had only known Andy for the short time since he had arrived at the base but he had taken to him straight away and was impressed with his stories of the Pebble Island and Plum Duff operations.

They had talked for hours about home and growing up and how they had entered the forces but it was only when Andy had mentioned Steve that he realised that they had a common mate. Angus had been sent to Punto Arenas as part of the small Royal Air Force and Royal Navy detachment primarily as security for his intelligence-gathering colleagues. Before joining the Royal; Marines two years ago, Angus had originally been a member of the Parachute Regiment but had left after four years when his father became seriously ill and he had returned home for a year to look after the family furniture business in Aberdeen. Angus had been on his third tour of Northern Ireland in 1978 and was operating down in what had become know as 'IRA bandit country' around Crossmaglen in South Armagh. He had been on patrol with three other colleagues when they came under small arms fire from across a field. They had then run to take some protective cover in some trees on the other side of the road but one of the members of the patrol had set off a booby-trap bomb by setting off a trip wire as he entered the shelter of the trees. There had been a huge explosion and the soldier was killed instantly. Angus had been thrown on his back by the force of the blast but other than being winded and concussed and temporarily deaf from the explosion he was otherwise unhurt as was one other member of the patrol. But the fourth man was lying by the side of the road with serious shrapnel injuries so they carried him quickly into the trees very warily in case they set off a second device.

As they propped him up against a tree they came under a sustained burst of small arms fire once again and were pinned down by fire coming in from two directions. They returned fire in small bursts but they could not see their targets clearly and the fire was wildly inaccurate. Angus crawled to where the injured man lay against the tree. He had been carrying the Clansman combat net radio system which fortunately had not been damaged. He had got through to control and was assured that a reinforcement team would be on their way as fast as possible and he had to hold his ground and not be taken but it could be at least ten minutes before they could reach them.

.Lieutenant Steve Barraclough had been visiting an observation post about a mile up the road and had heard the radio transmission and together with another trooper they had rushed to their Shorland armoured Land Rover. Whilst his colleague took the wheel, Steve had got behind the turret-mounted General Purpose Machine Gun. They roared down the lane towards the pall of smoke they could see hanging in the air and when they got to within eight hundred meters Steve had opened up with bursts of sustained fire at the hedgerows and fields opposite from the line of trees where he knew his colleagues were being besieged.

"*Drive on*" demanded Steve and they continued quickly to where they could see the troops holed up by the trees. Steve swung the gun barrel from side to side raking the fields in front of him with sustained bursts of fire kicking up plumes of dirt and mud as round after round had spat out of the end of the barrel with the brass casings cascading in a heap at the bottom of the foot well of the Land Rover. Angus had gathered up his deceased comrade and had made his way quickly to the rear of the Land Rover and placed the body of his friend inside and then turned to help the other injured man who was limping towards him leaning heavily on his colleague. They got in hastily and slammed the door closed. The driver didn't waste a second and pressed his foot hard on the accelerator pedal and the Land Rover surged ahead down the lane with Steve swivelling the gun behind him to keep up a rate of fire as they retreated.

Angus had never seen Andy look so serious. There was no movement in his face at all. His eyes were fixed and staring right at him, boring into his inner soul. Thoughts raced through Angus' mind in what seemed an eternity but a few seconds later, almost in slow motion, he found himself saying:

*"You crazy Yorkshire bastard. Of course I am. Let's go"*

The two of them walked briskly past the guys at the pool table.

*"What's with them?* said one of the snooker players

"No idea" replied the other.

Andy and Angus made their way quickly to the entrance to the crew room. Andy had said only a few words en route but Angus quickly had put two and two together.

*"He really is crazy and I must be too to go along with this. We'll both end up in jail or worse"* he thought *"but better that than a life of regret and remorse. We look after our own."*

As Andy went inside Angus said: *"I'll meet you in the heliport terminal in five. I've got to get a few things."*

Five minutes later Andy was in the single storey concrete building that served as the commercial heliport. He was dressed in his naval flying suit, his Browning pistol in a shoulder holster and carrying his flying helmet and a bunch of maps and charts. There was hardly anyone around, a lady at the check-in desk and a few civilians reading papers but they paid them no particular attention as they were all used to seeing military personnel come and go through the building all the time. It was only when Angus came running in carrying a bergen and his M16 assault rifle and a 7.62mm General Purpose Machine Gun that a few eyebrows were raised. But it all happened so quickly the two military men walked swiftly up to the departure gate and as Andy engaged the security guard in conversation, Angus felled him from behind with a blow to the back of the head. The lady in the check-in desk saw this and pressed a button which sounded an alarm but Andy and Angus were already racing across the tarmac towards the parked helicopter which Andy had seen landing only thirty minutes before. The helicopter was an ageing but still very serviceable American Bell Civil 204B. Andy had flown a military version during training some years ago. He knew that this model now fully fuelled would have a range of about three hundred nautical miles and a capacity of up to eight passengers which was more than adequate for the purpose he intended. The fuel truck had now departed and Andy quickly ripped away the remaining electrical connections and moments after scrambling aboard the rotors were starting to turn as Angus raised the ladder and closed the cabin door. Andy was focussed now. The control layout was different to a Sea King but there was nothing significantly unfamiliar with it. Training and adrenaline just kicked in, he was acting in an automated mode and nothing could break his composure and focus. He saw out of the port window a group of three soldiers running towards the aircraft shouting and waving their guns in the air followed some distance behind by an army jeep with a mounted machine gun in the rear, and from the starboard window he could see a service truck careering across the tarmac towards him but he was not concerned. The Lycoming T53 turboshaft engine was reaching the necessary take off power output and the forty eight foot diameter rotors were now roaring overhead and a few seconds later the helicopter lurched into the air and swung low over the terminal building heading east across the Magellan Strait avoiding the Chilean town and airfield at Porvenir and on towards the border with the Argentine territory of Tierra del Fuego.

It was a distance of about one hundred and eighty five miles from Punto Arenas to the Rio Grande airbase which lay thirty three miles from the border with Chile and according to the information that Andy had seen, Steve's beacon indicated that he was about two miles inside Argentine territory. It would, therefore, be 'touch and go' on the return flight to make sure that they had enough fuel. He doubted whether they would be pursued and certainly not once he had crossed the border. On either side the reception would now not be friendly but Andy just shrugged off the thought and refocussed once more.

After a while Angus climbed into the cockpit and said:

*"How long to go?"*

*"We are making about one hundred and fifteen knots which is near enough flat out for this old bird"* replied Andy

*"So I reckon we should be in the target area in about just over an hour"*

*"I'll get my gear ready then – give me a shout when we are five minutes out"* and with that Angus disappeared out of the cockpit back into the cabin.

Andy was flying fast across the Magellan Strait and the water below the aircraft was still and calm like a mill pond in complete contrast to the wave of emotions surging through his mind. He was, however in complete control and had switched into his professional mode and the training just kicked in.

*"I'll almost certainly get binned for this if we get back"* he muttered to himself *"But what the hell."* and he unconsciously looked down at his left arm and smiled:

*"And what's more it's been a great ride"*

Angus unpacked the Bergen. He took out the hastily gathered kit that he had managed to lay his hands on in the rush to get airborne. There were high explosive grenades, smoke grenades, flares, a spare barrel for the General purpose Machine Gun and two further ammunition belts, spare magazines for the M16 and a browning 9mm pistol and spare magazines.

# Chapter Fifteen

## Saturday 29th May 1982: Tierra del Fuego

Angus opened the door of the helicopter and the cold howling wind rushed in with a real vengeance. He took out the 7.62mm General Purpose Machine Gun and set it up on its tripod in the middle of the open aperture so that he allowed himself a good one hundred and eighty degree arc within which to fire. The GPMG or "Gimpy' as it is generally known by the troops has been in use by the British armed forces since 1958. It is a belt-fed, air-cooled weapon with a quick-change barrel. It can fire over six hundred and fifty rounds a minute at an effective range of eight hundred yards.

He then placed the spare ammunition belts on the floor next to it and the bergen with the remaining items just behind him. He crouched down behind the Gimpy and made himself as comfortable as possible and tied a scarf across his face to provide some protection from the cold wind.

*"Crossing the border in five"* shouted Andy over the noise of the wind

*"I'm ready"* Angus yeleld back

He took out the binoculars from the bergen behind him and started to scan the terrain below. After about five minutes he shouted in earnest:

*"What the hell's going on down there on the left"*

He could make out an upturned cart and a horse slumped down by it and a soldier in a distinctive disruptive pattern material uniform.

*"That's a British uniform"* he shouted towards the cockpit.

*"That must be Steve"* replied Andy his voice quivering a little with excitement and adrenalin.

Angus looked again and then he could see an army jeep with a mounted machine gun and four soldiers onboard approaching the group about eight hundred meters away and from the other side an

APC was going fast over the rough terrain bumping and charging along towards him

*"Oh shit"* he said *"Whoever he is, he's got some very unfriendly guys about to overrun him"*

The three soldiers from the first jeep that were crawling towards Steve looked up at the sound of the helicopter's engine.

*"What's that"* said one *"Is it one of ours?"*

*"It's not military"* said another

*"Don't know what it is but the pilot must be off course but nothing to worry about"*

Andy swung the aircraft round and descended and as he passed over the top of the advancing jeep at about eighty five feet Angus threw out some high explosive grenades. The grenades exploded around the jeep sending fragments of hot metal in all directions hitting one of the soldiers sitting in the rear of the vehicle.

Steve stared up at the helicopter incredulously.

*"What on earth was a commercial helicopter doing low over a firefight and then someone was dropping grenades on the advancing Argentines. I have no idea who those guys are but they are very welcome!"*

Andy took the helicopter up as the three soldiers from the damaged jeep had now realised that this was a hostile aircraft and had started to turn fire on it. As Angus sat on the floor crouched over the Gimpy rounds were whizzing above his head through the open door and slamming into the cabin on the far side and three windows had already been shot out scattering sharp fragments of glass throughout the cabin and increasing the wind noise. As Andy felt some of the rounds hit the aircraft his nerves tightened:

*"This is not a military aircraft"* he thought *"The airframe and skin is quite light and there is no protection anywhere. One lucky shot into the fuel tank or the engine and we're done for."*

To make matters worse now that they were engaging with enemy troops who had no doubt contacted their base, the ruse of being a commercial aircraft off course was now over and they could expect company in the air and that would be game over. They had to get this done fast and get the hell out.

He turned the aircraft round, dipped the nose and opened the throttle and shouted at Angus:

*"Sort them now"*

Angus trained the Gimpy on the advancing jeep and rounds came spitting out of the end of the barrel raking the jeep below and in front of him. The barrel of the Gimpy juddered and rocked on its tripod with each burst of fire. It is difficult for anyone firing a gun when airborne as it is not easy to see where the shot is falling relative to the target so it was vital that Angus kept an eye on the tracer rounds and one eye on the target. A tracer round has a phosphorous base which, when fired, leaves a red glow behind it enabling him to follow the trajectory of the rounds more easily thereby allowing him to adjust the point of aim as necessary to maximise the hits on target. Already the barrel was burning hot to the touch and Angus figured that he had to be a hundred rounds into that first two hundred-round belt and he knew that he had to conserve his rate of fire – one burst one kill. This was not the time to pull the trigger and get an empty click. Changing the ammunition belt was not an option as this was definitely not the time to stop getting the rounds down even for the couple of seconds it would take him to do so. He swung the Gimpy, taking aim carefully and kept his finger on the trigger chewing out the rounds and saw the empty cartridges spewing out of its breech onto the carpeted floor of the helicopter in a cascade of hot, smoking brass. It was a sea of spent bullets down there and he had to keep kicking them out of the way to maintain a balanced foothold.

A spray of bullets destroyed the windscreen of the jeep below him which then careered off to one side and turned turtle as it hit a hard ridge of rock on the track at the wrong angle. Meanwhile the three surviving Argentines from the first jeep had fanned out and were keeping close to the ground and very slowly advancing towards Steve's position and keeping him pinned down with sustained fire. Steve returned fire in short bursts and then decided to ever so slowly crawl to his right back to the cart about ten yards or so away. He stopped firing and just concentrated on trying not to be seen and keeping his head down.

On reaching the cart he shouted:

167

*"Are you alright"*
*"Yes" came a feeble voice from underneath what was left of the cart.*

The APC was now only fifty meters away on the right hand side and Steve steadied his aim by balancing the weapon on the edge of the cart. He checked that the 40mm grenade slung underneath the M203 was still in place. He waited for what seemed an eternity and then released the grenade and it arced through the air and exploded straight into the advancing APC. The rear hatch of the APC opened and six soldiers spilled out, fanned out and hit the ground flat down.

Steve was now in a pincer movement from the troops on the round on the right and the left. He took a smoke grenade that was attached to his webbing and threw it back to the position he had vacated just a moment ago. As the smoke billowed around, two of the three soldiers on the left put their heads up to get a better aim and Steve cut them both down with a short burst of very accurate fire. At the same time Andy was preparing for one more run:

*"Finish it this time Angus"* he yelled

Angus had just changed the ammunition belt for a new one and was holding the Gimpy rock solid in his hands. His shoulder muscles were burning from the pain and tension of swinging the weapon from side to side. He was used to seeing and hearing tracer on exercises but he'd never experienced anything like this as he sensed bullets tearing metal and smashing more glass windows all around him. He figured that the aircraft was taking some punishment and he just prayed that she kept going. As Andy flew towards the APC Angus kept his finger on the trigger of the Gimpy and rounds crashed into the ground all round the APC kicking up huge plumes of dirt and mud. It was lethal fire and the six men on the ground had no chance as they were raked with relentless fire from above. Steve recognised his chance and that the odds were now in his favour and he inserted his last remaining magazine into his weapon and loosed off the entire clip towards the remaining Argentine on the left catching him with two rounds and throwing him backwards.

*"Bring her down"* shouted Angus into the cockpit.

*"Let's go now!"* Steve yelled at Isabella but there was no reply.

He crawled to where she was lying under the cart and saw that she had passed out. With a Herculean effort he rose and pushed off the cart desperately trying to maintain his balance and not put too much weight on his left leg. He reached down and with all his remaining strength cradled her in his arms and lifted. He was not thinking now he was on automatic pilot he as he had been back in the Brecon Beacons making for the truck in its final destination. He moved painfully but very unsteadily forward towards the helicopter when there was a burst of fire and he cried out as a bullet passed through the fleshy part of his upper right arm. He steadied himself but did not drop Isabella and moved forward again. Angus had seen that the fire had come from the injured driver of the APC who had got out and was standing by the wrecked vehicle shooting. He loosed off a burst of fire and the soldier collapsed by the side of the APC.

*"Hurry up mate"* shouted Andy from inside the cockpit.

Steve made one final effort and Angus moved the Gimpy with its burning hot barrel to one side and reached down and grabbed Isabella into the cabin. *"Go Andy"* he screamed as he reached down to Steve to take his extended left hand and literally hauled him into the aircraft just as it started to lift off the ground. Suddenly there was another burst of fire and a number of rounds hit the aircraft fired from one of the soldiers from the first jeep who had rolled on to his back and was shooting upwards wildly. Angus instantly grabbed the M16 from behind him and sprayed the area with bullets and the shooting stopped.

*"Shit"* said Andy *"We're loosing oil pressure. One of those last rounds must have penetrated the engine cowling. This is going to be touch and go as the gearbox could seize."*

The helicopter dropped alarmingly and then picked up again as Andy wrestled with the controls. The main gearbox is the Achilles Heel of any helicopter. The role of the main gearbox which is situated just under the main rotor is to transmit power to the main rotor head and the tail rotor head and generate the power for the various accessories both electric and hydraulic. Andy had been taught that generally helicopters should be able to continue safe flight for at least thirty minutes after the pilot has detected a lubrication system failure or loss of lubrication and pressure in the main gearbox. This is often referred to as "the thirty minute run-dry requirement" but this was an old helicopter and Andy did not know if this standard safety feature had been incorporated into the design of its main gearbox. He just had to hope it had and decided to keep this information to himself.

Andy knew that it was a myth that a helicopter will drop like a stone if the engine fails. Helicopters are designed specifically to allow pilots to have a reasonable chance of landing them safely in the case of engine failure during flight, often with no damage which is accomplished via autorotation of the main rotor blades using the freewheeling clutch. This is accomplished by the main rotor of the aircraft turning by the action of the air moving up through it as with an autogyro rather than engine power driving it. This was all well and good when in descent and Andy had practiced this no-power technique many times in the past but this was a completely different situation as they still had to get across the border and there was still a chance of an Argentine aerial intervention and then they had to re-cross the open water of the Magellan Strait. Adrenalin was pumping through Andy's body as he concentrated on his task. He shut out everything that what was going on in the cabin behind him right now as he stared at his instruments and the sky around him and then back to his instruments over and over again. The oil pressure had dropped again but was not yet at the critical point so he slowed the engine down to reduce the pressure on the gearbox as he tried to coax it towards the border.

*"We're crossing the border about now"* he shouted over the noise of the wind to the cabin occupants behind him.

He didn't have to remind Angus to be ready. He had already re-opened the cabin door and he had reset up the Gimpy in the middle of the aperture. He had inserted a new belt of two hundred rounds and was now crouched behind it and swinging the barrel from side to side in case any contacts were suddenly spotted.

*"Would they follow them across the border?"*

He didn't know but he had to be as ready as he could be because there only option of survival would probably be to get in some serious fire first before they were taken out by a combination of cannon and/or air-to-air missiles. Andy descended and decreased his airspeed still further. The oil pressure gauge had now entered the red zone and a number of warning lights had now illuminated on the panel in front of him including the one that indicated that he was now very low on fuel. He estimated a further flying time of about thirty minutes.

*"Come on – we can do this"* he said out loud.

His mind drifted for a few moments back to the day he had been told that he would not pass the selection for the Royal Air Force. It had been the most shattering blow in his life. However, through sheer guts and determination he had proved that he could fly and would be forever grateful to the Fleet Air Arm for giving him his chance. Certainly during the last few weeks he had paid back that trust and investment in him.

*"But have I betrayed that trust now"* he thought. His career would almost certainly be over now and there would be recriminations and he would probably be an international embarrassment for his country and the Service he respected so much. However he dismissed these thoughts and returned to the issues in hand with the often used phrase of the British Prime Minister ringing in his ears:

*"There is no alternative."*

A few moments later the aircraft started to vibrate far more than was normal and Andy noticed that there was a grinding noise coming from above him from the main rotor. He reduced the power still further and dipped the nose of the helicopter. They were now only about sixty feet above the ground.

He contacted the control tower back at Punto Arenas and warned them of his situation and that there was a potential risk of a crash landing. He also advised them in a professional and matter-of-fact manner that he had two seriously wounded personnel on board. One Chilean national and one British national, both of which would require immediate emergency hospital treatment.

However, as he broke off the communication, he was also well aware that there would be more than emergency service personnel waiting for him when they returned. He looked back into the cabin and saw Steve slumped in a seat with blood dripping from his right arm onto the carpet. He looked in a real mess.

*"Hang on in there mate"* he said out loud" "Not long now."

Slumped in the seat next to Steve was a very good looking South American lady who was awake but sobbing and Angus had been applying a field dressing to a very nasty wound on her upper right shoulder blade.

*"Who is she"* thought Andy *"I have no idea but she needs to get to hospital pretty quick too."*

However, despite the serious trouble he knew he was in, Andy felt a strange sense of calm, as if a great weight had been lifted from his shoulders and a huge debt burden that he had been carrying for years had now been repaid. He just had to get this aircraft and all the passengers back down on the ground as safely and quickly as he could.

*"Focus"* he commanded himself.

The grinding noise was definitely getting worse and Andy noticed that the oil pressure gauge was now in its most critical zone. The aircraft was starting to shake and vibrate violently. Andy knew that he was now too low to disengage the main rotor unless he wanted to land now which was an option as they were now over dry land in Chilean territory but he wanted to return the aircraft back to its base. After all he owed that much to its owners. In the cabin, Angus had closed the outer door and was packing up the kit. He disassembled the Gimpy, took out the magazine from the M16 and tried to collect up as many as possible of the spent rounds and threw them into his bergen with the remaining unused items. He looked across at Steve and said:

*"I know that you would have done the same for me mate."*

Just as Andy thought that the aircraft would start to break up under the vibration the Punto Arenas airbase came into view. He reduced the airspeed still further and decided to descend at the edge of the airfield in case there were any difficulties.

As the helicopter hovered just above the ground Andy could see a procession of vehicles streaming out from the terminal buildings towards them. Fire engines, ambulances and military jeeps.

He brought the helicopter down in a soft landing and reduced the engine speed to an idle to shut the engine down in a controlled manner that would protect it the best that he could.

For him and Angus, as the American slang saying went: *"The shit was about to hit the fan."*

# Chapter Sixteen

## Saturday 29th May 1982: Punto Arenas, Chile

A few minutes after the helicopter had touched down and Andy had finally shut down the engine the aircraft was surrounded by vehicles. Two army jeeps carrying troops and military police were the first on the scene and they all got out and took positions around the helicopter with their weapons drawn. Angus opened the door and held up his hands and climbed out of the helicopter followed quickly by Andy. They both handed over the 9mm Browning pistols that had been in their shoulder holsters.

As they were led away by two military police officers medical staff boarded the helicopter and immediately set about getting Steve and Isabella out and onto stretchers and into the two waiting ambulances. Within a few minutes the ambulances were racing away from the aircraft with their sirens blaring. Andy turned and watched them go, his hands now handcuffed firmly behind his back.

*"Good luck mate"* he whispered. He just felt drained. After the adrenalin rush of the rescue and firefight and the nursing of the helicopter home his body now sagged as he sat in the back of the jeep next to Angus and not a word was spoken. Each of them lost in their own thoughts. Andy wondered about Jess. *How had she taken his letter? Could she forgive him? Would he ever see her again?*

The jeep pulled up outside the Military Police compound at the airbase and they were marched inside. Their details were entered on to forms and then they were quickly led away to separate cells where they were un-handcuffed but unable to communicate with one another.

Over the following two days they were intensely interrogated by both the Chilean Military Police, senior army officers on one occasion accompanied by Lieutenant Commander Carter, the most senior Royal Navy representative at the base:

*"You have put us in a very embarrassing situation Lieutenant Shaw"* he said *"Our presence here is supposed to be top secret, clandestine and delicate. Our remit here does not involve John Wayne–type, unauthorised gung-ho trips into enemy territory from a friendly neighbouring country. You could have caused a serious international incident and have put the British Senior Service in a very poor light with your undisciplined behaviour however well meaning."*

The owners of the helicopter were understandably irate. The aircraft had been substantially damaged and had now been withdrawn from service. It had sustained numerous punctures in the skin from rounds that had penetrated the interior and the exterior was pock-marked with bullet holes. Many of the glass windows had been shot out and the engine would have to be stripped down and rebuilt and the main gearbox replaced. It would be expensive to get the helicopter airworthy again. In addition the security guard felled by Angus was demanding that they be prosecuted and that he was properly compensated by these 'hooligans' who had been invited to share their base as friends.

A few days later Andy and Angus who were still not permitted to communicate with one another found themselves on a military flight to Santiago where they were held at the main army base for the next few weeks.

## Tuesday 15th June 1982: 10, Downing Street, London

Margaret Thatcher was in her private office in Downing Street and had been making telephone calls to both world leaders like President Reagan and British military commanders throughout the day. She looked at the next set of papers on her desk and digested them and then arranged for a call to be put through to General Augusto Pinochet, the President of Chile:

*"Good day Mr President "Thank you for taking my call."*

175

*She* was speaking deliberately slowly and clearly as she was aware that the call was being simultaneously translated for the President at the other end.

*"I am sure that you are as delighted as we are that the Argentine aggression against our territories of the Falkland Islands has not been successful although it has been at the cost of a significant number of lives of our servicemen. However, one cannot put a price on freedom and tyranny must always be opposed wherever it raises its head.*

*As you know the British people are enormously grateful for the assistance that you have given us in our endeavours over the last few months particularly in the invaluable intelligence information that you have been able to provide us with and for permitting a few of our personnel to be located at your airbase at Punto Arenas. In relation to this I wanted to discuss an embarrassing incident that occurred there which I am sure that you will be aware of. On 29th May this year a regrettable incident occurred caused by two of our Royal Navy personnel. I do think, Mr President, that it is in the best interests of all concerned that these two men are repatriated to London quickly and quietly – don't you?*

*I am sure that you will find that the British government will be very generous in our gratitude for your support and I do hope that we have the opportunity to meet face to face in the future. Good day Mr President."*

A few days after this call it was confirmed between the British and Chilean governments that the Chilean Air Force, the Fuerza Aérrea de Chile, could retain possession of the three Canberra aircraft that had been based at Punto Arenas and they also were to subsequently receive a total of nine Hawker Hunter jets and thirty spare engines on exceptionally advantageous terms.

# Saturday 29th May 1982: Punto Arenas, Chile

Steve and Isabella had been taken immediately to the hospital at Punto Arenas from the air base. Steve was in a bad way. He had lost a lot of blood and immediately underwent an emergency operation on his left thigh and right upper arm. Fortunately the rounds had penetrated straight through on both occasions missing main arteries and bone and had therefore not fragmented and caused further internal damage. However, Steve had undoubtedly made the wound in his leg significantly worse by the additional strain he had put upon it by escaping to the farm house and then travelling in the cart and crawling around the ground during the engagement with the Argentine troops as well as his final effort of carrying Isabella to the helicopter. It would be a long time before his leg would return to normal, if at all.

The following day he was lying in bed in a side room off a main ward. His leg was bandaged and raised on a support under covers and his arm was in a sling across his chest and there were numerous tubes coming in and out of his body. Outside the door he could see an officer of the Carabineros, the Chilean police. It was obvious that his presence here was not to be made known to the wider world.

*"Where is Isabella"* he had enquired weakly in Spanish of the nurse as she entered the room to check up on him.

*"The lady who was brought in with you has had a bullet removed from her right shoulder which is severely damaged but the surgeon believes that in time that she will recover with only a small loss of mobility."*

Unknown to Steve at this stage Isabella had been interviewed at length by the Carabineros earlier that morning. They had wanted to know who Steve was and what he was doing in Tierra del Fuego and who she was and how she had got involved with him. She had related to them everything that she knew.

A few hours later they had returned and told her sombrely that her father was dead and that his body had been discovered by one of his farm hands but the circumstances of his death were not known at this time. Isabella waited till the two officers had left the room and then covered her face with her left hand and just wept. Her hand dropped to the silver crucifix which had been a confirmation present from her parents which was hanging round her neck and she held it tightly and prayed quietly and then turned her head on the pillow and slept.

A few days later Steve was visited by John Cummins, the British Consul in Santiago. He told him that arrangements had been made to repatriate him back to the UK in the next couple of days as soon as he was strong enough to do so. It was clear to Steve that both the British and Chilean governments were keen to get him off Chilean soil before any leaks were made to the media which would incur a frenzy of investigative journalism and speculation.

Isabella had been visited again by the Carabineros who had told her that her story had been corroborated by various sources and that she would not be subject to any further investigation and could leave the hospital in the next few days as soon as the medical staff gave their approval. She was, however, strongly advised not to return to the farm as the Argentines would have a significant interest in detaining her and as a Chilean national this would not be in the interests of her country or government and indeed herself. The Carabineros would make the best efforts they could to recover her father's body and return it to Chilean territory where it would be buried.

*"But where do I go"* she thought *"There's nothing back at the farm for me now and I have no family other than my old aunt here in Santiago. Well at least that is a starting point."*

That afternoon after persistent requests, she was allowed to walk into the men's ward and into the side room to visit Steve. As the door opened Steve turned from looking out of the window to see who was entering the room and an uncontrollable broad smile beamed across his face which quickly faded:

"I am so sorry Isabella" he said *"I never meant to bring any harm upon you "*

*"My father is dead"* she replied.
*"How?"*

*"I don't know but it is suspected that he was shot by Argentine troops looking for us"*

"Oh my God" exclaimed Steve unable to know what to say next. Isabella shut the door and sat on the chair next to the bed.

*"It is not your fault"* she said

*"My father was a stubborn man and he had a vitriolic dislike of the Argentineans which had become more intense since my mother had died."*

*"What are you going to do?"* Steve asked quietly.

*"I am not sure yet. I will stay with my Aunt here in Santiago and then will visit my father's grave with her when we are told that it is safe to do so. After that who knows but I will probably return to nursing here."*

Steve thought for a while and then he slowly pushed his left hand over the top of the bed covers and reached for her hand which she extended readily. He squeezed it tightly and refused to let go but after a while he said:

*"They are always looking for qualified nurses in England"*

*"Is that an invitation?"* she replied

*"If you want it to be"*

They sat in silence for a few more minutes but they never released the grip on each other's hand.

*"I am going back home tomorrow"* Steve said suddenly

*"I know"* she replied.

*"I will be in touch Steve when I have sorted things out"* and with that she got up and lent forward and kissed him gently on the cheek and left the room.

Steve just stared at the window for a few minutes and involuntarily his left hand went up to his cheek and gently touched where she had kissed him.

*"Please do Isabella"* he whispered.

# September 1982: Yeovilton, Somerset

A couple of weeks after the war had ended Andy and Angus were formally handed over from the custody of Chilean authorities to British jurisdiction and were repatriated in civilian clothing the following day on a British Airways flight to London Heathrow. Andy returned to his base at Yeovilton in Somerset but was stood down from operational duty pending an investigation and a potential court martial hearing and was told to stay on the base. Royal Naval Air Station Yeovilton is one of the Royal Navy's principal air bases and one of the busiest military airfields in the UK. The base is located near Yeovil in Somerset and covers around one thousand four hundred acres with the main airfield in Yeovilton itself and the satellite, Merryfield at Ilton. Both 845 and 846 Squadrons were based here. Andy was confined to barracks and was due to face a Board of Enquiry as it had been deemed that he had a 'case to answer' and he was faced with the very real threat of being court-martialled.

He had now received the letter that his mother had written to him whilst he was in the Falklands but had never received because he had already set off on *Operation Plum Duff* and he had had a number of telephone conversations with them. He had also received a letter from Jess who had been updated on his situation by his mother. Andy had opened the letter with trepidation. He really did not know what it would say and how he would react to its contents:

Sheffield
14<sup>th</sup> August 1982

*Dear Andy*

*I am absolutely delighted that you have managed to get home safely particularly after all that you have been through and we are all very proud of you.*

*Thank you for your letter. I will not pretend that I was not terribly upset when you left and after the conversation we had that night in the pizza restaurant. I went through a very difficult time probably the worst in my life.*

*Unfortunately things have changed now but if you want to I would still like to see you. If you do too then call me but if you don't then I will understand.*

*Much love*
*Jess*

Andy stared at the letter and then reread it again.
*"What was she really saying? How did he really feel?* He simply did not know. His whole life was upside down now and in turmoil. That evening he found the courage to call her:
*"I am so glad that you are home safe"* she said
*"I am in trouble Jess"* he replied
*"I know"*
*"Did you get my letter"* he said
*"Yes"* she replied and then the phone went silent.
*"I suppose it was too late"* he said finally breaking the silence
*"In a way"*
*"What do you mean?"*
*"Well I did a stupid thing"*
*"I know"* he replied and once again there was silence between them.
*"I want to see you"* she said
*"I want to see you too"* he said quietly.

A week later Jess was on the train from Sheffield. It was a very long journey via Derby, Birmingham, Cheltenham, Bristol to Taunton and then eventually to Yeovil. It was too far to go there and back in a day so she had booked a room in a local pub. She had been given permission to spend a few hours with Andy on the base. Andy had never been more nervous in his life and had slept poorly the night before and was now pacing up and down his room.

*"This is stupid"* he told himself but he just couldn't rest. He just wanted to do the right thing and be true to himself but he simply did not know what that was. He did not know what Jess wanted either. There had been an awful lot of water under the bridge since that night in the pizza restaurant in Sheffield city centre nearly six months before.

At 14.30 he was informed that Jess had arrived and she was in one of the family liaison rooms on the base. Andy approached and knocked on the door and entered. Jess was sitting on a sofa in the small room drinking a cup of tea and there was a tray with a teapot, milk jug, sugar bowl and a second cup on the low table in front of her. As he walked in she got up and Andy walked quickly towards her. Nothing was said. He just put his arms around her and held her tightly and kissed her on the cheek. His eyes were moist and when he looked down he could see that tears were rolling down her cheeks. He squeezed her tighter still.

*"Mind the bump"* she said eventually.

They sat on the sofa and Andy poured out two cups of tea and gave one to her. For the next two hours they just talked as if they had never been apart. Andy relayed everything that had happened to him and she sat listening and every now and then reached for his hand which she squeezed gently. Eventually he said:

*"I am in serious trouble Jess"*

*"I know"* she replied. *"We'll get through it together. I saw Steve yesterday, he is staying back with his parents and I told him I was coming to see you. He is desperate to get in touch. Everyone in Sheffield is really proud of what you did Andy"*

*"How is he"* enquired Andy

*"He is ok. He has lost a lot of weight and still looks very pale but his mother said that she is going to feed him up on his favourite food. He has to walk with the assistance of a crutch at the moment and his arm is still all bandaged up. Did you know I think he has got a lady friend?"*

*"Who? Is it the lady who was in the helicopter that I brought back with him?"*

*"Yes. He is telephoning her a lot and I believe that she is coming to visit him soon. His mother told me that Steve will be paying all of the telephone bills from now on!"*

Andy laughed. It was the first time that he had laughed in a long time. It was quiet for a while and then Andy said:

*"Jess, I meant what I said in that letter. I would really like to make a go of it with you now. Do you feel the same way?"*

Jess said nothing and Andy could feel his stomach churning over and over. This was worse than any bad flying experience he had ever had.

*"Yes I do"* she replied *"But things have changed Andy. I have decided that I want to keep the baby"*

Andy was thoughtful and then said *"What about the father?"*

Jess turned to him, reached for his hand and then said shamefully without looking at him:

*"Andy you probably won't believe this but I don't even know his name"* and she hung her head sadly

*"But he has a right to know about the child"*

*"I made some enquiries about him when I found out that I was pregnant but no one knows who he is and evidently he had just come to Sheffield from London to visit a friend at the university for the weekend. So the baby does not have a father."*

*"Yes he does"* Andy replied.

*"Who?"*

*"Mr Andrew Shaw of Raby Street, Tinsley, Sheffield."*

Jess moved closer to Andy and they kissed long and tenderly not wanting it to end. Thirty minutes later it was nearly time for Jess to leave the base and Andy said

*"Will you be ok?"*

*"Yes I have got a room at the Phelips Arms in Montacute. It is really nice and I will be on the train back to Sheffield in the morning."*

*"I love you Jess"* he announced

*"I love you too"* she replied and they just held stood in each other's arms until there was a knock at the door. Jess was escorted off the base and as she passed through security and into the waiting taxi he suddenly felt very alone.

Two weeks later he was informed by the Base Commander, Commodore Jenkins that he had the option of not having to face the Board of Enquiry and the potential of being court-martialled if he took the decision to resign his commission and leave the Service immediately. Political pressure from very senior sources had evidently deemed that it was not appropriate and in no one's interests to pursue this case in the gaze of publicity. Angus had returned to his base at RM Stonehouse in Plymouth. He had also been confined to barracks and threatened with the sanction of SNLR or Service No Longer Required. However at the same time that Andy had opted to leave the Navy, Angus also opted to accept the opportunity to voluntarily discharge himself and he returned to his home town of Aberdeen.

## Tuesday 8ᵗʰ June1982: Aldershot, England

On returning to the UK Steve was immediately transferred to the Cambridge Military Hospital at Aldershot where he spent a further four weeks recuperating. During this time he was debriefed on Operation Mikado by a superior officer and a civilian he did not know who turned out to be a senior civil servant in the Ministry of Defence. *How many Exocet missiles had been disabled? How many Super Etendards had been damaged and in what way? How had he got separated from his patrol? How had he got away? How had he come to be involved with two Chilean nationals? How had he been rescued and had he had any communication prior to that with Lieutenant Andrew Shaw of the Royal Navy Fleet Air Arm and what was his relationship with him?* It had gone on and on for a couple of days and Steve had become drained by the experience.

However, it was not over. On release from hospital he was sent to Hereford and the whole process started again. Only this time in a lot more depth. Evidently relations between Britain and Chile had become strained because of what had happened and as Steve was to discover keeping them on side was vital to the war effort particularly in these later stages of the conflict. At one point during the interrogation debriefing process the door of the room opened and in walked De la Billière. Steve rose to salute but the Director SAS extended his hand:

*"Good job Captain""*

*"Could I have a word in private sir"* Steve requested

*"Five minutes only"* he replied and the other men left the room.

*"I know it's a mess Sir but there was no way that we could have achieved the objective without the engagement of enemy troops. I had no idea Lieutenant Shaw would try and rescue me. I thought I could cross the border on my own but the opposition was too strong and I would have most certainly been killed and the Argentines would have had the body of a British SAS Captain taken on mainland Argentinean soil which would have been a PR coup for them. I know what Lieutenant Shaw did was wrong sir but he saved my life and probably the life of the lady who had helped me. Is there anything you can do for him Sir?"*

*"It's a matter for the Royal Navy Captain Barraclough"* came the matter-of-fact reply

*"I know Sir but I just wondered..."*

But the words were falling on deaf ears because De la Billière was already leaving the room. However, unknown to Steve he did put in a brief call to Admiral Fieldhouse at his Northwood Headquarters.

A few days later Steve was allowed to return to his parents home in Sheffield for an extended period of rest and recuperation. He had to attend the local hospital as an outpatient for treatment and restorative physiotherapy but he did not have to return to Hereford until December when he would undergo a full medical assessment and decisions about his future career would then be taken. He had immediately telephoned Isabella in Santiago but not before assuring his parents that he would pay all the telephone bills during his stay with them. Although the line was crackly he was delighted to hear her voice again. He had been awake half the night before, wondering if she still wanted to talk to him and whether she was now blaming him for her father's death and her injuries. He needn't have worried as she had been driving her aunt mad with talk about this very handsome Englishman she had met and what had happened to them.

*"It is really nice to speak to you Isabella. How are you feeling?"*

*"I am ok. My arm and shoulder are very stiff and sore and there is not much movement at the moment but it is getting better all the time."*

*"How are you?"*

*"I am good and my mother is feeding me up with all my favourite food!"*

*"That's what mothers do"* Isabella said laughing

*"Isabella I really want to see you again"* Steve suddenly said quietly but seriously.

*"I want to see you too"* she replied *"I have taken a contract nursing job at the hospital here in Santiago for three months starting in January and I will be staying with my aunt."*

Steve bit his lip trying to hide his disappointment and went on to tell her about his few months of rest until the medical reassessment and how he was looking forward to Andy's wedding but not the fact that he had to make a speech.

*"I would like to come"* she said suddenly *"I would like to hear that speech"*

Steve nearly dropped the telephone receiver in surprise and excitement.

*"I am not starting my job for nearly three months so that I have time to recover and I have never been to England and I would like to thank Andy personally for what he did for us. You can show me the all the places that I would like to see in London particularly Buckingham Palace and the Houses of Parliament. That is if the invitation is still open?* She let the words tail off and drift across the nearly eight thousand miles between them.

*"Of course it is Isabella. You know that I really would like that more that anything else. You can stay here with my parents but the house is very small so I apologise in advance but I am looking for my own place to rent for a while perhaps you can help me find the right one? The flight will be very expensive though."*

*"That is no problem. You have seen my father's farm. It was certainly no grand estate. Also I have some money saved up and my aunt is now negotiating to sell my father's farm and so I will be inheriting some money in the near future."*

186

Since that first call Steve had contacted Isabella every few days and he knew that he had already run up hundreds of pounds in telephone charges but it didn't matter. He was still receiving his salary from the army and although he was contributing some money to his parents he still had plenty. He too had saved money. Over the last few years the army and the regiment had been his life and apart from his mess bill there had not been much else to spend it on apart from his beloved MGB. He had bought the Roadster sports car three years before. It was British Racing Green with wire wheels and chrome wheel spinners. It was an L registration 1973 model and one of the last models made before they had fitted the horrendous large rubber bumpers to satisfy impact regulations in the important export market of the United States. The car was stored in a garage at the Hereford base and he knew that it would be sometime before he could get into it again let alone be able to operate the clutch with his left foot.

The weeks had flown by and they had continued to call each other all the time. It was the highlight of the day for each of them. Santiago was four hours behind Sheffield so they had decided that the best time to speak to each other was 10.00pm GMT. By the end of September, Isabella's father's farm had been sold and she and her Aunt had travelled to Punto Arenas to sign all the necessary legal documents. They had also visited her father's grave which was in the beautiful four hectare cemetery of Punto Arenas situated between the streets of Francisco Bilbao and Angamos.

## October 1982: Sheffield

It was the beginning of October when Andy was walking down Raby Street in Tinsley having caught the bus from the railway station. It was a cold autumn day but nothing like the South Atlantic he thought. He had decided to surprise his parents with his homecoming. He knocked at the familiar front door and waited with a slight knot in his stomach. His mother opened the door and was overwhelmed to see him. She just screamed in delight and threw her arms around him and just held him till Andy felt all the breath had been squeezed out of him.

*"Welcome home son"*

said his father Tom coming out of the kitchen with a cup of tea in his hand and he too embraced him.

An hour later they were in the front room drinking tea.

*"What you did was wrong son but I can understand why you did it"* said his father *"but I think it was incredibly brave and I am extremely proud of you. Mr and Mrs Barraclough came over a few Sundays ago to thank us so much for what you did for their Steve."*

*"What are you going to do now though Andy"* his mother added.

*"Well as you know I am a qualified pilot with a lot of flying hours and experience behind me. My mate Angus contacted me last week and put me in touch with a company in Aberdeen where he lives. They run a fleet of helicopters carrying people to and from the oil rigs in the North Sea and it has really taken off and they are desperate for pilots who have experience of flying in challenging conditions. I am meeting up with them next week and staying with Angus for a few days. As you know he has left the Royal Marines and has now taken over the running of his family furniture business up there."*

*"Good lad"* chipped in his father *"There is nothing for you in Sheffield right now."*

*"Do you know dad they are offering to pay me more than fifty percent more than I was getting in the Navy. Now I have sorted things out with Jess we are going to move up there for a couple of years and see how it goes."*

After Andy had unpacked and they had had some lunch his father suddenly said.

*"Andy there's something I want to show you in the shed"*

So they went out the back door and into the small courtyard and next to the outside lavatory was a small wooden shed. His father opened the padlock and squeezed inside was a motorcycle covered with a tarpaulin. He pulled it off and smiled.

*"Looks good doesn't she"*

Andy stared at the 1962 350cc Norton Navigator twin cylinder machine that he knew so well. It was in absolutely immaculate concours condition.

*"Over the last few years since you've been away I have completely rebuilt her for you. They are starting to fetch good money these days. It's my wedding present to you."*

Andy turned and put an arm round his father's shoulders *"You are a genius dad."*

That evening Andy had walked up the road to Steve's parent's house.

*"Can Steve come out to play"* Andy had said cheekily to Mrs Barraclough as she opened the front door. She moved forward and put her arm around him and hugged him warmly. Just then Steve came out of the front room leaning on a crutch under his left arm.

*"Fancy a couple of pints mate"* said Andy with a smile.

*"Bloody hell mate what are you doing here?"*

*"I'll tell you all about it in the "Fox and Duck". I need to ask you if you will do me a favour"*

*"What's that then?"*

*"I want you to be my best man at my wedding in two weeks time"*

Two hours and three pints each of Wards Bitter later, which the landlord had refused to take any money for, they left the pub and walked very slowly back with Steve hobbling along calling at *Bennett's* to get a fish and chip supper. They hadn't spent so much time together for nearly ten years and as they had talked it was as if they had never been apart although there was so much to catch up on.

*"You know you are a complete nutter"* said Steve as they walked home down the narrow street with cars parked on both sides of the road

*"But I owe you a big one."*

*"No you don't. We are just even"* Andy replied.

Steve was about to question what he meant by that remark when a car pulled up alongside and a window rolled down and a voice said over the loud music coming from inside:

*"Good to see you back lads"*

They both waved at Ricky as he drove off in his company car, a Ford Cortina as he was now a sales representative for Tinsley Wire based at the factory on Sheffield road and covering all of South Yorkshire in his sales territory.

The wedding had been set for Saturday 17th October. Although Jess would be six months pregnant and would not be able to fit into a very glamorous white wedding dress she was determined to be married before the baby was born. It was going to be a relatively simple family affair. He had been to see Jess' father almost immediately he had got back to Sheffield and they had been absolutely delighted when he had announced that he wanted to marry their daughter, Jessica.

*"I've got an instant family"* he had said with a big smile as he shook her father's hand. Andy had rented a terraced house on Oversley Street in Tinsley for a three month period so that he and Jess and the baby would have somewhere to stay and get themselves sorted out. The house had come unfurnished so Andy had been visiting second hand furniture shops all over the city to get what they needed. Jessica's parents had been very generous and had promised them a new three-piece suite and a fridge freezer as a wedding present and his own parents were buying them a new gas cooker. He had rented a colour television and when it was up and working he sat in the front room watching *'Match of the Day'* very proud indeed of his new home. He had made the long journey to Aberdeen a few days before and had accepted the job that was *offered to him subject to the satisfactory completion of a flying test the following day.*

*"If I can land a helicopter on a ship pitching and rolling in the South Atlantic I am sure that I can do this ok"* he had said to the pilot from the company who was in the seat next to him in the cockpit as the aircraft neared the oil rig in the Forties oilfield in the North Sea.

He had stayed with Angus for the a few days and had told him about the wedding plans and Angus had been delighted to accept the invitation and he had also agreed to start to look for a house for Andy and his new family to rent for when he started his new job in January.

Meanwhile Steve had decided that his parents' house in Raby Street was too small to have Isabella to stay in for a few weeks as it would have meant him sleeping on the sofa and it was not fair on his parents. So he had set about finding somewhere to rent for a few months until after his medical assessment. Ricky had volunteered to 'schive off' for a couple of days and drive him around to look at potential properties. Steve had decided that he wanted a place in a more pleasant area of the city than Tinsley. Not that he wasn't fiercely proud of his neighbourhood it was just that he now wanted something different and this was a chance for him to branch out a little even though he was still staying in Sheffield unlike Andy who would soon be living in the north of Scotland. He settled on a small house just off the Eccleshall Road in the established residential district of Nether Edge. It was well connected with buses running up and down Eccleshall Road and when he was fit enough again he could walk into the city centre in fifteen minutes. Moreover, a fifteen minute drive the other way and he would find himself in the Peak District.

*'Perfect'* he said to the agent who had showed Ricky and himself around and he had signed the rental agreement that afternoon. The two-bedroom property was fully furnished and he took great delight in showing his parents around the house a few days later.

*"I will come and give it a good clean out'* his mother had said straight away

*'Don't fuss mother'* had been Steve's immediate reply.

He moved in straight away and brought his things over from his parents' house in Tinsley in two taxi rides. Pride of joy was his stereo which he set up in the lounge and immediately put the first record of the double album *'Quadrophenia'* on the turntable but he kept the volume down because he didn't want to upset his new neighbours to whom he had only just introduced himself that morning. He had arranged for the MGB to be driven down from Hereford and it was now parked outside the house. When he had mentioned it to Isabella she had screamed in delight at the prospect of being able to drive them both in the open top sports car saying:

*'I am sure that my shoulder will be ok by then'*

It was Monday 19th October and the British Airways flight from Santiago was due to land at Heathrow at six in the evening. It had taken sixteen and a half hours to fly the seven thousand two hundred sixty nine miles and Steve had come down on the train form Sheffield that morning. He had been at the airport for three hours now as he had wanted to get there early and he had already drunk four cups of black coffee by the time that the plane had landed and he was pacing up and down the arrivals hall in Terminal Three with a knot in his stomach constantly looking at the Arrivals board. He made his way to the arrivals gate and waited. Dozens of thoughts raced through his mind as he stood there leaning against his crutch and clutching a newspaper he had already read over and over. He had decided that he would 'play it as cool as possible' but all that went out of the window because as soon as she saw him standing by the gate she dropped her bag and ran towards him and threw her arms around his neck and kissed him passionately.

They talked animatedly as Steve led the way to the tube station and then to King's Cross station to get the train back to Sheffield. Within ten minutes of the train leaving the station she was asleep in the seat next to him with her head gently resting on his shoulders. Steve looked at her constantly and gently stroked her dark hair. He had never felt happier in his life. Suddenly the medical assessment had started to lose its importance.

*"My time in the regiment is over anyway now I am sure of that'* he thought *'and there is no way I am going to be returned to unit now or do anything else in the army. It is time for a change.'*

Andy and Jess' wedding was to be held that Saturday afternoon at the Registry Office in Sheffield which is at the rear of the town hall. They had chosen to hold the reception in the banqueting suite on the top floor of the Brightside and Carbrook Co-operative Society department store on Angel Street in the city centre with its separate street level access. Angus had agreed to play the bagpipes as all the guests entered the reception. Isabella was fascinated she had never seen a man in a 'skirt' before and playing this strange instrument which made such a glorious sound. After Jessica's father had spoken eloquently in his rhythmic South Wales accent about his beautiful daughter and the pride that he shared with his wife that she was finally married to her teenage sweetheart and the bride had been toasted, there was a sense of anticipation amongst the guests for the Best Man's speech.

Steve rose using his crutch to steady himself. He looked resplendent in his full dress uniform. He took a large sip of champagne, cleared his throat and began:

*"I am not sure about this Best Man thing"* he said *"If I am the Best man why is Jessica marrying Andy and not me?*

There was a ripple of laughter across the large room and he continued:

*"I have known Andy since we were five years old and throughout that time he has continually been getting me into scrapes of one kind another right up to a few months ago."* There was muted laughter and a lot of whispering in the room.

*"I am sure that you can appreciate, therefore, that I am absolutely delighted that Andy has decided to settle with his new wife in Aberdeen which is nearly four hundred miles from Sheffield which means that I should be safe in the future."*

Steve continued for another fifteen minutes recounting stories and events that he had shared with Andy as well as giving an outline of his career but not before recalling that fateful wet Tuesday night back in March 1971 when Andy thought that he would never have a flying career and it would be over before it started. He recalled how devastated Andy was when he had seen him soon after he had failed his medical with the Royal Air Force and how he had never given up on his dream and after a while he had just picked himself up and tackled the issues head on with determination and imagination.

*'But that's the measure of the man'* said Steve

*'I am proud to be your friend.'*

After raising a toast to the Bridesmaids he sat down to rapturous applause and a big pat on the back from Andy and Jess got out of her seat and kissed him on the cheek.

Isabella put her hand on Steve's knee under the table and gave it a squeeze consciously aware not to touch the wounded thigh.

*'That was really well done. I am very proud of you.'*

She had already made the decision that morning - she would not be sleeping in the second bedroom of the little house in Nether Edge that evening.

# Chapter Seventeen

## 28th April 1983 Cutlers' Hall: Sheffield

It was just about twelve months after the events in South America that the taxi dropped them off outside the hall on Church Street, opposite the Cathedral. So much had happened in the last year. It had been a difficult journey through police cordons and control points.

*"It's like being back in Belfast not Sheffield"* Steve thought to himself,

Steve felt uncomfortable in the *white tie* evening dress outfit; he had never been fond of ceremonial dress in the army. The front of the dress coat was cut as if it were double-breasted but designed so that it cannot be closed with a squared away front. His medals jangled from their bar on his lapel as he balanced himself on the walking stick that he was still using. He looked across at Andy and realised that he was thinking the same thoughts:

*"Do we belong here?*

As Steve and Isabella got out of the taxi in front of the Hall, they were met with a cacophony of sound as two thousand protesters were being held behind police barriers. They were however, trying to push forward violently and were shouting chanting and waving placards noisily. There was also a barrage of eggs being thrown which were landing on the pavement around him and two had splattered on the windscreen of the taxi as it had pulled up. Steve had never experienced anything like this and a myriad of thoughts raced through his mind as he took Isabella's hand and walked quickly into the Hall.

Ever since the invitation had arrived and the name of the principle speaker had been announced there had been vociferous debate within the wider Barraclough family. Yes they were very proud of Steve and his achievements and those of the rest of the British armed forces in the South Atlantic last year. And yes she had shown great leadership in that conflict and time of crisis but this was Sheffield in 1983 a year later. And according to Steve's uncle, Frank and his father and his brother, Paul, she was now:

*"Ripping the heart out of Sheffield."*

*"Sheffield is built of steel. We are the 'Men of Steel' and we will say no to the Iron Lady"* said Frank when they all sat in *The Fox House* pub in Attercliffe one Friday night the previous month.

"Do you know" added Steve's father: *"That since 1979 there have been fifty seven thousand redundancies in Sheffield and over eighty percent of them were in manufacturing"*

*"It's now getting worse"* chipped in Paul, *"It said in The Star the other night that since 1981 the rate of redundancies has been running at over one thousand every month. There are lots of rumours going round at our place."*

Steve sipped his pint of Wards Bitter and just listened. *"It was great to be home and his family had welcomed Isabella with open arms but they all just seemed a little parochial to him maybe it was his years in the army and the experiences he had been through not just in the Falklands but in Northern Ireland, Belize and the Middle East that had broadened his purview beyond 'the largest village in England' which was the reputation that Sheffield had garnered."*

*I went with my mate Dave to the Miners' Welfare Club the other night"* added Paul

*"There are lots of rumours starting to go round that the Tories are planning to close a lot of the pits in South Yorkshire."*

*"I don't know where it will all end"* said Steve's father with a sombre tone

*"I really don't but I am glad for your mum and I that I took that voluntary redundancy offer at Christmas last year, I've just had enough of it."*

*"That's ok for you dad but Linda and I have got a mortgage now and I am really worried."*Paul said quietly.

Steve listened intently and nodded occasionally but didn't speak. He had also read the article in *The Star* and he was aware that in the last twelve years Sheffield had lost over sixty percent of the steel jobs in the city and he was worried for Paul too because he knew that there was nothing else he could do. He also felt that in some ways Sheffield's tight knit community was also a potential source of weakness. Social and recreational facilities have all revolved around the works clubs, social, football and fishing and the working men's clubs all of which catered almost exclusively for the needs of the predominantly male workforce in the manufacturing sector.

*"But was this any different from the army and military life"* he pondered.

*"How was he going to fare on civvy street when he leaves the army next year? How many employers would want his skills?*

But he knew the mantra that had been drilled into him from his earliest days in the army *'there's no gain without pain'* and he would retrain, adapt and sell himself hard which he always had done.

*"You have to go Steve lad"* said his father when Frank had gone to the bar to get another round.

"Yeah you do" added Paul

*"It's just that she's only coming so it can be seen as a clear challenge to the local labour movement. Just remember to eat with your knife and fork"* he grinned.

The four of them, Andy with Jessica on his arm, Steve and Isabella looked up quickly at the front of the listed building built in 1832 which was the third Hall on this site. They entered the foyer of the Cutlers' Hall and the sound of the crowd outside started to fade.

*"Bloody hell"* Jessica whispered in Andy's ear as they entered,

*"I thought that I was quite clued up on what lay behind the large imposing doors of the Hall and I have done my homework on the Company of Cutlers"* but Jess was not prepared for the impact that it had on her as they moved through the entrance. The four of them were directed to climb the main staircase with its plush red carpet, ornate columns and cedar wood hand rails and after climbing the nineteen steps of the first tier they were faced with an enormous mirror and a painting of her Majesty the Queen whose portrait hangs in pride of place and as a reminder of her last visit to the hall which was in 1975.

As they slowly climbed further they stared at enormous beautiful paintings and portraits of all the previous Master Cutlers and benefactors of the Hall itself, the Duke of Wellington mounted on his horse and the wife of the man who set up the first ladies and maternity hospital in Sheffield. They were just too many to take in so they just kept on ascending slowly.

The Cutlers' Company was established by a parliamentary Act of Incorporation in 1624 when it was given jurisdiction over:

*'All persons using to make Knives, Blades, Scissers, Sheeres, Sickles, Cutlery wares and all other wares and manufacture made or wrought of yron and steele, dwelling or inhabiting within the said Lordship and Liberty of Hallamshire, or within six miles compasse of the same'*

For almost four hundred years the Company had sought to maintain the standards and quality of Sheffield manufactured cutlery and steel products and to promote the name and proud heritage of the City of Sheffield. The most important function in the Hall's calendar is the annual Cutlers' Feast which has been held every year, with only a few exceptions, since 1625 when it was simply a dinner after the annual account taking. By the late eighteenth century, the celebrations lasted for three days – the Feast on the first day was for gentlemen, on the second day ladies came to the Hall, and the third day was for employees and servants. All work stopped in the town during these three days and tents and stalls were erected on the land separating the Hall and the Parish Church (now the Cathedral) for the sale of food and drink.

By 1983, the Feast had become firmly established as the premier event in the Master Cutler's year and gave him opportunity to entertain representatives of both national and foreign governments, leaders of business and industry and members of the Armed Forces.

The group of four were greeted first by the doorman and then by a Guard of Honour standing to attention on the steps leading up to the reception rooms and the main hall. Half way up the grand staircase they had all been given a booklet containing the details of the night's events including a table plan. Tonight in line with tradition, it would only be gentlemen, about three hundred and forty of them, who dined in the Main Hall. Isabella and Jessica were amongst the twenty ladies who were specially invited guests of the Mistress Cutler and who were to dine in the Lower Hall, although they would be allowed to troop up to the Ladies Balcony of the Main Hall to hear the main speaker. On reaching the top of the stairs a toastmaster presented each of them to the three dignitaries waiting to receive them, the Master Cutler, William J.D. Carr who was their host and both his Senior and Junior Wardens. After the introductions they were shown into a reception room. There are three reception rooms and with their invitations had come a coloured card which indicated which room they were allocated to. They each took a glass of champagne that was presented to them on a silver salver by two waitresses one either side of the door as they entered the Drawing Room which was their allocated room. They stood together but did not make much conversation but looked around and smiled at everyone in the room and only occasionally engaging in casual conversations as the guests started to mingle.

Slowly the room began to fill up and suddenly at about quarter to seven there was a flurry of movement outside the room and seconds later the Prime Minister strode in with a big smile on her face with the dignitaries and others in tow. She was immediately surrounded by different groups and entered into animated discussions presumably about the gauntlet that she had just run outside thought Steve. After about ten minutes she broke free of the group and advanced across the room towards Steve and the other three:

*"Ah Captain Barraclough"* said the Prime Minister as she extended her hand

*"I wanted to remake your acquaintance. I believe we briefly met in London a couple of years ago. I know that all the people of Sheffield are very proud of you as is the rest of the country. We can all celebrate in the magnificent achievement of our armed forces in the South Atlantic last year. The forces of freedom must and always will conquer tyranny and evil wherever it presents itself. Thank you for your contribution."*

With that she turned and was ushered away to another group on the far side of the room. Steve squeezed Isabella's hand and she just looked at him and beamed:

*"I can't believe that that just happened"* she whispered.

*"Nor can I"* he replied.

At the appointed hour the announcement was made that guests should make their way into the Main Hall and find their places as quickly as possible so that they were all ready for the main procession. Steve and Andy said goodbye as Jessica and Isabella made their way downstairs to the Lower Hall

*"Behave yourself"* Andy said to Jess *'And don't neck the wine!!'*

Andy took his place in the hall midway down one of the sprig tables that lay across the hall.

*"It's a bit of a tight squeeze"* he thought to himself as he managed to manoeuvre himself into the right position. Steve had been given the honour of being seated at the top table as one of the Master Cutler's principle guests and was therefore part of the procession. The toastmaster banged his gavel and the hall went quiet as he announced welcome to the Master Cutler and his principle guests. On the balcony, a trio of trumpeters played a suitable fanfare to accompany the entrance of the procession.

*"Pray silence for the chaplain to the Master Cutler who will now say grace"*

The main course was a Cutlers' Feast favourite – Steak and Kidney pie with the addition of oysters brought that day from the fish market at Whitby on the North Yorkshire coast. The caterers at the Hall had learnt how to perfect this dish even for nearly four hundred discerning guests. The secret was in the nurturing of the meat so that when they cut through the wheaten gold crust, the gravy clung to the chunks of meat before oozing out across the plate. The meat divided with just a little pressure from a fork.

*"There's something very English in the way that all these different flavours blend together don't you think?"*

Steve said to the gentleman on his right who was the veteran Member of Parliament for Sheffield Park, Fred Mulley who famously as Secretary of State for Defence in 1977 fell asleep during the Queen's Jubilee Review of the Royal Air Force at RAF Finningley when there was considerable noise around him. Having a small sleep during exercise was referred to by members of the RAF as having a 'Fred Mulley.' Steve chuckled internally as he remembered the pictures in the papers the following day of the politician asleep next to the Monarch who clearly could not have been 'amused.' This representation of the classic English dish however, was a far cry from that produced by his mother in their small kitchen at the back of the terraced house in Tinsley with the cheap cuts of beef that had to be cooked for hours to tenderise them, that she had bought from the local butcher when he was a boy.

It was time for the speeches. But it was the turn of the principle speaker, the Prime Minister, The Right Honourable Margaret Thatcher MP that had been the most eagerly awaited. She got to her feet and Steve looked up and saw that the ladies had now taken their places on the balcony and there was silence around the great hall. She presented a typically forthright, confident and upbeat speech commencing with:

*"Lord Lieutenant, Lord Mayor, High Sheriff, Senior Warden, My Lords, Ladies and Gentlemen. It is a pleasure for me to be your guest on this great occasion of the Cutlers' Feast with its long and famous history..."*

She made a comparison between the two institutions of parliament and the Cutlers' Company and how each had gone through 'turbulent times' and in an oblique reference to the demonstrators outside the Hall she recalled that the Cutlers Feast in 1756 had had to be postponed for a fortnight because of rioters and a rowdy mob demanding changes that they thought were appropriate to the Company's laws. She then stated with a slight smile that she was glad that this had not been necessary on this occasion. The Prime Minister then referred to the very direct speech that had been made earlier by the Senior Warden who had laid the blame for the current woes of the steel industry on the problem of cheaper steel imports. In her typical confident way she thanked him for his plain speaking that is the trademark of a Yorkshireman but then moved on to discussing the performance of Britain as a trading nation in a much wider context.

Steve listened intently as she went on to discuss the country's performance as a trading nation, and of particular interest to so many of those in the room – the steel industry. The Prime Minister argued that the health of the steel-producing industry critically depended on the health of the steel-using industries with which it had a symbiotic relationship, with the latter employing fourteen times the size of labour force. She countered the proposition from the Senior Warden that the ills of the steel producers began in the aftermath of the steel strike in 1980 but that the real blame for the surge in imports during the decade of the Nineteen Seventies lay with the fact that the costs and prices of domestic producers had risen faster than those of their foreign competitors.

After then talking about industrial costs, rates, the challenge of change and recovery she concluded that it was impossible for anyone to stand in this Hall on such a splendid occasion and not have a strong sense of history, pride and tradition. The source of that pride, she argued, was the quality of workmanship done by all their forbears who had gained a reputation for Sheffield and for England in general that could not be surpassed by any other nation. She continued by stating that Sheffield had to rise to these standards again today. In the past success had come for Sheffield and the rest of industrial Britain by continuously fashioning new products, in order to remain ahead of competitors through design and innovation and commitment. Once again, she argued, we must use our skills and craftsmanship to win new and future markets. The mantra must be *'to adapt and prosper.'* Britain is undoubtedly on the move again but we can all maintain that momentum by our own individual efforts and enterprise. She concluded by saying that this great room was full of wise and entrepreneurial businessmen and that she had every confidence that like their forbears before them, they would succeed and flourish.

There was widespread applause throughout the hall and everyone rose as the Prime Minister then left at quarter to ten. As the applause rang through the hall Steve's mind went back to the conversation he had had with his family in the pub a few weeks before:

*"Two opposite positions, two different approaches. Which was right?* He didn't know and perhaps the solution was as always somewhere in the middle but the words *'adapt and prosper'* had found a resonance within him."

Steve could not see Andy amongst the rows of well-dressed gentlemen from where he was sitting but he knew that he was somewhere in the Hall. He glanced up at the coat of arms on the wall and the motto of the Company of Cutlers in Hallamshire in the County of York beneath it:

*'Pour y parvenir a bonne foi'* he knew from the booklet that they had been given earlier that this roughly translated as

*"To succeed through honest endeavour'*

Something that the two sons of Sheffield had tried to do since their childhood. He smiled to himself and whispered:

*"Not bad for two Tinsley scallywags!!"*

It was time to settle back in Sheffield for good. He was leaving the army next year with a pension and was rehabilitating physically and going to join courses that would better prepare him for life and a future career outside of the military.

*The Owls* were playing Fulham at home on Saturday, it was the last game of the season and he was going with his brother Paul and his two nephews. There simply was nowhere else better. Sheffield was going through hard times and would continue to do so for some time and they probably would get worse before they got better. But we are resilient, we are resourceful and we will adapt and prosper. The *'Made in Sheffield'* endorsement is still a global mark of quality, strength, consistency and craftsmanship. These attributes apply to the people who are born and grow up in this great city as well as the produce of their labours and any Royal Navy warship that carries its name he thought.

# Epilogue

## February 1984: Sheffield

Steve opened the formal looking envelope over breakfast one morning. He pulled out the stiff white card it contained. It was headed by the words:

*'The directors of Swan Hunter request the pleasure of Captain Stephen Barraclough at the Keel Laying Down Ceremony of HMS Sheffield on 29th March 1984 at the Wallsend West Shipyard in Wallsend, Tyne & Wear"*

As the *laying down* of the keel is the initial step in construction of a ship, in British shipbuilding traditions the construction is dated from this event. Steve knew that only the ship's launching is considered more significant in its creation. A structural keel is a large beam around which the hull of a ship is built. The keel runs in the middle of the ship, from the bow to the stern, and serves as the foundation or spine of the structure, providing the major source of structural strength of the hull. The keel is generally the first part of a ship's hull to be constructed, and *laying the keel,* or placing the keel in the cradle in which the ship will be built, is often a momentous event in a ship's construction — so much so that the event is often marked with a ceremony, and the term *lay the keel* has entered the English language as a phrase meaning the beginning of any significant undertaking. Modern ships are now largely built in a series of pre-fabricated, complete hull sections rather than being built around a single keel, so the start of the shipbuilding process is now considered to be when the first sheet of steel is cut.

Steve looked across the table at his new wife, Isabella

*"Why me?* He said staring at her with a genuine quizzical expression on his face.

*"Don't you know?'* She replied without a moments thought, a thin smile parting her lips

*"Its all about the restoration of pride my darling."*

Just over two years later on 26<sup>th</sup> March 1986, HMS Sheffield (F96) was launched at a traditional ceremony at the shipyard which was attended by the relatives of the twenty Royal Naval personnel who lost their lives when the previous bearer of the name was hit by an Exocet missile fired form an Argentine Super Etendard aircraft during the Falklands campaign on 4<sup>th</sup> May 1982. Also attending the launch were HMS Sheffield's former Captain, Sam Salt, the Lord Mayor of Sheffield and the Master Cutler.

Many months later Steve was interested to read a passage written by the new Master Cutler that had been reproduced in the local press.
*"Couldn't have put it better myself"* he said smiling to himself knowing full well that literary proficiency was definitely not one of his core skills.

*"Some months ago I had the pleasure of going to sea on the new HMS Sheffield to see her put through her paces during sea trials. It was an exhilarating and reassuring process.*

*This may be a nuclear age but Britain has found more than once in the last couple of decades that the Royal Navy still has a vital role to play in the defence of our country. Just a few hours on board your fine ship was enough to convince me that this third in line to bear the name of Sheffield will uphold a proud tradition.*

*For fifty years the links between the first and second HMS Sheffield and the City that I represent as Master Cutler have been strong and deeply valued by all of us. I am sure that this special relationship will continue and be strengthened through your Ship's Company.*

*Since it was incorporated in 1624 by a group of far-sighted men who were determined that the expanding new industry of that time, the manufacture of cutlery, would not allow shoddy workmanship to tarnish the city's reputation for producing quality goods, the Company has never wavered in its defence of the good name of*

*Sheffield. And though the cutlery industry itself has contracted, the Company is still on its guard to ensure that foreign manufacturers do not cash in on the guarantee that goes with 'Made in Sheffield' by using spurious trademarks.*

*As Master Cutler one of my most important responsibilities during my year of office is to represent the city, to uphold the traditions of the past, but also to safeguard the future prosperity of and happiness of its people – just as you will be expected to for the nation as a whole.*

*I am sure that this city and this Company will have every reason to feel proud of the new HMS Sheffield and our thoughts will be with you wherever you serve."*

Printed in Great Britain
by Amazon